SCORPION ISLAND

Long Bay

Black Cay

For Mac & Zach.

Alison.

East End

West End

Sunset Cove

KAMARIA

New Town

The EYE of the STORM

A NOVEL

ALISON KNIGHTS BRAMBLE

This book is a work of fiction. Names, characters, places and incidents are products of the author's imagination or are used fictitiously. Any resemblance to actual events or locales or persons, living or dead, is entirely coincidental.

Copyright © 2011 by Alison Knights Bramble
All rights reserved.
Published by aLookingGlass Ltd.

No part of this book may be reproduced or utilized in any form or by any means, electronic or mechanical, including photocopying, recording or by any information storage and retrieval system without permission in writing.

Inquiries should be addressed to
aLookingGlass
PO Box 3895
Sea Cows Bay, Tortola
British Virgin Islands, VG1110
www.alookingglass.com

FIRST EDITION
First Printing 2011

Catalog-in-Publication Data
Bramble, Alison Knights
The Eye of the Storm
p.   cm.
I. Title
ISBN 978-0-9569697-0-5

Publication Design copyright © 2011 by aLookingGlass Ltd.

Cover Illustration copyright © 2011 by Daniel Worth
Cover Design and Map Illustration copyright © 2011 by Nick Cunha
Shell Museum title font copyright © 2011 by Nick Cunha

Prepress in the British Virgin Islands

Printed in China

Acknowledgments

Thank you to my first reader, the man I trust most in the world, my husband Colin. Thanks also go to my friend and colleague Lorna Dawson, together with the Kinkead family who were patient enough to read my story while it was still a rough copy.

My biggest thanks go to my editor, Traci O'Dea, who convinced me to pursue the venture and then in her spare time took on the mammoth task of rounding my words into a real novel.

I would also like to thank our sponsors, LIME, INTAC, Caribbean Insurers Limited, Rotary Club Sunrise of Road Town, Rotary Club of Road Town, and Victor International. Without them, this fundraising project would not have been possible.

For all the young people I have had the
privilege accompanying as we have explored
the land and sea of the British Virgin Islands,
may you continue your adventures.

Eye of **the Storm**

FOREWORD

As a young man, I had an accident in the British Virgin Islands which would change the direction of my life forever. One minute I was a fit, healthy 18-year-old yachtsman with the world at my feet. The next, I was paralysed from the chest down, facing an uncertain future. The only certainty being a lifetime in a wheelchair. Someone sent me a get well card whilst I was in hospital which said, "When life gives you lemons, make lemonade." I didn't understand what that meant at the time. Twenty five years later, after arriving back in Tortola, having just become the first disabled person to sail the Atlantic Ocean, I was reminded of that get well card. Finally, I realised what it meant. In the quarter of a century I had indeed made lemonade—plenty of it. But I would not have achieved a fraction of what I have were it not for two things: the love and support of my friends and family and the freedom of sailing. My accident brought to an end my budding career as a yacht skipper but not my love for the activity itself. With the support of my loved ones, I was able to sail again. And over time, I was able to play a part in helping provide opportunities for other disabled people to experience sailing and enjoy the same sense of freedom that I get when I'm out on the water. Regardless of their ability, any sailor will tell you how special that feeling is. It's truly the one time when I do not feel disabled. I leave my disability on the quayside with my wheelchair. On the water, I regain my freedom.

Freedom is one of the main themes of *The Eye of the Storm*. The young characters achieve it not only through sailing but also through the sense of safety that exists on an island where kids can explore the streets, the bush, the sea and the beach without adult supervision, allowing them to discover their own limits.

Geoff Holt, MBE, Disability Sports Ambassador

CHAPTER 1
THE BEGINNING OF THE END

Ben knew at that moment that they never should have left Sunset Cove. Their small fishing boat struggled as the fuming sea made fools of them all. The light vessel was being tossed about—the stern lifting precariously before being hurled down the steep slope of the next wave. The propeller screamed as it spun, fighting to keep its grip on the water.

"Man, we need to go back. The engine, she won't make it through this!" Isaac had to shout to be heard over the noise of the gathering storm. Ben grappled with his rising panic, trying to keep it under control, mesmerized by the white water crashing on the corner of Scorpion Island—each wave managing to climb higher than the last, spray bouncing around the seabirds that were forced to abandon their perches.

As his friend started to turn the thrashing boat back for home, he yelled over the relentless noise. "That way is upwind, Isaac. If we try and drive back through that squall, we'll be turned over for sure."

Charlie had frightened tears in her eyes, and looking at her made Ben want to cry, too. "Then what?" she asked. "Please do something!"

Kai was frantically bailing with the sadly inadequate plastic water bottle, his other hand pointing in the direction they had been going. Although unable to speak, the boy was demonstrating his determination to go on. Certainly they were closer to land now than they would be if they tried to turn back. Ben had to agree with him.

"He's right. Let's keep going. We'll find some place to get ashore to wait it out. If we go back, we'll risk capsizing." As the word "capsize" came out of Ben's mouth, he realised two things: they had no lifejackets on board, and, even worse, Isaac couldn't swim. How had he gotten so sloppy? Just over one month in the Caribbean and he had disregarded everything he'd ever been taught about being safe on the water.

Six weeks earlier, just days before the end of term, Ben was unaware of this extraordinary chapter in his life. The day he'd found out that he'd be going to the Caribbean, he'd been much more excited about something else. Straight after school, Ben had cycled down to the watersports centre. On arrival, he'd found his mentor covering up dinghies in the yard as a local school group traipsed back to their waiting bus.

"Hi, Ben. Give me a hand with this and then we can go up to my office."

With the boats tidied, Ben and the principal sat in the tiny room overlooking Ben's favourite place in the world—the water he sailed on.

"I have the dates and group numbers booked in for the first five weeks of the summer holidays, and I would like your help for as much of this as possible. Would you be willing to work for us this summer?"

Ben tried hard to look serious but the edges of his mouth flickered as he pictured the scene. For five glorious weeks he would be hanging out with his friends, sailing any boat he chose and to cap it all, getting paid for the privilege. "That would be great," he said, not trying to sound too excited.

"I do, however, need your parents' permission. Take these forms home now, and kindly ask your mom or dad to sign them for me."

Pocketing the forms and thanking the smiling sailing principal, Ben mounted his bike like a circus performer and rode home singing at the top of his lungs.

He walked in through his back door, still half expecting to be greeted by the big paws and wet tongue of his ancient golden retriever Painter who had died two months earlier. Instead, the familiar scene of a kitchen floor covered in plastic toys and the residue of a toddler's dinner stretched before him. As he shrugged off his jacket, he watched his mum juggling his baby sister Ruby, something in a saucepan on the stove and a telephone tucked under her ear.

Still talking into the cordless phone, completely oblivious to his presence, she said, "We can't put it off any longer. We must tell Ben what's going on." Before he could overhear any more of the conversation, his mum spun around and rather too brightly said, "Oh, hello, Ben," then hastily announced to the person on the other end of the line that they would talk later.

Ben wasn't sure whether to continue to pick his way over the minefield of discarded Fisher-Price items on the way to his room or wait to be filled in on whatever it was he didn't know about.

"That was your dad. He'll be home early tonight. We wanted to have a word with you."

"Okay, sure. What about?"

"Well, why don't we wait until Dad gets back then talk it through together?"

"I have some news, too. I just came from the watersports centre, and guess what?

"Ruby! No!"

The runny dessert that his sister was supposed to be eating splatter-sprayed in an impressive arc, from table to floor, to a substantial amount of wall as the yellow plastic bowl clattered to a rest at Ben's feet.

After the reverberations of the spinning bowl had died away, Penny looked up, "Sorry, what were you saying, Ben?"

Raising his voice to carry over the now impatient drumming of a spoon on the kitchen table, he said, "It's brilliant. I am going to—"

With hands pulling at her roots, not even glancing in his direction, she interrupted his excited flow for the second time, "What a mess. Why don't you tell me later, darling."

Back in the relative sanctuary of his room (at least Ruby couldn't climb the stairs on her own yet), remembering the overheard telephone call before World War III had broken out, Ben began to go through all the recent incidents, unfinished homework, the odd broken window and anything else slightly sticky that his parents may be holding against him. He couldn't think of much he'd done wrong lately, even the computer thing seemed to be more or less forgotten now. Besides, it wasn't his fault. One of the boys in his form had sent the link, and all he had done was click on it. So maybe he was being too hard on himself. For all he knew, they were going to give him something for being a wonderful son. Well, perhaps not. But wait a minute, he thought, maybe we are getting a new puppy. Or, better still, maybe Dad has finally seen the sense of buying him his own Topper!

Ben's mood perked up considerably at the thought of his own boat, but even so, there was a niggling little feeling stopping him from bothering to log on to chat as he had promised his mate Tony he would. Hearing his father's car pull up in the driveway outside his bedroom window, Ben began to panic.

Not sure whether to rush down and greet him or act aloof and totally unaffected by this pending announcement, Ben hung around at the top of the stairs and tried to listen in on any conversation coming from the kitchen. He couldn't hear anything, and as his heart seemed to be going twice the speed it should, he thought he may as well get it over and done with. The final thought that struck him as he got to the bottom step was, "Oh no, my mum's going to have another baby!"

Ruby was okay, as little sisters go. In fact, his sister was sometimes quite useful at tying his mum in knots so she gave him a break. Unfortunately, though, Ben was old enough to be useful, too. Somehow, he had been awarded the dubious responsibility of designated picker-upper of toys and other household objects used for Ruby's basketball practice (or that's what he assumed she was doing by the way they were hurled everywhere). He knew he was fast approaching babysitter age which would entail having to stay in while his parents went out at the weekend. He had wondered for a while if this may have an upside, as he had heard that babysitting jobs could pull in some serious revenue.

As he entered the kitchen, he saw both his parents sitting at the table.

"How was your day?" his dad asked.

"Okay, thanks." Suddenly remembering summer sailing, Ben continued quickly, "Guess what happened to me today?"

"Sit down, Son. You can tell me your news in a moment."

At this, Ben swore he could actually see his heart trying to punch its way out of his sweatshirt.

"We have a surprise for you."

The voice inside Ben's head cheered, "Yes!" as he quickly scanned through all the potential presents his dad could be referring to.

"I have been offered a new job."

He was instantly disappointed at not hearing the words "dog" or "boat."

"I guess that's good. So what's the surprise then?"

"Well, the new post is overseas."

Although Ben took his dad for granted like all nearly thirteen-year-olds, he did like him to be around occasionally. And as the main form of transport, he was essential to Ben's sporting and social life. The idea that he was going away was not great news.

"How long will you be gone for?"

"It's not a permanent move," Frank Johnston explained. "I have been asked to set up a new office for the firm in a developing area, so we can be the first to benefit from some expected offshore business there."

The word "offshore" was bantered about a lot when his dad was with his cronies from the office, but Ben just mentally filed it with all the rest of the legal jargon he associated with his dad's job. He was a lawyer, after all.

"That's cool."

"Actually, it gets much better. We are all going."

Once realising he wasn't in deep trouble or that he obviously wasn't the recipient of a shiny new Topper dinghy, Ben's heartbeat had more or less returned to normal. Now it seemed to stop.

"What do you mean?'

His parents continued to rattle on for almost an hour, getting embarrassingly enthusiastic about moving to some Caribbean island, miles from civilization (or at least Ben's civilization) for the whole summer, leaving home at the end of next week, to spend all of July and August on Kamaria, which was apparently a small, lightly

Eye of **the Storm**

populated island in the West Indies. Every time he heard about the so-called "delights of the Caribbean," Ben thought about the plans he had already made, in stone, for this summer holiday. Besides, they couldn't even get their facts straight, were they going to Kamaria, the Caribbean, or the West Indies, for heaven's sake?

In between chat about palm trees and multicoloured fish, Ben told his parents about the principal's offer of a five-week job, which they didn't seem that concerned about, nor did they seem to care about the sailing club's Open Week Regatta or, even more importantly, the Zone Squad training session in August (that he was convinced he would qualify for).

Just when he thought life couldn't get any more depressing, they hit him with the last piece of stunning news. They actually suggested that at the end of this tortuous, but admittedly sunny vacation, they would stay in Kamaria for two years, and he was coming back to England on his own!

Taking the helm back from Isaac, Ben increased the speed of the idling engine and headed further into the gap between the two pieces of harsh land, Scorpion Island and Black Cay, both bordered with unforgiving rock faces. He watched the narrow channel force the sea into a funnel-like space building taller, whiter, waves that climbed on top of each other to reach the other end. They were in the worst place possible right now, but if they could just make it through, it had to be a little calmer on the other side, didn't it?

Without warning, a rogue wave hit the four teenagers. A wall of blue water broke over the side of them. Kai was propelled head first across the small dory, and then there was a noise missing. The three others turned and stared at the silent motor, its throttle still in Ben's hand. Isaac leapt up and reached for the starting cord. He pulled and pulled, pumping the choke and the revs, but the outboard engine was waterlogged.

Charlie's face was grey with fear, her hair plastered to her cheeks. Kai continued to fiddle with the engine, but they all knew it was pointless.

Isaac turned to Ben, "So what now, eh? You the clever one, you got us here, now you get us drowned!"

"It's not my fault. You didn't have to come, anyway. You were the one that was calling us back, remember? Not wanting to be left on the beach."

The ridiculous argument pulled Charlie back to her senses.

"For heaven's sake, pack it in, you two. Fighting will not help. We are not going to drown! Let's calm down and decide what to do."

Both boys stared at the petite, blonde girl shouting at them and immediately fell silent.

Eye of **the Storm**

CHAPTER 2
GONE SAILING

Ben Johnston, for the most part, was a pretty cool kid, at least that's the impression he worked hard to maintain. He played most sports well, hung out with a good group at school and spent a substantial amount of time chatting online to his friends about girls and music. He was successful with his teachers; his grades were usually good. The rest of the kids liked him because he was the best at heading off a couple of the more gullible teachers onto a completely different subject until the class couldn't help but start to giggle, then eventually the room would collapse into fits of laughter when they knew that they'd managed to do it again.

Ben did, however, have a secret problem. One that for weeks at a time he could bury at the back of his mind and not think about. Sometimes it would rear its ugly head, but so far he had been able to deal with it. Nothing disgusting or terrible–just the fact that he had never slept a night away from one or the other of his parents.

Sleepovers were one sided; his friends always came to his house. The boys didn't mind or even really notice that he always found an excuse not to go round to theirs. His mum was pretty laid back, and she cooked great burgers or was happy for the guys to order in pizza and even eat in Ben's bedroom, so no one minded spending time at his place. He was pretty lucky with his electronics, too, owning some serious computer hardware and PSPs that Tony's family couldn't afford to buy. His iPod was docked into a set of Bose speakers that blasted out rock, pop or hip hop.

So why was it such a big deal? It wasn't like he was afraid of the dark, or he thought that vampires were going to come and swallow him up in their drooling mouths and torture him to death. Even he couldn't explain it out loud. He just wanted to sleep at home. No matter how tired he was, and even if he was with Tony or his aunt and uncle, he didn't want to stay. He knew that it made things difficult for his parents, and he was running out of believable excuses to convince his school friends that he wasn't totally lame, but he couldn't help it. He'd tried a few times to get over it and had twice fallen asleep at his grandparents' house when his mum and dad had driven him and Ruby over to be babysat while they went out. His grandmother had put him to bed thinking he'd be fine, but he'd woken up and felt so alone and unsafe. Ben had cried both nights until his dad came and picked them up.

It wasn't really that he needed his bed or room or stuff, even. It was almost like he imagined claustrophobia might feel like. He'd get this crushing feeling inside him to the point where it made him want to throw up. Each time he tried to face this in his mind, he felt like such a dork that he changed the subject quickly.

So far, he had gotten out of all school trips that involved overnight stays, faking sickness or just "forgetting" to tell his mum until it was too late to go. Hiding letters sent from his teacher and avoiding bringing his mates home in case they inadvertently talked about the trip in question were other tactics.

One time last year, faking an illness had backfired on him when he managed, completely unbeknownst to him, to pick a set of symptoms indicating impending appendicitis. This prompted his doctor to perform the classic examination for a suspected appendix ready to burst. You have to go through this personally to know how totally gross and embarrassing the procedure was. When the GP began pulling his rubber gloves on, and Ben realised what was about to go down, he had quickly changed his story about the acute pain in his right side and decided it was on his left lower abdomen after all. Unbelievably, this actually encouraged the guy. Suffice to say, Ben was fully examined in a way he hoped never to repeat and was found not to be in grave danger of an exploding appendix. The things he had to do to avoid sleeping out amazed even him sometimes.

Other than this secret fear, life was pretty good for Ben. Together with listening to music and messing with his PC, he had his sailing which right now was a big part of his life, and he intended on making it much bigger. Strangely, his secret fear had actually gotten Ben into sailing in the first place.

Two years ago, when he was 10, his form had been asked to pick a compulsory adventurous activity as part of their PE timetable. The choices turned out to be a watersports day at a local sailing school or a rock climbing experience at an outdoor activity park. Climbing sounded fun, but it involved a weekend trip with an overnight stay in accommodations at the park. Watersports it was. There and back in one day was much more convenient.

The day had turned out to be windy and wet. Most of his group wasn't very impressed with their drenched jeans and trainers under the naff, bright yellow waterproof trousers that they had been given to wear. They were taken for rides on small sailing dinghies by the staff in the morning and then sat around eating their packed lunches in very damp clothes, looking pretty pathetic whilst it poured with rain. The afternoon session involved one-person boats, and most of his mates easily cried off as their accompanying teacher seemed to have quietly slipped away for some peace and quiet, letting the sailing instructors take control. Ben didn't see the point of hanging around doing nothing any longer, so he took some notice of the guy's briefing and climbed precariously into a very small, completely unstable bathtub.

An hour later, he was hooked. At the time he wasn't sure why. He was a good swimmer and had gone fishing a few times with his grandfather (not that he'd ever actually caught anything). Fishing, that was an activity that defied all understanding. Standing on a pebbly beach in the middle of the night, in the middle of the winter, in the middle of a blizzard was not his idea of fun. Chucking a lead weight on the end of a line, baited with disgusting worms that he had to actually thread up the shaft of the hooks whilst this gross liquid oozed out of their squishy bodies was really beyond him. Especially when within spitting distance there was a local fish and chip shop with its lights blazing and steam coming out of the door each time a customer opened it, serving the best cod and chips in the world. Still, Granddad seemed to have fun, and Ben did like the old codger.

Sailing was completely different than riding in a fishing boat. The little sailboat he learned on was called an Optimist and designed for one kid to operate. It was really difficult to make it go in a straight line, and even the instructor didn't seem to have completely grasped the concept as only half of what he warned would happen actually did. Ben was sure from where this guy was standing—in a nice, stable, powerboat—everything was quite simple. There was something cool about being in charge, if only barely in control, of your own vessel, though. When Ben finally managed to maneuver this very small ship back to the jetty and not wrap it around two of his mates' boats that didn't seem to be doing quite so well, he was told by Tom, the instructor in the powerboat, that he had done great for his first time and should come back and do some more.

That was the start of a new sport for Ben. When he had asked his dad about sailing lessons on Saturday mornings, he had not gotten a great reception. The under-11s football team seemed to need him more, and Frank was into his footie. But Ben eventually convinced his dad to allow him to sign up for a set of six lessons, and while feeling the odd-one-out for the first couple of weeks, he increasingly enjoyed the freedom of sailing. During that summer holiday, he spent three weeks at the centre, earning some certificates and a logbook which recorded his time on the water and instructor's ticks in the boxes as he learned more stuff.

There were some perks to this sailing lark, too. Some of his new friends had parents that owned big boats and even yachts. They all hung out at the local sailing club next door to the watersports centre. He had been invited out for the day on Jason's dad's cruiser during that first summer, setting off really early in the morning and sailing to the next harbour along the coast. He'd discovered on that first trip that, unlike Jason, he didn't get seasick and could happily go down below and retrieve their lunch and drinks and any other errands Jason's dad asked him to do.

Gradually, the following spring, Ben plucked up the courage to enter his first race at the club. It was the same piece of water, and using a borrowed "Oppie," he thought that it couldn't be that different to what he normally did on a Saturday. He knew how to get around the buoys that were out there, so what could be so hard? He had kind of learnt some rules about who had the right of way in boats, but obviously these rules didn't count in this particular race, as if you were bigger and could shout loud, you got to go exactly where you wanted. At least this is how it seemed to Ben, and he may not have tried to race again—just gone back to poodling around on Saturday mornings, if he hadn't met Charlie. Charlie was a girl and was racing her souped up Oppie in Ben's first botched race attempt.

In fact to this day, she still gently teases him about his first race. Dead last and feeling incredibly small, he had gotten wrapped around the underwater line that held the buoy in place on the last lap. This meant that until he could do something about it—ideally like doing a Harry Potter and disapparating to the comfort of his lounge at home, trying to forget that he had ever seen a stupid dinghy—he was now the new race mark. As he sat in the bottom of his spinning tub, the rest of the fleet that started their race 20 minutes after his junior class came at him from all sides. He was completely surrounded by huge, fast, sleek white boats, all with frantic crews yanking out poles and shouting at each other and him as they hauled on pieces of string and brightly coloured spinnakers popped out of (or in some cases wrapped around), the sharp ends of the boats.

Charlie had seen Ben's plight, and after it was safe to approach the offending orange buoy, she'd doubled back on her course and sailed up to him, suggesting that he may like to lift his dagger board up a bit higher and all underneath would miraculously detach itself. Embarrassed, but very grateful that he wasn't going to have to send scuba divers down to untangle the mess, he obediently did as he was told by this girl who had already thrown her boat around in a tight circle and was on her way again waving, a little too confidently it seemed to him, in his general direction.

Hoping desperately that a sea monster would appear in front of him before he got to the finish line, putting him out of his misery once and for all, he sailed the last lap. Sadly, the sea monster didn't eat him, and he and his Oppie did come last. He was inwardly surprised, however, that hoards of the racing kids didn't come up to him afterwards and mock him, laughing at his predicament. One older sailor, who Ben had quietly hero-worshiped that summer, actually made some passing remark about "how awesome was that, being stuck in the middle of the Dragon fleet."

Whilst Ben was packing his boat up that afternoon, the girl came over and introduced herself as Charlotte, "but I preferred to be called Charlie," she said.

Ben made a show of being unperturbed by the battle with the buoy but did manage to get out a muttered "Ta for coming back," before she rejoined her crowd in the clubhouse.

Since then, Ben and Charlie had become friends. He hung out with her crowd in the clubhouse when he was there. She was the one who persuaded him to try again in the next junior race, giving him a pair of her old sailing gloves to use. Whilst trying not to make it too obvious, Ben followed her boat around that day and soon realized that maybe he did know a bit more than he thought. The following Sunday, he finished ahead of Charlie which made him feel so huge he could have burst. By the end of that series of races, he had worked his way up into the top five of the club Oppies and was spending most of his weekends messing around in boats at the watersports centre.

Last year, Ben's second summer as a sailor, he all but lived at the water's edge. Hanging at the sailing school got him chances to sail other dinghies, like the Toppers and two-person boats called Mirrors. He was growing tall and wasn't likely to stop any time soon as his dad was six foot three, so he soon much preferred the longer and more powerful Topper dinghy to the cramped Optimist. The Topper actually looked like a boat and resembled the ultimate in sailing as far as Ben was concerned—the Laser. They screamed in a breeze and were sick to sail.

Ben desperately wanted a boat of his own like some of his friends, and he frequently daydreamed about naming it something cool, upgrading the sail controls and plastering rock band stickers all over it. The dinghies used at the sailing school were battered and slow. So far, however, his requests for funding from his dad had fallen on deaf ears.

All his hard work and training had finally paid off and been rewarded when he was offered the job at the watersports centre. But now, instead, he was going to have to spend his summer on some island in the middle of nowhere. He hoped they had sailing there.

CHAPTER 3
VOLCANOES AND THE INTERNET

Losing his summer to some hot, sandy, mosquito-ridden island where he knew no one was bad enough, but he couldn't believe his parents were still seriously contemplating a boarding school for him in September. How could his own mother do that to him? It wasn't like she didn't know about his secret problem. It was her fault probably, he thought. Something she had deprived him of when he was a baby had to be the answer. Maybe he had been dropped on his head or something? He didn't know or care, but he was going to make sure that he was such a pain in the butt all summer that they wouldn't dare send him home alone.

Ben's determination definitely not to enjoy his summer was fueled not only by missing out on his sailing and earning power but also by the thought of not seeing his friends. He really didn't need any new ones as his father kept suggesting. He had plenty already. If his parents were so interested in dumping their only son in a boarding school, part of him wanted them to simply leave him in the UK now and be done with it. Although having said that, the other half of Ben was desperately trying to put off the insurmountable problem of how he was going to sleep at night on his own in this new school. At least going to Kamaria, or whatever the place was called, would delay that particular situation, and maybe in the meantime something would happen that would change his dad's work plans, or maybe the island would get hit by a hurricane, and all the new offices would be completely flattened.

Looking up Kamaria online hadn't enlightened Ben too much. Evidently, it was within the Caribbean chain and seemed to be set away from anywhere interesting. It had no satellite or cable TV although they were apparently coming soon. So was Christmas, right? He had been allowed to carry a laptop which his dad had brought home for him, but he soon realised that there were not going to be multiple Wi-Fi hotspots for him to tap into. How was he going to email Tony or Charlie? Chat and instant messenger probably hadn't even been heard of on this rock.

Judging by the limited images online, the island seemed to be surrounded by palm tree lined beaches, which even Ben had to admit looked amazing, with the Caribbean Sea on one side and the Atlantic Ocean on the other. This had struck Ben as weird. How did anyone know where one sea stopped and another ocean started? Was there a strange line of waves where the two met? Was one colder than the other? If you swam across the line would you get sucked into the Bermuda Triangle?

Kamaria was 26 miles long and kind of bent like a banana. According to the map that his dad had pinned on the kitchen wall, there seemed to be other tiny rocks quite close by. The website said that it was a volcanic island which sounded pretty dodgy to Ben, but the site went on to explain that it was formed millions of years ago out of volcanic rock from eruptions beneath the sea bed. Glad all that was done with, Ben could only assume that the smaller rocks or "cays" as they were called, were bits that had broken off or just flown a bit higher in the sky.

Whatever happened, this was not going to be a high-tech summer. Perhaps his granddad's fishing experiences would finally come in handy. Either way, at least it would be hot. His mother had talked non-stop the past week as they were packing about the clear blue sea and how she was going to get a wonderful tan. Big brother Ben had been nominated to teach Ruby how to swim. Actually, he had some quite novel ideas about that, one involving a pair of arm bands, a long piece of bungee cord and a palm tree!

Of course, the first thing the twelve-year-old had searched for on the internet was dinghy sailing. Unbelievably, there wasn't one mention of anything that floated apart from a few references to secluded bays where visiting, cruising yachts anchored overnight. No clubs or sailing schools—nothing! How could you live on an island and not go sailing? Ben's instructor Tom and the principal of his watersports centre had both tried to reassure him, telling him to go and have fun and not to worry about missing anything. They said he could still make use of his new assistant instructor status later in the year, and the south zone were hosting an open meeting for the junior classes in October just down the coast from his home club, so he still had the chance to make the squad.

He was secretly looking forward to a few things, like trying snorkeling for the first time. Maybe he'd have to make do with being under the water rather than on it. From what Ben could make out, most of the people lived at one end of the island around New Town. The word "town," Ben thought, was used very loosely, as there were no megastores, one post office (depicted as looking like his uncle's garden shed), no cinema, no bowling alley, no gym, one hotel, a small collection of industrial type offices—one of which his dad was going to work in—and a market that sold food. Heaven knows what sort of food. Let's face it: how could he live somewhere that had never heard of McDonald's?

Two Springer Spaniels, tongues lolling and the docked stubs of their tails comically wagging, leapt in relish over the bags and cases by the feet of the cued passengers. Ben asked one of the handlers what they were looking for, and she explained to him that these two dogs were trained specifically to sniff out explosives.

Frank, Penny, Ben and little Ruby were sitting at the departure gate waiting for someone to tell them to board the jet. Actually, Ruby wasn't sitting; she was hurling her cuddly frog at anyone who dared to pass within five metres of them. Ben had decided that being a toddler definitely had its advantages—she wasn't getting told off, and every time she got a direct hit, everyone (including the target) laughed, which obviously was the only encouragement any two-year-old was ever going to need to try harder and throw further.

The woman in the funny uniform at the front of the room brought Ben back to reality as she called the Johnston family's flight. Collecting up the hand luggage, which, of course, consisted mostly of Ruby's stuff, they obediently lined up.

The captain announced the flight time to Antigua as 7 hours and 48 minutes. Being jammed between his dad and some giant-sized guy in the outside seat was going to make this a very long trip for Ben. How come adults figured they had full rights to the arm rests? His dad had already commandeered the left arm and the giant was practically sitting on the right hand one. So where, exactly, was he supposed to put his elbows?

After an uneventful takeoff which reminded him of his sailing instructor who was always going on about "take offs and landings are the tricky bits," Ben figured that there may be an escape route to some personal space three aisles down the plane. He was still locked in, but with his fingers poised on the release of his seatbelt, determination to be first to leap for freedom and stretch out somewhere away from his dad and the massive guy making him sweat, he waited impatiently. Finally the bing sounded to let the passengers know that the seat belt sign had been turned off. Ben shot out of his seat like a 100-metre sprinter with a mumbled "excuse me," not, however, hanging around to be excused, and with his flailing iPod coming close to removing one of the flabbergasted guy's eyes, Ben hurdled the barrel-sized thighs and was free.

Pirates of the Caribbean: At World's End, seemed like an appropriate choice of in-flight movie. With three seats to himself, Ben spread out, making the most of the time away from his mum, who was currently further up the plane with a wailing Ruby, and his dad, who was now alone with the hulk. He figured they could both do what they liked with the arm rests now.

CHAPTER 4
FLYING HIGH

Captain Jack Sparrow flitted in and out of Ben's dreams later on that day, just before he was tersely awoken by a flight attendant looking down her nose at his feet propped up the third seat. Ben reluctantly returned to his assigned seat for landing. Squeezing in front of the behemoth's legs, he sat next to his dad and peered out of the window. Antigua was a fairly large island; he could see harbours and boats and rough-looking scrubland rushing past beneath him. Landing on a runway a fraction of the size of the one that he'd left behind was more worrying than he let on. He managed to resist the urge of gripping his dad's hand as his stomach kept trying to join his feet.

When he walked down the steps of the jumbo jet onto the tarmac, Ben could taste the air. It seemed chewy and thick. A hot breeze blew on his face. They had one and a half hours to wait at Antigua airport. The airport lounge was busy and cramped. No one in transit was allowed to go outside, and by the time they were ready to line up for the next flying lap, Ben had walked around the confining room what felt like five hundred times, getting to know intimately a bar that sold hotdogs and a collection of tiny stalls displaying magazines and books, rum and t-shirts and one that had hundreds of CDs for sale, which, after examination, all seemed to be reggae.

The last plane of their day was not at all impressive; it had only seven seats in it. The pilot was very chatty, a bit too much for Ben's liking, especially as Ben wasn't totally convinced that he hadn't been smoking something stronger than your basic cigarette before the flight. This particular flight was almost completely dedicated to the Johnstons with the exception of one man who boarded behind the family. The man demonstrated familiarity with the pilot and destination.

Ben had been informed that small planes were safer in the case of engine failure and that if they needed to, the things could glide to a safe landing. There was still something comforting, however, in the feeling of a Rolls Royce-powered, high performance, jumbo jet with hundreds of people onboard, cruising at a much higher altitude. Who cared if, ultimately, the monster aircraft would explode on impact, killing the entire passenger list and crew, not to mention anyone hanging around minding their own business in the vicinity of the crash landing, at least he wouldn't know anything about it.

He was just beginning to get his head around all this too close for comfort flying stuff as they were taxiing to the end of the runway for take-off when the guy in charge addressed him, "Close the door, man." Ben was speechless. Who in their right mind asked a twelve-year-old to take a huge responsibility like that for heaven's sake? What happened if he messed up that task? What if the door didn't close properly? What if someone fell out? But he did as he was asked and closed the door.

Apparently, the pilot was determined to develop this interactive flight technique. Soon after the shuddering vibrations caused by the steep climb over the sea below eased, he proceeded to ask Ben's father if he wanted to take the controls and fly the thing. Ben had known it was a mistake when he watched his dad climb into the front seat as they boarded. There were hundreds of dials and switches just waiting to be fiddled with by a nosy lawyer. Come to think of it, his dad had always fancied himself as a bit of an aviator; he'd even loaded a flight simulator game on to Ben's PC at home once, but fortunately gave up after a couple of attempts, complaining, "It's too complicated. What does it think I am, a pilot?"

Next thing he knew, his dad had his hands on the joystick thing between his legs, and the pilot's hands were off the one in front of him. After what felt like a lifetime later, Ben relaxed a little as the happy pilot took the controls back from Frank Johnston and turned to the rest of his passengers pointing out Kamaria below.

As the tiny aircraft lined up its approach with a runway that didn't appear to be visible to the naked eye, Ben craned his neck to look down on what was to be his home for the next two months. It looked small and green.

Bumping gently between three wheels, the island hopper landed gracefully on a rough piece of concrete with dirt and bushes along one edge and rocks covered in lapping waves lining the other. A wooden structure served as the terminal building. Bizarrely, on its flat roof, people stood waving, presumably not at him as they had fizzing bottles of champagne in their hands. Judging by the way they were celebrating the arrival, by the time their buddy joined them on the roof, there wasn't going to be much bubbly left.

No moving carousels carried luggage from their light aircraft, just two guys throwing bags from the back of an open jeep onto the wall which ran alongside the customs and immigration room. One large man in a dark uniform sat behind a desk looked in turn from them to their passports as they traipsed through. The unsmiling official then got up and walked very slowly to the next chair which was placed behind a yellow line painted on the floor. Here he took a form from Ben's dad and asked them where they were going to stay. The Kamaria Hotel was, in truth, the only visitor accommodation on the island.

As the family walked past the immigration and customs officer, he nodded and said, "Enjoy our island, and be careful, Benjamin."

Feeling just a touch spooked that the huge man had noted his name, let alone spoken to him personally, Ben stuttered, said, "Thank you, sir" and caught up with his mum and Ruby in a hurry.

The lone passenger that had silently shared their plane from Antigua was apparently the recipient of the celebration on the roof. As they watched, three of the welcome party rushed to take bags from the man, and a woman gave him a rather overbearing hug.

Surveying his surroundings with his knapsack strapped to his back and a larger bag between his ankles, Ben saw flat open land in the foreground, encircled by tall, green hills. He suspected that they may even be classed as mountains. There were no buildings other than the one behind him that he'd just walked through. The ground was rough; a combination of sand, rock and dirt. Any grass was sparse and unkempt. The light was rapidly turning warm and soft, the sky responding by displaying blue, orange, red and black broad brush strokes. The dwindling sun threatened to disappear behind a rock on the water. Or maybe that was a cay? There was no noise, well perhaps that wasn't entirely true; rather, there was no familiar noise. No traffic, music, people, telephones or industrial work in progress, but there was something. Ben assumed he could hear birds, but they had a very strange call, a high pitched chirp. Then he realised he could hear a grasshopper. No, two or three or maybe hundreds.

CHAPTER 5
THE FISHERMAN

At five in the morning, local time, Frank Johnston had already left for his new workplace. He figured he might as well take advantage of his jet-lag affected sleeping patterns by getting to work early. In two minutes, he walked from the hotel to the building leased by his British-based firm. His office had a picture window framing the harbour, a view to die for anywhere in the world, let alone a fledgling law subsidiary in a newly developing territory. He wasn't sure how this offshore facility would pan out, but he could see no reason why he and his family should not take advantage of a two-year contract. With his home in England already housing a tenant and his own salary reflecting the "inconvenient" overseas move, he would actually end up making extra money, too. He did worry about Ben, however, who, after his summer in the Caribbean, would be taking a huge, independent step by enrolling in a boarding school in the UK. Knowing that Ben worried about this and the anticipation of being away from him and Penny, Frank prayed that the next two months would provide new experiences and a safe freedom for his son that sadly no longer existed for young people in the modern, so-called developed world. Ben would be fifteen when the foreign posting ended, which meant that he would probably stay in his boarding school until after he'd finished his GCSEs. It was certainly going to be an important time for them all.

Still working on UK time, Ben's watch said ten minutes past ten in the morning. A five hour time difference meant that it was actually only ten past five local time. Adjusting his watch, he gazed out of their rather small hotel room window. A pale blue sky was emerging over a harbour with a handful of boats swinging with the wind, not one the same size or shape, and most of them looking like tired fishing vessels. They had pots made from chicken wire stacked one on top of the other and tall floats tied along their sides.

Holidaying in Cornwall had partially prepared Ben for the view, but this harbour was larger and less congested. A jetty pushed into the sea across the street almost dead opposite his window. A couple of the fishing boats were moored alongside it, moving back and forth with the gentle swell. A building stood close by within a rough car park, and even at this time in the morning, a hum of activity was emerging from it, people meeting and talking in anticipation of the coming day. The jetty seemed to be the centre of attention. As Ben lifted his baby sister up to the window, he watched an open-topped blue passenger boat come into view from around the corner of his horizon. A minute later, it was mooring up on the opposite side from the fishing boats to what was, in fact, the main dock on the island.

The sea was a deep blue with gentle waves sliding up and down boulders on either side of the town dock. Just like on those West Country holidays in England, he immediately wanted to climb and explore the rocks and the pools he imagined were hidden amongst them. Further around the water's edge was a sandy beach with a few sailing yachts anchored off of it. Ben ached to climb his way to that beach. Beyond were the two headlands of New Harbour. Their edges, resembling snow, were made from soft, fluffy wave crests, surging on the high, rugged cliffs that rose up to green hills and down into the depths of the Caribbean Sea. As the boy and his little sister watched, the ferry spewed out people from somewhere else and waited while passengers that had been chatting on the dock stepped aboard.

Have you ever noticed that sea gulls always stand head to wind? Well this particular species in Kamaria certainly did. Ben had never noticed this phenomenon before at home, but these smart birds stood like soldiers on parade, incredibly immaculate and completely identical. All pointing directly into the breeze, they were much smaller than the birds from the south of England. Ben mentally christened the one closest to him "Humphrey." He wondered if he'd see him around again, sniggering to himself that he wouldn't know if he did. Time to get out of this hotel room, he thought. He was talking to himself.

After a lot of persuasion and conversation with his mum about the usual boring stuff—safety on the roads, safety on the rocks, safety in the water…blah blah blah, and a makeshift breakfast from the café-type place next door, Ben had been given a pass. He was free! But in which direction was anybody's guess. He was standing at the bottom of the U-shaped natural harbour and was probably equal distance from either headland. He had a bottle of water, a packet of crisps, two snack bars, a towel in his backpack and until lunchtime to explore. Great, he thought, that's three hours without Ruby.

Setting off on the sea side of the road, which he guessed at some point had been tarmacked, he followed the dirt edge. The traffic was light and slow moving. Most of the vehicles were 4-wheel drive, and all of them had definitely seen better days. The gulls had flown from the dock and were patrolling the inner harbour's skies. He could also see larger seabirds circling higher. Ben ended up opting to walk to his left, east, he thought. Up ahead, he could see the end of the road where the town transformed into open land with just a few individual homes scattered along a rough track. They were low houses that had balconies around them. Nothing more than two stories high appeared to be the fashion here.

Although not a particularly shy boy, with the exception of when he was around teenaged girls, Ben had never been on his own out of the UK before. Sure, he'd visited other countries around Europe, where they spoke different languages and dressed and acted differently, but he'd never walked around alone in another country, especially one where the people, culture and climate were so different from England. He heard snippets of conversation between the islanders as he passed by, and although he tried, he had difficulty understanding their dialect. He could maybe make out one in twenty words. He wondered if they'd be able to understand his UK accent. Also, several adults had said, "Good Morning" to him as they strolled by him on the street, as if they knew him. This confused him even more.

He was getting further away from the town now, and the track began to move a little inland away from the water. He was determined to stay by the rocks, so that's what he did. The climbing was easy enough—just boulders to scramble over— the yellow beach didn't seem to be getting closer, though, and Ben was already wondering if he was going to make it there and back in three hours. Walking in just his shorts and trainers as the sun grew stronger, he had already drunk half his water supply. Stopping for a swim off the boulder-strewn coast was becoming very appealing. Although the swell was not harsh, he could see that it would be tricky to get in and especially climb out from the rocky edge. The water displayed so many different shades of blue and green as the morning went on, and Ben could see the bottom clearly now. No sand, just more rocks and what he thought had to be reef. Even to his untrained eye, it looked exceptionally sharp.

He was debating risking the plunge into the sea to cool off, wondering if his mum would kill him if he kept his trainers on when he spotted a boy standing on a large flat rock ahead. The boy was peering into the water below his feet, holding a long sack of string. Abruptly, the boy launched the sack over his shoulder grasping a rope attached to the head of the bundle, swinging it like a cowboy's lasso. Then, right before Ben's eyes, he let go, and the spinning white sack opened in the air beyond the rocks before gracefully landing, having spread out into a perfect circle, stretching at least two metres across. As it hit the sea, it was dragged below by tiny lead weights sewn around the edge of what was obviously a net. The contraption sank from the outside in, being held just underneath the surface of the water by the rope that the boy was still holding. While Ben continued to watch, fascinated by this display, the young fisherman hauled on the line in his hands, and the net gathered together from the middle as it was dragged up and towards the rock that the boy stood on.

Ben, though becoming a little self-conscious that it looked like he was spying on the kid, was reluctant to move from his spot as he continued to watch the net exit the water carrying hundreds of tiny passengers. Some of the fish managed to fall free, but most were trapped inside. The boy continued to drag his haul up to a bucket standing beside him before dropping the net and its contents inside.

To Ben, that seemed infinitely more sensible and rewarding than the way his grandfather fished. The catch was huge in number, but the squirming fish were small. It reminded him of one time when he went to a restaurant with his parents, and he'd watched with disgust as his mum ate a plate of tiny fried fish including (unbelievably) the heads! He wondered now if that was the way they had been caught. He certainly couldn't imagine catching each individual fish on a rod and line. It looked like a cool thing to have a go at; he figured he could do it easily. As he was considering this, the boy turned and waved at him.

The next thing Ben was aware of was being very wet. How lame can you get? When he raised his hand to wave back, he had lost his balance, fallen off his perch and was thrashing around trying to regain his footing on something slippery. About the same time, it occurred to him that, yes, his mum would kill him if he got his brand new trainers wet.

Laughing, the boy with the fishing net leant over a rock, reaching out his hand close to where Ben was trying to get some traction on the rocks. Hoping he could pretend it was an intended dip in the sea, being the new kid on the block, Ben was reluctant to take the offer of a helping hand from this still giggling dude. Eventually, having to admit he wasn't making much ground up the slippery face of the boulders on his own, Ben grasped the boy's arm and was pulled to his knees on the shore, grazing all his exposed skin on the way.

"Thanks," Ben said, looking bedraggled but much more in control of his arms and legs now. He grinned lopsidedly at his rescuer. "I'm Ben."

"You on vacation?" The boy asked.

"Kind of. Well, I had to come with my parents for the summer. My dad is working here now."

"Cool, man. You wanna fish?" Ben realised the boy hadn't told him his name yet.

"Wicked. But I don't have long. I have to be back in town in an hour, and it'll take me that long to walk it."

"We catch a ride. Me have to go see my uncle in West End." Ben assumed that catching a ride meant with a friend or his parents or someone. He wanted to act cool and not too concerned about getting back to his mum on time in front of this kid, but he also knew in his heart it would be unfair to let his mum worry about him. Besides, if he messed up on his first day, he'd risk being grounded, and he had too much exploring to do to lose his freedom so soon.

Eye of **the Storm**

"Look, the bait fish there." The local boy was pointing over Ben's shoulder into the water.

"How do you know?"

Making a weird sucking noise with his teeth he said, "'Cause the pelicans are diving."

"Right," he said, then to himself, asked, "How was I supposed to know that?"

The boy held out his net, and Ben, realising that the thing was much bigger up close, wondered if it was going to be quite as easy as it had looked. The birds were definitely trying to tell him something—they were crashing into the sea from amazing heights, beak first, some of them more elegantly than others. What if I catch a pelican? he thought.

"Look there, throw, throw."

Ben heaved the bundle above his head and made an attempt at throwing it towards the feeding frenzy underway in front of him. He needn't have worried about catching a pelican—just as the net had begun its flight upwards, it stopped abruptly like someone had pressed freeze frame, and instead of spinning weightlessly through the sky to land on hundreds of waiting fish, it dropped like a stone directly onto Ben. It seemed like he was destined to be the butt of this kid's fun today, as peering through the net wrapped around his face, he could see the kid rolling around holding his stomach, killing himself laughing again.

Getting a little tired of being the entertainment of the moment, Ben ripped at the disgusting smelling mesh around him, trying to throw it at the grinning boy.

"Okay, okay. What's so hilarious? It's not like I need that useless skill to get through life. I'm out of here. I have things to do." Ben stomped away from the fishing rock back towards town. He was hot, thirsty and angry. His trainers squelched with every step, and his backpack was still dripping down the backs of his legs. Determined not to slow down, he heard the black kid yell at him.

"It didn't work 'cause you were standing on the rope!"

Ben kept clambering, ignoring the kid, and then he heard, "You wanna ride?"

Still fuming about being made an idiot, he hesitated at that question. His shoes had been rubbing at his heels for a while before he fell in the sea, and now the salt water was making the raw spots sting like crazy. He'd love a ride, but was he going to get laughed at again and in what would he ride? he wondered. In the end he gave in and yelled in a cocky voice, "In what?"

"Soon come," was the only reply.

According to the kid, who still hadn't told Ben his name, hitchhiking was the normal thing to do on the island. Apparently, that's how most of the kids got to school. An old pickup appeared in a cloud of dust from behind them as they waited by the side of the track. It slowed to a stop and the kid leapt in the back. He motioned Ben to follow, and before he had both legs in, the truck was moving again. No one had said anything to anyone at all, but now they were bumping around in the bottom of the vehicle sliding around on some old sacks. Taking off his soggy trainers, he looked out into the harbour and watched as the clumsy pelicans crashed into the sea popping back up with bloated throats. There were two other types of seabird feeding other than the gulls he had seen earlier.

For something to say he asked, "What are those birds called?" He was pointing towards some very sleek birds, diving like arrows, barely breaking the surface of the water as they disappeared for a few seconds before coming back up head first instead of the Pelican's butt-first technique.

"Boobies."

"Excuse me?" Ben questioned with a smile developing on his face, not sure if he had heard right.

"Boobies. Brown ones. Brown boobies."

Ben had heard right and began to giggle.

The boy looked at him straight faced and said, "What's up?"

From this reaction, Ben decided not to elaborate on why he thought "brown booby" was a hilarious name for a bird.

Almost frightened to be told what the other species of bird gliding over the harbour was named, he didn't bother to inquire. New Town was up ahead, and he could see the ferry dock. It seemed that was where the guy driving the truck wanted to go, too, as the pickup pulled into the makeshift car park. Ben jumped out quickly in case the driver took off again without all of him being safely away from the wheels and then turned to look at the boy still sitting inside.

"So, you staying there?"

"Go to West End to my uncle's house. He wants bait to catch pot fish from his boat."

"Okay, I'll see you around then. What's your name?"

"Isaac. See you tomorrow."

The truck driver finished talking to another man through a glassless window, revved the rattling engine and drove off. Wonder how he figures he's going to see me tomorrow? Ben thought. As he turned to look across at the hotel, his thoughts turned very rapidly back to how loud his mum would shout when she found out his new trainers were drenched.

Eye of **the Storm**

CHAPTER 6
CREEPY CRAWLIES

Ben spent the rest of the afternoon watching Ruby while his mum shopped in the market. He pushed his sister around the shop in a battered trolley, not overly impressed with the items on the shelves. In fact, he really couldn't find anything that he particularly recognised; it seemed that it was mostly American food, and the rest was labeled in Spanish. He did throw a box of Cheerios into the shopping basket because this morning at the hotel, his choice of breakfast was a chocolate muffin or a meat pastie.

They were all planning to go and see their new rental home when his dad finished work that evening. The next day, Ben and his mum would start cleaning and sorting out the rooms. That way, they would be out of the hotel by the following night. Ben was trying extra hard to be cooperative since he had gotten back from his aborted fishing adventure. His mum had, of course, gone ballistic about his shoes which were presently stationed on the tiny hotel balcony with paper stuffed in them, drying out. Scoring points keeping Ruby amused in the food market was a start, but he knew he would have to toe the line at the new house tomorrow. At least he had an excuse not to actually participate in the housework as he was a great deal more valuable as a babysitter than a cleaner.

Frank turned up around 4:30, just after Ben had given up trying to get online from any Wi-Fi hotspots around the hotel. He had resorted to playing Magic Ball 2 on the laptop when he noticed his dad climbing out of an ancient pickup truck on the street outside. He surreptitiously pulled the newspaper out of his trainers, hoping to not have to go through that conversation again and ran outside to meet him.

"How was your day?" his dad asked.

"Good, thanks. Do you have internet set up at your office yet?"

"No, the telephone company is coming in on Friday to hook us up."

Ben's face fell. That was two more days away. How was he supposed to survive until then?

"Come on, get your mum and sister. Let's go look at our new house."

Driving west from the ferry dock, they headed along the coast road before turning right at the edge of town, onto a steep, rough track. The old truck began to crawl upwards. From the open bed of the vehicle, where Ben was sitting, he had a spectacular aerial view of New Town and the harbour spreading out below. He could see where he had met Isaac on the rocks and the beach he had been aiming for that morning. As they climbed, he watched the blue ferry leaving the dock and heading back out to sea again. With miniature passengers sitting on the top deck, the ferry looked like a toy far below them. On the peak of the mountain, Ben could see a complete three hundred and sixty degrees around him. The island, with its many shades of green, dense forest, appeared to float on a carpet of still, blue ocean.

Sailing off the far side of the island was a yacht with three masts and lots of sails. He thought this may be a schooner. He had seen a similar one at home, used as a sail training ship. The school kids that crewed her slept in hammocks and ate around huge wooden tables where there once stood loaded cannons. The proud schooner could have easily been a pirate ship. He thought of Captain Jack Sparrow again, with that useless compass that only pointed at what the owner most desired. If this place had internet and Pizza Express, that's where his compass would be pointing right now.

Driving along a ridge, high on the hilltop, the family could see amazing bays on both sides of the pickup. Thousands of metres below, Ben could pick out the vibrant colours of the coral reefs that lined the seabed. In some cases, the reefs protected the bays by forcing the swell to break away from the beaches, creating flat, perfect, turquoise lagoons that were just begging him to dive into their crystal clear depths. Ben physically ached with the need to get down to one of those beaches and swim. He didn't want to see any stupid apartment.

Being thrown against the rear window of the truck was not fun. His dad really should have given him some warning before he braked like that. Straightening himself up and rubbing his shoulder, he saw the reason for the emergency stop—goats! Loads of them wandering around in the middle of the not very wide road.

"You okay back there?" shouted his mum.

"Yeah, fine. Aren't they supposed to be in a field somewhere?"

"I don't know. I think they're probably allowed to roam around on Kamaria."

"Great. Maybe someone should teach them to look both ways before they cross the road!" (Ben was the only one that thought this amusing).

Every now and again, there were residences along the way, set back in the trees with people sitting around on old chairs or wood piles, unwinding at the end of their day. A man with a machete was chopping the tops off a pile of coconuts as they drove by. There was a group of young children crowding around him, presumably waiting for their share of the fruit. None of them wore shoes. Neither had Isaac, now that he thought about it. Ben liked coconut. At least the ones in Sainsbury's anyway. But they were brown, and these things were bright green. He figured he'd climb a palm tree tomorrow and pick one himself to try.

Eye of **the Storm**

Turning down a left hand track, the vehicle bounced and groaned over a narrow lane. They followed tight, switchback corners, the view below now completely obscured by impenetrable trees and shrubs. After several painful minutes in the back of the truck, Ben's jaw dropped in sheer wonder as the most gorgeous bay appeared.

"Hey, are we going down there, Dad?"

"Yes, I think so. I hope I turned in the right place. This map David drew seems a little vague. Look out for a house on the right hand side, Ben."

"Okay," Ben said, but he couldn't take his eyes off the beach. Reef filled the bay, dotted with stretches of sandy bottom as it wound its way to shore. He could make out every type of blue imaginable in the water together with the washed out purples, oranges and yellows of living coral resting beneath. The beach was lined with tall palm trees all bending the same way—pointing their heads towards the lapping shoreline. Behind the pale sand, low scrubby bushes gave way to rock faces that etched the boundaries of the oval bay.

The truck was nearly on the beach when his mum yelled, "There. Is that it?"

"You mean, we're living here?" Ben squeaked not quite in control of his excitement. His dad veered off the track onto an even narrower one that actually was a driveway to a squat, rather neglected house. It had the now familiar veranda all the way around the front, with a hammock hanging precariously from the roof at one end. The windows were small and shuttered closed, but the door was open. Actually, there was a framed mesh, extra door that came first, which was shut. Ben and Ruby had discovered the delights of mosquito bites in bed last night, and she was nursing some nasty inflamed bumps today. He guessed this screen was to stop the buzzing insects. His dad double-checked the map and description on the paper in his hand (there were no addresses on Kamaria and apparently no postman either). Having done the trip personally now, Ben could well imagine why any mail for him was not going to be personally delivered to this particular gate.

Pulling open the screen door, his dad walked inside. The rest of the family followed. It was not like his home in England, that was for sure. This place was a bit tatty. Flowery patterned, thin curtains drooped from grubby elastic stretched over windows that were made up of narrow pieces of glass that overlapped, flattening onto themselves. A rusty fridge and cooker stood in a kitchen area, and some cane settees faced each other around a rather scratched-up coffee table. Three doors led off the main room, two bedrooms and a bathroom.

"It smells weird," Ben muttered to himself.

His dad threw open a back door that led down two steps to an overgrown yard, littered with broken stuff, including what looked like a very old outboard motor with no propeller or engine cover.

As Ben peered over his dad's shoulder at the back garden, a scream came from behind them. They swung around to see his mum clutching a cupboard door in the kitchen. The cause of the outburst, a very large, black cockroach, ran across the tiled floor towards the front door, followed in hot pursuit by Ruby. The insect neatly ducked the bottom of the screen door and disappeared. Although the screen didn't seem to be very effective at keeping insects at bay, it did stop the toddler.

"My heavens, that was disgusting."

"It was just a cockroach. They don't hurt you. It's to be expected. The place has been empty for months. We'll get some spray tomorrow and fumigate."

Ben checked out his room, it smelt the same—musty. There was nothing in the room except a double bed and a built-in wardrobe. He turned the handles on the side of each of his windows and the panes of glass sprang away from each other letting in some air. They faced the west side of the bay. Not a bad view, he thought. His parents' room was bigger and had an extra single bed for Ruby. At least it was to be them that would share with her.

Bored of the house, Ben stepped back onto the front porch gazing over coarse grass and scrubby bushes that gave way to almost white sand that, in turn, disappeared into the sea. On the horizon was an orange glow, enclosed by a pink and blue sky so big it threatened to squash him. This aerial display, he was to discover, was caused by the daily process of the sun going down.

"You can see why this is called Sunset Cove, can't you?" asked his dad from somewhere close behind him.

Penny Johnston locked the door on the way out. Ben wasn't sure why she had bothered as there was no other living sole around and nothing to steal. Maybe she was trying to keep the cockroach from returning to its cupboard.

The return journey was less interesting as it was dark. Ben rode inside the pickup cab, squashed up between the front seats and the rear window. His mind had switched off. He only vaguely listened to his parents' conversation while he daydreamed about pirates.

"I like it, but it's a bit cut off, isn't it?" his mom asked. "Once you leave for the office with the car, we are stuck."

"You can come with me in the mornings if you want the car then come back at the end of the day and pick me up."

Penny was uncertain about being so cut off from civilization. She was none too sure about the local wildlife, either. Ruby had a bad habit right now of putting everything in her mouth. Penny couldn't bear to think about what would have happened if Ruby had caught that grotesque roach.

"What if we have a problem? What if the kids are taken ill?"

Eye of **the Storm**

"Look, this place is getting its wireless communication sorted impressively quickly. I will have two cell phones for us by tomorrow night. The cottage hospital and the single ambulance are going to respond in just the same way wherever you are. We discussed this before we left home, remember? We agreed to think of it as an adventure. The children are going to spend every day playing on a safe beach. Ruby can learn to swim, and Ben will love exploring the cove. You did say you wanted some peace and quiet, right?"

"Okay, okay, we'll try it. Maybe I'll write that book I've always talked about."

The next morning, Ben still woke up early but full of ideas about exploring Sunset Cove. Even if he had to drag Ruby along while his mum did the cleaning (and boy, did she have some cleaning to do), it would be fun.

Pulling on his shorts, he padded over to the unopened box of Cheerios on the counter. Ripping the cardboard at the top of the cereal packet, Ben tipped a large portion of cheerios into the milk waiting in the bowl. While watching Ruby play with her favourite plastic truck, he absentmindedly scooped up an overflowing spoonful of his breakfast and opened his mouth. As the spoon was about to disappear into the gateway to his starving stomach he glanced at the bowl. The contents were moving.

During the same split second that his lips closed around the loaded spoon, insects flew from the Cheerios box in front of him. Fortunately for all concerned, Ben was standing next to the narrow balcony, and as he spat the contents of his mouth in a style not dissimilar to a firehose on full blast, he managed to direct most of it out the open door.

"Ben! What are you doing?"

"The Cheerios are alive! Look!" Pointing at small black creatures making their escape from the innocent looking box still standing on the counter, Ben continued to spit imaginary insects from his mouth.

"Frank! Look at this." She yelled at her husband.

"What is all the fuss about? I'm trying to shave and get to work." Grimacing slightly as he peered into the offending cereal box, he admitted, "Oh I see, I think they may be weevils."

"That's just charming. You can't even get a decent breakfast in this dump!"

"Ben, calm down, they are harmless. In the olden days, the crews on the galleons used to find them in their dry biscuits and eat them as desperately needed protein."

"Thanks, Dad, but if I discover myself in need of extra protein I'll boil an egg."

Penny threw the box in the bin and washed her hands.

Eye of **the Storm**

CHAPTER 7
SUNSET COVE

Having picked up more stuff from the market in town, Ben and Penny loaded the truck with supplies and swimming gear and belted Ruby inside the cab. They used the same directions as yesterday afternoon, but this time, being much earlier in the day, the sun was brighter and the colours even more vivid as they retraced their route to the family's new summer home.

Knowing that he would have full responsibility of keeping his little sister happy while his mum worked in the house, Ben mused over the idea involving palm trees and a bungee cord. Trouble was, he hadn't noticed any elastic in the shop in town, so that wasn't going to work. It couldn't be that difficult to keep Ruby amused in this setting. She liked to dig holes, and she could make a giant sandcastle. That would take her all morning.

After they arrived and unpacked everything out of the truck, including an ice box full of cold drinks, Ben held Ruby's hand as he wandered over to a big log that used to be a coconut tree and sat on it. Ruby could walk pretty well, although she always seemed top heavy, falling flat on her face every now and again. Sitting on his perch with Ruby on her hands and knees in the sandy dirt in front of his feet, he noticed activity close to the dive bombing sea birds. Something was emerging from the water, small triangles flashed around the edges of the darker blue area. If you blinked you missed them, but they were definitely there. Then he saw it, a big fish rolling around a floating pelican. The shiny triangles were fins and tails belonging to these monsters–they must have been at least a metre long, each. Ben realised as he stood on the log for a better view that the birds were feeding on the same breakfast as the prowling life below the surface—bait fish. Memories, mostly embarrassing ones, of yesterday's encounter with Isaac and the net came flooding back. As he watched, the drifting pelicans digested their brunch whilst the boobies continued to dive. They were so fast and streamlined as they simultaneously pierced the sea in search of live food swimming below that they reminded Ben of the Red Arrows display team with their perfect synchronization.

Along the coastline to his left, Ben could make out the pink rooftops of a couple of big houses on the hill and just one small dwelling on the opposite side of the cove.

This one was almost on the sand and had what looked like a fishing boat moored close by. The sun was getting stronger. His mum had insisted in plastering Ben with sun block earlier, and judging by the burning sensation on his exposed skin, that was probably a better idea than it had seemed at the time.

The backdrop to the perfect beach was the now-familiar low, untidy shrub and a kind of grass that prickled your feet. Behind this, palms swayed in the hot breeze before dense, dark green trees took over, leading up the mountain. It reminded him of the *Treasure Island* movie he'd seen. He began to wonder what secrets that thick, mysterious, undergrowth was hiding.

Torn between swimming in the inviting, clear, cool sea and exploring the uninhabited land behind him, Ben walked back to the house with Ruby who was dragging a stick she'd picked up. Getting wet was definitely up first. Apart from his accidental entry off the rocks yesterday, he hadn't had a swim since he'd arrived. He found his new surf shorts and persuaded his mum that Ruby needed a cold drink. While she had that, he would just go for a quick dip.

Ben ran the width of the beach and dived underwater. It felt so good. He swam, ducking under the surface like a young seal, and then lazily treading water, gazed towards the place where the dark blue of the ocean met the pale blue of the sky. For the first time, his mind registered a small island interrupting the perfectly straight line of the horizon. Half closing his eyes against the intense morning light, he could see no buildings or signs of life. Maybe that was Treasure Island.

Turning to look back at his house framed by palms and smaller, round-leafed bushes, he could see his mum waving at him. It wasn't a 'Hi, hope you're having fun in the sea' wave; rather, it was a 'Come and get on with your babysitting job' kind of wave. So, reluctantly, he waded out of the shallows, feeling the powdery sand shift between his toes with each slow step. As he walked to his front door, he noticed a dog bounding around further along the cove, seemingly on its own.

Retrieving Ruby and some plastic buckets and spades, he trudged back down to the water's edge and began showing her how to make sandcastles. Each one he made, looking so perfect when he carefully lifted the bucket clear of the molded sand sculpture, Ruby promptly jumped on. His little sister definitely had a destructive streak in her. After the first dozen crushed castles, he turned his back to collect some more water in the bucket when a high pitched scream struck his ears. Jumping out of his skin, he turned back to see that Ruby had been frightened by a wet, hairy nose planted unceremoniously on the back of her neck.

The dog Ben had seen earlier had obviously decided to join in the sandcastle demolition project. It was quite tall, but not as stocky as Ben's old retriever Painter. Its short coat was uncannily close in colour to the surrounding beach. A long tail held high wagged at the children as his handsome white-cheeked head panted and seemed to laugh. Ben knew to be wary of strange dogs, and he looked around again for the owner, but there was no one in sight. The animal sat down next to Ruby as she ignored him and returned to the hole she was digging. Speaking quietly, Ben offered his hand for the dog to sniff, the dog responded then jumped up and trotted off towards the sea. Ben watched as he waded in waist deep (if dogs have waists) and then stood very still as if in a trance staring at the water just below his snout. Looking comical as he remained completely motionless, evidently braced for something, the dog struck, thrusting his head underwater and frantically wagging his tail. His head emerged dripping but without any sign of a prize. For ages the dog continued his game in the shallows. Curious to catch a glimpse of what the canine eyes could see, Ben got closer, but all the boy could imagine, after studying this display for a while, was that he was trying to eat shadows.

The young dog hung out with Ben and Ruby as they played on the beach, and it splashed around in the warm sea with them each time they needed cooling off. Eventually Penny called from the shade of the house, broom in hand, letting them know that she had made sandwiches. Ben picked up the toddler, threw her over his shoulder and ran up the hot sand, eager for lunch and something out of the cooler. Ruby loved it when her brother carried her like that, and by the time Ben dumped her off his back onto the log she was giggling madly. The dog had followed at a respectful distance; his casual gait making his movements look totally effortless.

"Where did the dog come from?"

"He just appeared. He's really friendly. He's been playing with us all morning."

His mum frowned. "He must belong to somebody. Don't encourage him around here. You don't know what he'll do."

"He's fine. He'll probably go home soon." Already subconsciously attached to the dog, Ben wondered why he didn't have a collar or anything.

The children munched on ham and cheese sandwiches made with strangely sweet-tasting bread whilst their new companion sat smartly at attention on the sand, gazing longingly at the food. He didn't get close enough to make it look like he was begging, but rather left enough distance to be polite and not to be immediately regarded as a nuisance by the adult. It worked. Surreptitiously, having glanced over his shoulder to make sure his mum was not looking, Ben threw the crusts of a sandwich towards the patient animal. After gratefully retrieving the tidbits, the dog sat again, and wagged his tail, brushing a pattern in the sand.

This would have all gone unnoticed by Ben's Mum if Ruby had not decided to join in and promptly (without looking over her shoulder to check the coast was clear) hurl a whole sandwich towards the dog. Ben couldn't stop her in time, and it would have been way too much to ask the dog not to grab and devour the gift in one slick movement.

"What are you doing? Do not feed that stray!"

"Thanks, Ruby. That's me in the doghouse again," the boy muttered.

Smelling tension in the air around these new human visitors and sensing it may well have something to do with him, the young dog trotted off up the beach and lay down under a coconut tree.

That afternoon, Penny managed to get Ruby to lay down for her nap which released her son from his brotherly responsibilities for a couple hours. She knew he was dying to explore further than he could with a two-year-old in tow. Smiling to herself, she watched as he leapt to his feet, spinning in circles as he grabbed his backpack and the flask of iced Coke she'd prepared for him. The screen door crashed in the wake of his delight at being free.

Ben wanted to walk the beach to the right-hand side of the cove. He was vaguely interested in the lone house on that end, wondering who owned the fishing boat and thought he would venture into the backdrop of shady trees on the way. He'd been in two minds as to whether to even bother to bring his trainers as shoes didn't seem necessary but then thought he may want to climb some rocks or something, so he had tied them to his backpack.

Leaving the beach and walking carefully through deep layers of dry and decaying palm fronds, he felt like he was stepping on crispy, cotton wool. He was aware of birds singing although when he looked, he could see none. He wondered if they had wild parrots here; they would be amazing to see. Brown coconuts lay strewn everywhere. When he picked one up, it felt much lighter than it looked. Those were the empty husks. High above his head, he could see large green fruit the size of footballs hanging in clusters at the tops of the palms. Not wanting to be directly underneath when the next one decided to fall, he kept moving. Some of the more normal looking trees had massive black growths attached to their trunks. He hoped they weren't hives built by killer bees. Ben and his friend Tony had seen a movie about them. Although the story was set in Africa, Ben gave them a wide berth to be on the safe side.

Hiking further inside the undergrowth but still heading east, he could see what looked like a pile of old bricks ahead. As he got closer, the sunlight filtering through the canopy above made everything look like a spooky wilderness that hadn't been penetrated for centuries. As Ben's eyes adjusted to the muted light, he realised he was looking at ruins, seriously old, looking like they had been deserted hundreds of years ago. Feeling slightly jumpy now, he stood still and gazed at the scattered walls strewn with bits of old black iron machinery and the remains of glassless windows in the stonework. Everything was covered in creepers that climbed down from the trees and branches that hung overhead like a makeshift roof. He thought of some old black and white Tarzan movies he'd seen on Saturday afternoon TV when he was younger. This Tarzan dude had lived in a jungle and swung from tree to tree using hanging vines like ropes. Not convinced that these Caribbean creepers would hold his weight, he resisted trying it personally. Besides, he then began to imagine that they looked like snakes and made himself shudder.

The window openings were very narrow, but the walls were built about half a metre thick. Was it a hideout or a fort, maybe? He conjured up images of soldiers lying on their stomachs, peering down their musket barrels or even cannons poking out of the openings waiting to fire upon invaders entering the bay. Dropping his pack, Ben plucked up enough courage to step over a low pile of stones and found himself inside the ancient ruin. Creatures scuttled in all directions as he jumped onto what once was a floor. He saw loads of lizards running up the moss-covered stones. He didn't mind them; they were quite appealing, but he was still hoping that the snakes were all in his mind. Inside the old room lay black, conical, metal things that looked like they had been beaten into shape by hand.

Disappointed not to find any cannon balls lying around, he climbed back out, still without any shoes on. That was a mistake. A tiny cactus obviously waiting just for him stabbed the bottom of his bare foot, offloading hundreds of minuscule spines into his skin as he unthinkingly grabbed at it. It was almost sticky. As his fingers closed around the plant, it attached itself to his hand. Hopping on one foot, whilst shaking his hand frantically in the air for a few minutes got rid of the broken piece of cactus but left Ben with spines everywhere. He could see them and realised that sitting down and removing them rather than forcing them deeper into his flesh was a more sensible solution. As soon as he had picked them out of his sore foot he would go back to wearing his trainers that were tied to his—

"Wait a minute, there's only one there!" exclaimed Ben out loud. He looked under and around his bag for the lost shoe, but it was gone. Now what was he supposed to do? Heading very gingerly back to the soft sand, he threw off his pack, the single trainer and his t-shirt and fell into the sea. It eased his aching cactus wounds as he let the buoyant, salty water lift his body and support him. He floated on his back, blinking repeatedly as he watched large sea birds circle high above him amongst white, cotton wool clouds.

Rolling over, he faced the beach and there, right in front of him, were two familiar sights—the dog and his shoe! Having dug a hole, his mischievous four legged friend then dumped the shoe into it and was now industriously pushing the loose sand back into the hollow with his nose. Ben ran out of the water and up the beach shouting. The dog saw him and, wagging his tail, grabbed the half-buried Nike and trotted to the boy. As Ben got close, the dog sat high on his haunches and, looking incredibly proud of himself, presented Ben with his shoe–minus the laces. It was really hard to be angry as the tan-coloured animal wagged a very long, flagpole-like tail.

"Okay, I'm going to call you Sandy," Ben said, "Got any bright ideas about how I get a new set of laces without Mum finding out?"

Sandy woofed at his new friend then trotted off up the beach towards the house with the boat. He gave every impression that he wanted the boy to follow him as he repeatedly looked back over his shoulder. So Ben did.

Eye of **the Storm**

CHAPTER 8

SANDY AND THE MACHETE

The home appeared to be made from everything except conventional building materials. It wasn't much more than a shack at first glance, surrounded by what looked like the contents of a small scrap yard together with a woodshop and boatyard thrown in. Sandy the dog picked his way through the debris and disappeared from view around the back. Having run out of beach (the rest of the cove ahead was rock face as the cliff rose up to dense forest), Ben paused, just in time to hear a yell a fraction of a second before a yelp, both noises coming from somewhere behind the shack.

Sandy came charging back, dodging a big stick flying through the air. Still motionless, Ben spotted the owner of the big stick in hot pursuit. The big man was attempting to give chase to the nimble animal whilst stumbling and swearing continually as he tripped over everything lying in his path. Sandy had obviously decided that Ben was going to help out as he cowered behind the boy, having first dropped at Ben's feet the object of the ensuing dispute—a lump of cooked meat. Aware that he was now a conspirator in the attempted theft of the guy's lunch, Ben began backing off, only to fall over the quivering dog hiding behind him. Spluttering an undecipherable, explanation about simply minding his own business and not having the faintest idea why the canine had dumped the stolen goods in front of him, Ben's eyes fixed on the hefty machete in the man's fist.

"Uncle Beck! It's the kid I told you about yesterday. He new here."

Relieved at the sound of a familiar voice, Ben stammered, "Isaac, um, I'm sorry. I was just walking on the beach, and San…I mean the dog, just ran in and grabbed this."

"Yeah, he a beach dog. Always theifing stuff," Isaac said, but he pronounced "theifing" with a hard T sound instead of a TH, so it sounded like he said "teefing." Isaac examined the sand-encrusted, slightly mauled leg of pork. "Chicken feed now, uncle."

The big man continued to mutter incoherent phrases in a language Ben simply could not fathom. This was probably a good thing as he was still far too young to be exposed to the language that he guessed was being spoken.

"So you living in the old place up the beach?" Isaac asked as Ben got up and brushed himself down.

"Yeah, my mum and dad rented it for the summer. You live here?" Ben asked.

"My Uncle Beck lives here. Me live over the hill."

"So was this where you were going yesterday afternoon with the bucket of baitfish?"

"Uncle and me went out last night and caught shark."

"Shark?" The word blurted out of Ben's mouth before he had properly engaged his brain.

"Yeah and dolphin and…"

Before Isaac could finish the sentence Ben screeched this time "Dolphin? You caught dolphin?"

"Chill man, dolphin fish not Flipper!"

"Oh, right," Ben said meekly.

"So if you caught all that fish, why is your uncle cooking pork?"

"He sell the fish in New Town, so we eat one of his pigs. That piece the dog thiefed was for my mother." At the mention of Sandy, Ben looked around to see if he was still nearby. The hungry dog was lying down out of range of any potential low-flying weapons, watching the boys intently.

Isaac surprised Ben by inviting him around the back of the dwelling. His huge uncle had already returned to his seat on an upturned crate under the shade of one of the trees with big, round leaves. Clambering over discarded engines, nets, coils of thick rope and what looked like an old cart, Isaac opened a dirty white cooler, containing iced bottles of Presidente beer and cans of orange Fanta. As Ben passed by the door, he caught a glimpse inside the one-room shack which held a single bed, a table and chest of drawers. Outside, half an oil drum held off the ground by a metal frame on legs puffed smoke as it cooked more chunks of meat, all black on the outside, sizzling above the heat of the coals. It smelt great.

Conscious of being late for his mother yet again in the presence of this local boy who seemed to have total freedom and be in no hurry to achieve anything, Ben downed the rest of his Fanta and thanked the man for the drink. He considered making an attempt at an apology for the incident with the leg of pork and the machete but decided it was best to let sleeping dogs lie.

The two boys walked along the cove together, not saying much. The beach dog bounded up in their path.

Ben asked, "Do you know who owns that dog?"

"He live with the people at the place your family rent, but they left him behind when they leave island."

"Really? Do you know his name?"

"Me, no. Why? You name him?" Ben immediately felt self-conscious as he knew he had named him but didn't want to seem like even more of a dork than he already did in the eyes of Isaac, so he hesitated before he replied.

"I figured maybe Sandy. What do you think?"

Isaac laughed and agreed, "Well, he sure is sandy."

"I have to go back. My mum will want me to look after my sister so she can get on with the house."

"Sure, man. I have to check my uncle for a ride home." Isaac turned and walked in the shade up the beach. Sandy, who had been shadowing the two friends, chose to follow Ben across to the tree stump outside the dog's old home.

As an afterthought, Isaac turned and called after Ben, "Hey, man, come to my uncle's tomorrow. Me and my cousins go fishing."

Ben opened the screen door to find Ruby playing with a cardboard box and his mum still scrubbing away at the cupboards in the kitchen. Wanting to stay out of the sun for a while, he chatted to his mum about meeting Isaac and his uncle, carefully leaving out the episode with the machete. He told her about the ruins he'd discovered and then about Sandy being abandoned.

Penny had that tired, tolerant motherly look on her face as she let him finish the bit about the dog. Knowing what was coming next, she preempted him. "He has a name now then, this stray?"

"Well I just thought it suited him. He's really good and doesn't jump up or anything, and I think he's hungry."

"There was some cheese and meat left over from lunch. It will just go soggy in the ice water until I get this fridge clean. Give that to him—outside. He's not to come in the house. Do you understand, Ben?"

"Yes, Mum, of course. Thanks." Without being able to stop the grin on his face, he took a bowl of water and some scraps out to the tree trunk. Sandy sat and waited until the boy put the food and water on the ground in front of him then tucked in, wagging his tail the entire time.

When the children and their mother closed up the beach house late that afternoon, they left the cleaning gear and cooler and returned for one more night's sleep at the hotel in town, planning on packing up the suitcases and bags of Ruby's toys the following morning. As his mum drove the pickup back up the hill, Ben couldn't see Sandy and was suddenly sad for the dog who was being left alone again. He wished there was a way that he could explain that they would be back tomorrow. Then as the truck climbed higher, he spotted the animal lying under a palm behind the house. Ben resolved to pay closer attention to the shelves in the food market in the morning, determined to find a can of food for his new friend.

Having been brought up to speed with the day's activities and discoveries by his family in Sunset Cove, Frank presented his son and wife with a new cell phone each. He explained that Kamaria's wireless provider seemed to be surprisingly advanced, and their technology made up for the lack of a more traditional landline network. He also had a second surprise for Ben.

"This is an EVDO card," he announced.

"What's it for?"

"It is short for Evolution Data Only, and it provides a fast, wireless, broadband internet service directly to your laptop. It'll work all over the island and apparently up to 20 miles offshore, so now you can talk to your friends online whenever you feel like it without plugging in to anything."

"That's so wicked. Thanks. I'll go try it out right now."

That evening, Frank and Penny walked outside the hotel and sat in a roadside bar from which they could see their balcony window. Ben was deep in cyber-conversations with his friends and without taking his eyes from the computer screen had acknowledged that they were going for a drink across the road, and he was in charge of a sleeping Ruby.

Frank explained to his wife, "I thought it was a good idea to let Ben have his own mobile so all three of us can be in contact. If he is away from the beach house, he should have a means of emergency communication and with you. Actually, the deal was perfect as all three cell phones talk to each other for free. But for heaven's sake, don't let him call the UK. It'll cost an arm and a leg!"

"Keeping it dry may be the toughest task for Ben. In the past couple days he seems to have dropped everything he owns, including his new trainers, into the sea. That internet thingy seems to work well though. I think I'll give him my camera tomorrow morning, and he can email his grandparents some shots of Sunset Cove. That'll save me having to call them again so soon," she said. "There's a lot to be done in the house if we are sleeping there tomorrow night—not least of which is some more fumigation!"

CHAPTER 9
ONLINE CHAT 1

Ben says:

hey wass up?

Tony says:

hi whats happenin

Ben says:

just got a card for laptop so i can get online wireless

Tony says:

cool bet that was loads of $

Ben says:

Dunno think dad is tryin to keep me happy

Tony says:

So wass it like?

Ben says:

cool, very hot and the beach is really great we have a beach house in sunset cove a place over the hill from the town noone else lives there except this old guy and I know his nephew his names isaac.

Tony says:

u got tv?

Ben says:

no only in hotel but its just loads of american adverts

Tony says:

its boring here now but my mums got me a job in tescos stuffin ppls bags at the checkout

Ben says:

lol do you get tips?

Tony says:

some old bid gave me some coppers yesterday I get 3 quid a hr

Ben says:

i would have got 3.50 at the watersports centre if theyd let me stay at home

Tony says:
    So do u hate it?
Ben says:
    sometimes but it would be good if it was a holiday
Tony says:
    later ben
Ben says:
    yeah later

After catching up with Tony, he noticed that no one else, not even Charlie, was online. Probably, he thought, because it was five hours later at home than here, they were asleep by now. Pity, he felt like telling Charlie about Sandy the dog and other stuff. Ben was lying on his stomach (his back was surprisingly red and sore) with his PC on the bed beside him, vaguely surfing the net—pretty impressed with the speed he was getting. The next thing he knew his parents were waking him and making him get under the sheet to stop the mossies scoring hits on him.

CHAPTER 10
THE SILENT SWIMMER

Excited about getting back over the mountain to Sunset Cove, Ben had no problems getting motivated to get up and dressed. In the grocery store, they loaded the shopping carts with supplies. Now that his mum had declared the fridge sterile and the kitchen cupboards free of cockroaches, it was safe to shop.

Ben wondered if Sandy would be waiting for him when they got to their beach house. For all he knew, the dog may have just wandered off. Although he tried not to talk about him too much to his mum that morning, he secretly prayed he would still be there under his favourite palm tree.

Ben had furtively found a bag of dried dog food and dropped it into the trolley he was pushing with Ruby riding shotgun on the front. His mum had made no comment as she pushed a second trolley around. When they did get to the checkout, Penny smiled when she noticed the item.

The day was stunning again: bright, hot and blue. So far, rain had only fallen at night which Ben regarded as very civilized. The Johnston family's only water supply was to be from the sky, and so although Ben appreciated the need for rain, it was very convenient when it only did it under the cover of darkness and didn't spoil his exploring.

Riding in the truck's open back was becoming normal for the boy who was used to a car at home with seatbelts and airbags. He had quickly discovered, however, that if he sat on anything that wasn't fixed to the vehicle, he tended to slide around the bed of the pickup each time his mom turned a corner. This was kind of fun, but any severe braking shot him into the rear window (as in when goats decided to migrate slowly across the road in front of oncoming traffic). Also, once on the way up the mountain, Ben had come a little too close to being catapulted over the back as the gradient increased without any warning. After this episode, he no longer sat on the slippery cooler and stuck to the wheel arches.

Driving around the switchbacks down into Sunset Cove, the boy's eyes were straining to catch a glimpse of his canine friend waiting for him. He couldn't see him anywhere. As they pulled into the track in front of the beach house, Ben's heart sank, but he jumped out and pretended not to be totally gutted that Sandy wasn't there to greet them. Unloading took much longer than the day before, a never ending stream of grocery bags to carry in and then their own bags and Ruby's toys. Scanning the area as he traipsed back and forth through the screen door, Ben resigned himself to giving up on the dog.

'So what, anyway,' he thought to himself. 'He got me in to trouble yesterday and wrecked my trainers. He would just be a nuisance all the time.'

Penny didn't bring up the subject of the stray. She could see Ben's face was set in a resolute frown as he helped her with the unloading. She knew how much he was looking forward to seeing the animal, and she also knew her son well enough to not speak about it until he volunteered something on the subject.

Hands on hips, with a sheen of light sweat on her face, Penny Johnston gazed around her home for the summer. The island was beautiful, but she was not entirely comfortable in the basic housing that the residents seemed to accept as normal. She had worked so hard yesterday cleaning the floors, surfaces and cupboards, but she couldn't actually say that the place looked welcoming. Penny supposed that part of the strangeness of it all was that so much in her home in England was not needed here. Central heating, airing cupboards, thick carpets and surround sound media centres just were not part of this culture. People did most things outside, including preparing meals on barbeques in the gardens or on decks. She was also concerned about the water supply after Frank had shown her the cistern the day before yesterday. She just couldn't get her head around how they could drink anything that came out of that hole. Then there was the journey the water took after it had hit the tin roof and passed through the rickety guttering full of heaven-knows-what type of creepy wildlife and bugs. Needless to say, taking no chances, the large boxes that were now stacked on the floor beside her contained bottled, drinking water.

Deflated, but trying to get over his disappointment, Ben took Ruby down to the water's edge with her buckets and spades. His mum had said that if he amused her for a while, he could go and swim on his own until lunchtime. Ruby had developed a slightly worrying new habit of crawling on all fours into the sea. She didn't seem to appreciate that wading in head first was not necessarily a sensible option for a two-year-old that could not swim. Being remarkably nimble, she moved amazingly fast into the depths, insisting (judging by the coughing fits that always followed), that she did this with her mouth wide open. Ben decided that permanently attached water wings were a safe solution to the problem. Bobbing up and down with her face above the waterline was definitely a happier option for both children than the alternative of her sinking from view. He kept on his t-shirt, after realising a little too late the day before that the sun really did burn.

After Ruby's first swimming lesson was completed, he thought that maybe later he would try and persuade her to kick her legs, although he had this feeling that teaching his little sister how to move in the water whilst being held up by floaty things was simply asking for trouble. He suspected that she would much rather chase a pelican out to sea than stay by him.

Depositing Ruby back with his mum, he grabbed a cold Coke and headed up the beach towards Isaac's uncle's shack. He had a cell phone and a digital camera in his (now dry) backpack with the threat of eternal grounding if he "so much as dreamt" of getting either wet. Ben stopped by the ruins and took some photos. It crossed his mind that he could send a picture file to Charlie on MSN if she ever deemed to talk to him again.

Reaching the end of the beach, he saw activity ahead. Isaac and some other boys were hauling in the boat that had been moored off the beach the day before. It was what they called a dory at the watersports centre. Although longer than the one used for safety cover there, it was still an open, flat boat with an outboard engine on the back. The boys had dragged the front onto the sand and were loading it with buckets and coolers. Feeling a little self-conscious again, Ben wasn't sure whether to go any closer or not. Isaac had invited him to come around when he'd left yesterday, but the other boys all looked older than he was. One of the tall youths spotted Ben and pointed towards him. Now it was too late to make an escape.

Isaac yelled, "Hey, come."

Feigning disinterest as if he was just passing through would be pretty lame (especially since the only thing ahead was a steep rock face), Ben walked up to the group. He could see the contents of one of the buckets now; the essential bait fish were lying there, eyes bulging, reminding him again of that plate of crispy fried, miniature fish he'd once seen his mum eat.

"What's up?" Ben asked.

"Going fishing. You coming?"

"Dunno. Where you going?" Ben glanced at the three other boys, who were all unashamedly staring at him.

"Out to the point. Fish feeding there." This information came from the tallest of the trio.

Conscious of having to make some pretty swift decisions if he was going to save any face at all here, Ben looked at the dory again and saw the handlines wrapped on plastic rings, a dirty cooler that was full of ice and the ever-present cans of Fanta, a fuel tank, an anchor and rope thrown into a muddled heap, and one long wooden oar.

Over the past two years, the English boy had been trained to never go near a small boat without wearing a buoyancy aid. Actually it was so ingrained in him, it was all he could think about right now. There were none in sight. Fighting the urge to ask if they had any, he instead said, "Sure, can I leave my bag at your uncle's, Isaac?" his subconscious remembering the threat of what would happen to him if the electronics in his backpack settled themselves into the bottom of this very damp boat.

The kid that had pointed at him leapt over the front of the dory, clambering over the contents to reach the engine. He pulled at the starting cord and, at the third attempt, the motor sputtered to life. As he gunned the throttle, it roared, black smoke gushing from its insides.

"Let's go," said Isaac as he jumped over the side, and the other two followed. By the time five of them had found a space to sit, there wasn't much boat left. Reversing a little too enthusiastically with the engine partially lifted to keep it clear of the bottom served to fill the rear of the small powerboat with seawater. This prompted the rest of the crew to issue several exclamations of disgust and disapproval, mostly in the form of: "Man, watch it!" or "Man, you can't drive!" The tall boy ignored the complaints, reached over to click the engine all the way down and aimed the boat at the right-hand point of Sunset Cove.

Isaac volunteered the names of his two cousins while they motored away from the mooring. Their captain today was called Jehiah, and the other shorter, much stockier teenager was Shamoi. Ben wondered if his full name, Benjamin, would seem as foreign to them as theirs did to him. The third youth Isaac introduced as his cousin, Kai. This person hadn't spoken since they had left the beach and seemed fascinated with what was flashing past underneath the boat. When Ben looked for himself, he could understand why. It was surprisingly shallow, and as they cut through the crystal clear water, the coral reef lay below enticing him to reach down and touch its razor sharp edges.

"He don't hear or speak," Isaac explained.

"Really?"

As if to demonstrate that fact, the quiet boy sprung to life, waving his arm and pointing to something ahead. He didn't speak, but he could make noise. He had spotted a turtle peering around at them. It was the first one Ben had seen, and he couldn't stop himself from pointing and grinning as well. The comical sea creature took one look at the approaching vessel, bowed his long neck and dived back below the surface.

As they traveled further away from the shore, short chop replaced the glasslike surface of the water, and spray occasionally came over the front of the fishing boat. The reef was no longer visible, and ahead they could see the giant rocks being struck by meter-high waves. Jehiah navigated them close to a tiny, white polystyrene buoy bobbing up and down. Isaac reached for it, tying up to what looked like a very flimsy piece of line rising from the seabed underneath the buoy.

Once the engine was quiet, the team busied themselves with slowly rotting bait fish and large hooks on the ends of the handlines. This sight reminded Ben once again of his granddad. He tipped his head back and stared at the rocks. Close up, they were pretty scary–slippery black, scarred white in places where sea birds obviously liked to rest. There was what looked like a cave set back in the darkness of the craggy scene in front of the boat. Letting his imagination go back to *Treasure Island*, he wondered what was hidden in there.

Shamoi, who seemed to be called Sham most of the time, passed Ben a handline baited with dead fish. Watching the others, he gathered that you simply threw the line out and let it sink.

"So how deep is it here?" he asked.

"Maybe forty feet," replied Jehiah. "Look you can see the bottom."

With a quick piece of mental arithmetic Ben converted the alien measurement back to metric using the basic method his dad had explained last night to his mum, that there's about three feet in a metre.

Looking into the dark depths, Ben could make out huge coral heads and fish moving around in thirteen metres of water. After he'd watched the other boys toss their lines effortlessly over the side of the boat, he thought he'd better get rid of his. Trying to mimic the others, he threw his into a space, taking care to throw downwind knowing this would help. The local boys watched as the line travelled just clear of the boat then abruptly dropped. Hanging just below the surface, the dead bait fish looked pathetic as it dangled uselessly underneath them. Shamoi scoffed, then said

"Turn the thing around, boy!"

Rewinding the line, Ben looked up at him lost. "What do you mean, turn it around?"

Taking the reel from him, Shamoi turned it around then returned it to Ben's hand. "You check?"

"Okay." Not seeing what difference this was possibly going to make, Ben tried again. Incredibly, it worked! The line rushed off the black ring as the now very battered fish flew through the air and plopped into the sea, sinking steadily as the line continued to pay out. Looking once again at the simple disk in his hand, Ben could now see a subtle difference. One side had a raised edge on it that would stop the line from falling away, the other side was flush. Obvious, really.

The only crew member not fishing now was Kai. He just sat looking intently over the side of the boat. "Doesn't your cousin like to fish?" Ben asked Isaac.

"No, he likes to swim. He think he a fish."

Almost at the same time, three things happened. Isaac and Jehiah got bites, and Ben caught the bottom. The two older boys pulled in fighting silver fish with yellow lines on their backs, bucking all the way as they fought their hunters. Ben's line was definitely stuck. As he watched the suitably named Yellow-Tailed Jacks being dragged over the gunwales, he had a sinking feeling that he would have to own up and cut his line, losing the hook.

"Hey man, you under a rock," Isaac said, stating the obvious as he saw Ben's fingers turning even whiter than they already were, as the blood was cut off by the fine, strong fishing line.

"Yeah I think so. Do you have a knife?"

"No knife, just Kai." After being signaled by his cousin, Kai became animated. Already gripping an old face mask in his hands, he pulled it over his head and was over the side of the dory before Ben could say anything. Kai sank gracefully straight down, head first in the direction of Ben's trapped hook. It took moments for the swimmer to reach the coral head, and Ben, feeling the tug, wound up the loose line, watching as Kai looked up and slowly ascended. With one, lithe movement, he was out of the water and back in the barely rocking boat. Ben naturally went to say "Thanks" then realised this was futile, so reached over and patted a strong arm dripping with salt water. There was no doubt by the grin on Kai's face that this was exactly why he was on the trip.

The friends continued to fish until early afternoon, filling the iced cooler with pot fish of all sizes and colours, even adding a couple of "Old Wives" that Ben had finally managed to catch, much to the approval of Kai who kept patting Ben on the back with delight. Getting hungry and uncomfortable, they stowed their catch and gear whilst Jehiah, who seemed to be the designated driver, returned the fishing boat and its young crew to shore. When he killed the outboard engine in the shallows, the cousins jumped off and larked around, throwing water and jumping on each other, then ran up the beach and collapsed on to the hot sand, rolling around coating themselves in sugary grains until they looked like grey ghosts. Ben swam around them, grateful for the cool water, then helped carry the cooler up to the shack.

Knowing yet again he was on a time limit, while they didn't seem to be under any rules at all, Ben said goodbye, turning walk back to his waiting mum.

"Hey, man, you want your fish?"

"Um, I dunno."

"Here." Jehiah gave Ben a plastic bag with his share of the catch in it. Very unsure if he would actually want to eat this prize or even if his mum knew what to do with it, Ben figured it would be easier to take the offering then worry about these issues later.

"Thanks. See ya." Backpack retrieved, Ben jogged up the beach, hoping he wasn't in trouble again.

Eye of **the Storm**

"Hi. I'm back."

"I called you. What's the point of us giving you a mobile phone if you don't answer it?"

"You did? Sorry, I left it behind when I went fishing. I thought—"

"You left it behind and went fishing?"

"Well I didn't want to get it wet"

"What's in that bag?"

"Fish."

Peering inside as if she was expecting the dead fish to jump out and grab her by the throat, Penny took the bag from her son. "I think this is dog food"

"Huh?"

Smiling she continued, "You had a visitor when you were gone. He's out back asleep. I gave him some of those biscuits you bought this morning; he looked hungry."

Without hesitation or composure, Ben yelled, "Sandy!" The young beach stray strutted through the open back door wagging his long tail and thrust his nose right into Ben's face as the boy bent to welcome the dog.

"Not in the house."

"Sorry, Mum. Come on, Sandy, let's go outside."

The boy and his four-legged friend trotted out to their tree trunk, both of them grinning from ear to ear. Ben spent the remainder of the daylight playing with Sandy and Ruby on the beach. Having the young dog around made spending time with his little sister much more bearable. Later, Ruby was getting bathed and Sandy was lying outside on the deck underneath the hammock that Ben was swinging in. It was amazingly comfy. He could see why seafarers in the old ships slept in them. From his laid back position, he followed the sun going down, turning the quiet island that sat on the horizon a glowing red. It seemed to be almost beckoning him to come closer. Ben grabbed his camera from his backpack and flipped through the pictures of the ruins he'd taken that morning. He again pondered what had happened there so long ago.

Ben's dad had come home and was attempting to fix several items in the tiny house that Penny had briefed him about on the ride back over the hill. Ben knew better than to get in the way unless asked to help and even then, through experience, he knew it was always healthier to be obedient and mute when his dad was in do-it-yourself mode.

Waiting until Frank came out on the deck with a beer in his hand, Ben showed him his shots of the ruins. His dad thought it must be a very old dwelling, maybe a hideout of some kind, but it was obvious that he was guessing, too. Ben resolved to ask Isaac and his cousins in the morning what they knew.

CHAPTER 11
RUM AND MOLASSES

Frank drove himself to work the next morning, leaving his wife and children in the most idyllic setting he could ever have imagined. His working days so far had been spent establishing his side of the company's activities, adding to the basic formation that had already been put in place by his colleagues who had arrived on-island a year or less before him. Looking forward to the weekend, he imagined himself sitting on a sun chair with his toes being tickled by the ocean, a cold beer in his hand, doing nothing more than watching Ruby play with her buckets and spades. In the meantime, he was off to the office—if only a fairly basic one.

After breakfast, Ben was pleased to see that his mum had settled herself on a towel on the sand with the toddler digging holes nearby. The emergency cleaning was obviously over, and Penny had a jug of water, a book and a bottle of sun block lined up within reach. She intended to work on her tan today; this meant Ben was free.

With Sandy in tow (the dog had slept on the deck directly underneath Ben's bedroom window the previous night), Ben walked along the line of the gently lapping Atlantic Ocean, gazing out at the island on the horizon and watching Sandy occasionally stop to stare at a shadow in the shallows. Eventually, the dog would thrust his head under, come up drenched and gallop around in circles before he rolled in the sand, coating himself, then shaking his entire body as close to Ben as possible.

As they drew near to the shack at the end of the beach, no signs of life could be seen, and Ben considered turning around and heading over to the opposite side of the cove. None of the boys were hanging around, but Ben still kind of wanted to talk to Isaac's uncle, so he kept going, conscious that he shouldn't let Sandy go rushing around the back in case the old man was more accurate with his machete this morning. Ben called out as he reached the threshold of the home, no one replied, he walked to the side, but could only see the usual cluster of chickens pecking at the dirt. Fortunately, these didn't seem to faze Sandy. Ben could only assume that if you are born in a place where chickens are everywhere, you don't have any inbred instinct to hunt them. He'd even seen a cat lounging in the sun in town with a hen and her chicks happily clucking around it. Now that was one laid-back cat.

"Mornin'."

Ben jumped at the voice then said, "Hello. Sorry. I was wondering if Isaac was here."

"No just me and Kai. What's that dog doing back here?"

"It's okay. He's good, really. I'll make sure he's not a nuisance"

"Keep him away, or he'll see my cutlass again."

"Yes, of course." Ben motioned Sandy in the direction of the water. Fortunately, the dog gave no indication of needing to push his luck anymore. "I was wondering if I could ask you a question, sir, well actually two questions."

"Sir," the old man chuckled, "haven't been called that in a while."

Feeling pretty edgy about being around the old codger, but with a strong hunch that he may have some fascinating information, Ben stood and waited. He'd caught his granddad a couple of times like that. Sitting in his favourite chair, he had begun to recount some really scary stuff about being sent away from home at the end of the second World War.

The old local turned, walking slowly back to the dirty cooler under a tree in his back yard. Ben followed at a respectable distance, after having ordered Sandy to wait outside. Sitting down, dressed the same as he had been two days before in long, frequently mended trousers, a white vest and no shoes on his huge feet, Beck Hamilton picked up a net and a shaped stick and began repairing holes with the twine at his side. "What you want to know, boy?" He asked without looking up from his task.

"Well," he began, "the ruins in the trees back there, what did they used to be?"

"Ruins? Oh you mean the old sugar mill."

"A sugar mill?" Ben questioned.

"A rum distillery."

"Oh, I see, so it wasn't a fort or anything like that?"

Chuckling, Beck explained, "This island like, others around here, grew crops of sugar cane. The slaves, they worked the land, bringing the cane down the hill to distillery in them carts. That was the trade in them days, boy. I not been there for years, but last time me passed, the tall chimney, she was standing. That's one of them column stills. The copper pots are there, too, ya know. They boiled the sugar juice in them. The mill was worked by donkeys and sometimes slaves, too. Molasses was taken from boiling pots and used to make rum. The children, them used to wait for the mixing rods to be left lying, then they'd lick at the sweet sticks."

Ben was listening quietly to Isaac's uncle, not wanting to interrupt in case he stopped his story.

"They had to be clever not to get caught, for there was a whipping waiting for them if they did."

Ben asked, "Was it really worth the risk just for a lick of molasses?"

"You tasted that stuff boy?"

"I don't think so, sir."

"It's sweet like nothing else. They didn't have candy like the youth now. That was their treat, ya hear?"

"Yes, sir. I guess so."

"Not 'Sir.' My name is Beckford Hamilton. Mostly folks call me Beck."

Ben was impressed by such an important sounding name and wasn't sure whether to ask the man where it came from. He decided that he would try. "That sounds like an English name, sir. I mean Mr. Hamilton."

"It's a Kamarian family name. There are a few of us Hamiltons still here. We all related somewhere. This island was run by the British in plantation times, so the slaves took their names from their owners. After emancipation, most of them kept them." Beck looked at the white boy and did a strange thing—he made a sucking noise through his teeth—and then with a sly grin, he said, "Looks to me like the British are back."

"What's emancipation?" Ben asked, trying not to feel personally responsible for the slavery that was being described to him.

"Boy, you don't know nothing. In 1834 they were set free. That was when the rum finished. Once they were on their own, the African slaves, them took a while fighting among themselves, getting drunk and liming, so the crops went bad. No one wanted to do the hard work of cutting and loading and grinding the sugar no more. The white owners, they already fled the country, scared for their lives, so most of the cane fields were left to go back to bush."

"So what happened after that?" Ben was itching to hear more.

"Well, some of them free slaves got passages to other larger islands like Antigua and Barbados where there was still work. The rest lived off the land here, making their way. There were big hurricanes back then, and the crops of cotton that were still being grown were destroyed. Then the sickness came and killed hundreds of the people. The small pox was the worse. People built boats and sailed across to the sister islands and cays to escape the disease, but most carried it with them or couldn't survive with no food, so came back." Beck had put down his net and was staring up into the hill behind his home. "Most families that survived fished. Some raised small farms, growing vegetables and rearing goats and even cows left behind by the white men. Most were Christians by then, and they built churches. That's one up there." Following the angle of the old man's pointing finger, high and to the other side of the Cove, Ben could make out a wall in the trees. "That up there is an old fort." Beck had turned and was now pointing directly behind the shack and high up the hillside. All the boy could see was dense bush and trees.

"There's a fort up there? Really?"

"It used to defend Sunset Cove from invading ships. The soldiers, them and the reef did a good job of scuttling most of the privateers."

"So are there wrecks in the bay?" Ben was starting to fidget, unable to contain himself, letting his imagination conjure up images of magnificent, square-rigged galleons filled with pirates on the water and cannons and soldiers in the hills.

"Sure, boy, but they were wooden ships, wrecked in hurricanes and battles. You won't find them under there now. They rot away and are buried by sand and coral. Some people have found metal things—musket balls and such."

"Have they discovered treasure here?"

Beck chuckled. "Well not that I know about. You wanna know about treasure, you should talk to the Frenchman."

"Who's he?"

Sucking his teeth again, Mr. Hamilton looked at Ben and nodded out to sea. "The Frenchman, he live on Scorpion Island."

The second question burning in Ben's mind was answered. It was called Scorpion Island. The name seemed to add to the already mystical and slightly threatening image the island projected.

"Someone lives out there? Wow, that must be so cool."

"His family has lived out there for hundreds of years. They are the only ones that wanted to. They're all crazy."

"Oh." Was about all Ben could think of to say to that. "Is he French then?"

"He think he still a buccaneer. They say he live exactly like his ancestors did. No one goes over there except the Rastas. Them sometimes trade he lobsters for the vegetables they grow."

Ben's imagination started running riot again. "A buccaneer. That's a type of pirate, right, Mr. Hamilton?"

"Yeah, they did their fair share of raiding they say."

"So what does he do now?" Ben was conjuring up a picture of a lone pirate sitting on a barrel under a palm tree with black, knee-high boots and a three pointed hat, looking at his compass. (Captain Jack Sparrow's influence had gotten him again.)

"Well he crazy. Ya hear?"

Not satisfied with this answer Ben insisted, "Yeah, but what does he do out there?"

"I guess he gets enough to eat from fishing and the fruit and rum that the Rastas take him. There used to be wild boar on Scorpion Island. Maybe there still are. His place is around the far side. Me used to see it when we fish off the deep drop. There's a bay that's protected when the north swell gets up, except what's doing the protecting is a long reef, deadly to boats. Many tried to get in but misjudged the entrance and sank on Dog Leg Reef. The Frenchman, he the only one who knows the switchback under the waves that leads safely into the bay. He always have a fire burning."

"Does he have a boat to come over here when he needs to?" Ben pushed.

"Years ago, he wife was heavy with child, and she got sick. The Frenchman brought her to town in he sailboat, but the doctor's medicine couldn't save her or the baby. He swore he would never return. To my knowledge, he hasn't used the sloop since that day."

Saturated with information, Ben got up from the back step he had been settled on. He still had a hundred more questions but thought he had better let Mr. Hamilton alone for a while.

"If you're leaving, boy, go and get Kai. He up the back somewhere, doing nothing useful as is customary for him. I need some work done around here."

"Okay. Thanks for your time, Mr. Hamilton. I'll let him know."

"Beck, call me Beck, boy."

Ben wanted to point out that his name wasn't 'Boy,' but somehow he didn't think that would change much, so he left it, just nodding an acknowledgment as he climbed up the steep foundation of the hill behind the shack.

Rough, low bush scattered less and less with rubbish gave way to a grove of coconut trees and then beyond that, dense forest. The trees grew closer together here, and the filtering sunlight gave everything a strobe effect. As Ben walked, he realised that he couldn't call out for Kai any more than his old uncle could have done from the yard. He would have to actually spot him and attract his attention. A few metres more, and he was high enough to see over the roof of the shack, straight to Scorpion Island. He thought he'd borrow his dad's binoculars this afternoon and search for any smoke trails from a fire on the far side.

Turning back to continue his pursuit of the deaf boy, he was suddenly not alone. Sandy came bounding up behind him, tongue hanging out, frantically wagging his flag-pole tail. The dog had obviously seen Ben from his station, faithfully doing as he was told and waiting outside the front of the shack.

"Sandy, you're a good boy," he said. Rubbing the dog's head, Ben had an idea. "Go find Kai, Sandy. Find him." The animal looked at him, full of enthusiasm for whatever the boy was trying to explain, but confused, to say the least. Ben waved his hands up the hill and kept saying, "Find Kai. Find him!"

The dog bounded around then shot off through the trees to the left. Thirsty and very hot now, Ben thought he'd look for a couple more minutes then give up. Waiting for Sandy to come into view again, he sat down on a rock. Immediately, there were weird, large, red ant-like things running around his bare feet. He pulled away but they didn't seem to bite. Some of them were joined together end to end as they scuttled around the rock. Very strange.

The sound of barking brought Ben back to reality, and he jumped up and jogged in the direction of the noise. Amazingly, there on a large bolder were Kai and Sandy. The dog licking Kai's face obviously did not impress the teenager, and he leapt down, landing nimbly like a gymnast dismounting a beam. Grinning and waving a limp hand at Kai, feeling rather silly, Ben began the tricky message translation from words into signals. Kai quickly gathered what the visitor was trying to tell him and reassured Ben of this with various pats on the shoulder and thumbs up signs, putting him out of his misery.

As they were about to part company, Ben noticed something in Kai's hand. It was a sketch book, the pages folded back to the one that he had been working on. Gesturing to have a look, he saw as Kai offered it to him that this was not your average doodling. This quiet young man was a very talented artist. It was a landscape, a picture of their current surroundings, but it had incredibly detailed birds in it, one Ben recognized as a hummingbird. Somehow doubting that Kai or his brother had a camera, he could only wonder at how Kai could retain such information in his mind and transfer it to a drawing without a photograph to copy. Ben knew these tiny birds were present on Kamaria, but so far he'd not spotted any. It was Ben's turn now to pat Kai on the shoulder pointing at the book. The boy smiled sheepishly, took the sketch book back and ran down the hill.

"A swim, I think. Don't you, Sandy?" Ben and his dog slid down the hillside, sprinted across the hot, white sand and splashed their way into the sea.

Eye of **the Storm**

CHAPTER 12
ONLINE CHAT 2

Ben says:

    Hi hows it going?

Charlie says:

    Hey I thought youd forgotten me

Ben says:

    Lol ive been trying you for days and I had to get an evdo card first

Charlie says:

    Oh well I haven't really been here much

Ben says:

    So where have you been?

Charlie says:

    just at the club its been really windy and I've been out on a 4.7 laser

Ben says:

    cool, now I'm jealous I want a laser out here, you would love it the sea is
    so clear and warm you can see the bottom when you're on it

Charlie says:

    So you been sailing there?

Ben says:

    Well no a dory actually some guys here have it on the beach we went
    fishing yesterday it was cool

Charlie says:

    Sounds sick

Ben says:

    Yeah I have a dog called sandy hes a beach dog but some one left him
    behind on sunset cove so hes been alone for months hes really cute and
    bright I think hes young less than 2 maybe

Charlie says:

    So send me some pics

Ben says:

    Ok I'll send some files now wait

Charlie says:

> k

Ben says:

> These are of sandy and the cove and our beachhouse and some very cool
> ruins of a rum distillery! Its hundreds of years old and noone goes there

Charlie says:

> Wow sounds spooky

Ben says:

> Well just a bit theres lizards and stuff there

Charlie says:

> Yuk!

Ben says:

> I have to go mum's calling me to look after ruby
> later

Charlie says:

> Yeah talk to me soon

CHAPTER 13
JUMBIES

After the previous day's revelations at Mr. Hamilton's place, Ben's head was full of buccaneers and birds, soldiers and slaves. He was desperate to know more about the Frenchman but couldn't think of any even slightly sensible way of getting out to Scorpion Island. Looking through his father's binoculars had not helped as the highest peak was blocking the view of anything on the other side. Ben had cautiously asked if there were any shops in town selling charts of the local waters, and although his dad had looked at him funny, he hadn't asked why his twelve year old son would want a chart. Grunting, he had promised to have a look. Ben decided to ask Mr. Hamilton when he saw him again if he was planning a fishing trip to the Deep Drop, as he had called it, any time soon.

Ben had walked up to the other side of the cove with Sandy at his side. He could see the old church that the freed slaves had built at the top of the hill. Its congregation must have had quite a view. The building had been reduced to another ruin; he assumed that being so exposed on the top of a mountain in a hurricane had not been good for the church.

After lunch the devoted pair, boy and dog, trotted and swam their way to Mr. Hamilton's shack. Sandy had gotten the message by now about not being invited inside and retreated into a shady hole at the bottom of a nearby palm and closed his eyes. The cousins were all there, eating chicken and rice and drinking Fanta.

"What's up?" Isaac called.

"Not much, just hanging out. You?"

"Yeah, liming man."

That was the second time Ben had heard that word "liming."

"You want some food?"

"No I just ate, thanks. I was wondering about hiking up the hill to look for the old fort your uncle told me about. Have you been there before?"

"No, man. You don't want to go there!"

"Why?"

"Jumbies," interrupted Shamoi who had been listening but unable to interject before, due to the amount of food he'd stuffed into his mouth.

"Excuse me?" said Ben.

"Jumbies. You know, jumbies," replied the still munching face of the chubby, black boy. Ben looked at Isaac.

"What are jumbies?"

"Nothing. That's just silliness."

"Have you been there or not?" Ben insisted.

"Not exactly," Isaac muttered evasively.

"So, you wanna go? It should be wicked discovering a real fort. Maybe we can find something the soldiers left behind."

"No, man. I have to do work for my uncle."

"What kind of work?"

"Er, well, just stuff, you know."

Mr. Hamilton came into the front garden of his shack. He had been listening to the conversation between the boys. "Isaac and my boys are scared of jumbies."

"Mr. Hamilton, what are jumbies?" Ben was getting frustrated now, why wouldn't someone just explain what they meant.

"Boy, they spirits. Dead people's spirits"

"Oh, I see, you mean ghosts."

"I mean jumbies. They don't hurt you, mostly"

"So how do I find the fort Mr. Hamil… I mean Beck?"

"Easy. Follow the ghut."

The language barrier was starting to close in around Ben. "What's' a ghut, sir?"

"Boy, you don't know nothing!"

"I know, you have pointed that out a number of times." This, Ben took care to whisper under his breath.

Isaac explained that a ghut was like a stream, a natural or sometimes man-made way of leading rain water off the mountain to the sea. The old man cut in, "The fort was built next to a ghut 'cause they had no cistern to store drinking water. So when it rained, they had running water to drink and wash in." Now that sounded sensible, Ben thought. He could just follow this ghut up the hill until he came across the fort. He and Sandy could manage that.

Giving up on the cousins and trying not to ponder on the possibility of jumbies, he left the shack, called Sandy and put his trainers on. His backpack was loaded with water, sun block, a camera and his cell phone. He was ready, even if the boys were scared. All he had to do was find the end of the ghut at sea level, and the rest would be easy. Pity he'd forgotten to ask the specifics about that bit. Well, there was no way he was going back. They could "lime" or whatever they wanted to do; this place needed some challenges, or it was going to be a very boring summer.

Eye of **the Storm**

Mr. Hamilton had told him the fort's remains were right behind his shack and high up, so Ben started to walk up the mountain, climbing around palms and over boulders that randomly appeared from the ground—some of them the size of a dump truck. The going was fairly easy, but up ahead dense, heavily leafed trees overshadowed scrubby-looking bush that offered no obvious direction to follow. Sandy bounded around, sniffing and frequently cocking his leg, marking territory like he traveled this route everyday. Periodically, he sprinted back to Ben as if checking in on his companion, thus covering five times the amount of ground necessary.

With no evidence of what he imagined a ghut would look like and reaching the edge of the thick forest, Ben slowed down, beginning to doubt his resolve of finding this elusive fort on his own. For all he knew, it was just a story told by the local family. While still seriously considering heading back to the beach house, Ben heard a noise behind him. Spinning around just a tad quicker than was cool, he caught sight of Kai jogging nimbly over the rough terrain, clutching a machete in his right hand.

Extremely pleased to see a friendly face, Ben waved at the approaching figure, already getting used to not being able to use his voice to greet him. Kai, with his usual innocent grin, patted Ben on the shoulder and pointed into the forest to the right of where the white boy was standing. Not waiting for further conversation of any kind, Kai began climbing using his machete in short, strong strokes, deftly clearing the way for both of them.

Most of what the huge knife (that Mr. Hamilton had referred to as his cutlass) hacked through were creepers hanging in clumps from the trees. Ben followed Kai as he beat his way through the bush. Kai, in turn, followed Sandy, who seemed to have taken on the role of exhibition leader and was leading his small pack of two, with his flagpole tail held high, as if he had any clue of where the humans desired to go.

After ten minutes of crashing through undergrowth, Kai made a happy noise as he stood by the side of a crevice in the mountain that looked just like a dried out stream. The ghut. It had to be. Looking around, Ben could now see a narrow but recently trodden path following the side of the rocky cleft. They followed the path much slower now, scrambling on all fours as much as they walked on two feet, as it was extremely steep. Ben looked down once but couldn't see more than four metres before the forest closed in behind them. Vague glints of sun broke through the treetops providing just enough light to continue. Kai seemed very fit; he moved easier then Ben in this terrain. Desperately needing a drink, Ben reached forward for the back of Kai's white vest and motioned him to stop and rest.

With a small rock each to perch on, they all sat, Ben and Sandy panting more than Kai. Ben fished in his pack for the water bottle, drank some and held it out to Kai. The boy's eyes were staring above him through a break in the canopy, he was watching something. Then Ben heard the cry—a high pitched, sad shriek above their heads. Kai had already pulled out of his pocket a scrunched up notepad. Sketching for less than a minute, he produced a line drawing of a bird of prey, its name written in childish handwriting at the bottom of the page. Kai handed it to Ben. "Red Tailed Hawk," it said.

The eerie screaming sounds were obviously from the hawk depicted on the paper. Ben's camera suddenly seemed very inadequate. You couldn't produce a photograph if you could not capture the subject in the lens. After catching one glimpse, this boy had shown him what it was Ben could hear high above, without Ben seeing anything.

As they moved on, Ben tried to gauge how far up the mountain they had traveled. He realised it was probably not as far as it seemed. Walking on the vague track, he wondered who had trodden it before them. Whoever it was seemed very short as the way was clear of prickly bush around his legs but not his face. Of course, it was a goat path! Feeling silly at the obvious conclusion and studying his feet so as not to fall over, he walked straight into his friend's back. Kai had stopped and was looking smugly into a clearing around an out of place piece of level ground.

In front of them was spread a collection of crumbling walls of varying heights, some forming complete rooms and some partially surrounding open areas. All the ancient walls were broad just like the sugar mill ruin. None had roofs. Trees grew in and around the old buildings, and creepers were thick and matted, connecting the stone walls to the green foliage.

Ben guessed that this was not the first time Kai had been here; he had known where he was going. Even if he could have talked to his friend, at this moment he couldn't find anything to say that was useful. He was in awe of a place that was so old. Ben had visited castles at home, even the Tower of London with his school, but those historical places had tourists crawling all over them. You knew that you were one of millions that had stood and tried to imagine the history. Here on the mountain, there was no noise other than the rustling of lizards in the leaves and a dove calling to a mate.

The sugar mill had small windows, but the openings in these walls were really only slits. The boys climbed over a low pile of stones into an area that was open and flat. Stepping carefully, Ben turned and was now facing out to sea. Even though the trees were obscuring a lot of the view, there was still a natural break in the way they grew here, and he could see parts of Sunset Cove. They had to be halfway up the hill. No ship's cannon was going to reach this stronghold. The invaders would have to attack on foot, leaving themselves vulnerable while they scaled the mountain as he and Kai had.

Kai made his "come here" noise, and Ben spun around, at first not seeing him. Walking back into the rear of the ruins, he spotted the boy behind a wall. Kai was

Eye of the Storm

brushing at the stonework with his fingers. With closer scrutiny, they could make out what looked like graffiti. However, this was not your average swear words or some kid declaring undying love to his girlfriend carved into the wall. It was a ship—a ship with two masts and square sails—a pirate ship!

"Wow," he said out loud. "This has to have been drawn by a soldier on guard here who was looking at a ship in the cove!"

Kai guessed what Ben was saying, pointing towards the sea and using both his hands, dancing about when necessary, he portrayed a sailing boat, with guns and cannons and aggressive intentions.

Leaving the deaf boy (who Ben was gaining more and more admiration for as the day went on) copying the illustration on the stone wall into his sketch book, Ben found a high place from where he could sit and look out to sea. Because of the height, Scorpion Island was a different shape. More of the contours could be seen as a landscape rather than just an outline. Still no signs of life, though.

A movement in the bush behind him made Ben jump. After a few moments of silence, he relaxed, only to hear it again but this time from a different direction. He could see Kai still drawing and knew that he would be oblivious to any alien sounds anyway. Telling himself to stop being a scaredy cat, the English boy called Sandy to him. The dog trotted over from where he had been scratching at the earth. Feeling better for the company but still uneasy, Ben started to hanker for the open, sunny expanse of the beach.

Sandy began to growl. It began way down in his throat and was so low it was barely audible. The hairs on the dog's neck and back stood up with fear and aggression. Ben leaped to his feet as concerned that it was the first time he had seen this young dog show any sign of anger as wanting (or maybe not wanting) to know what was the cause of the display. Scanning the tight forest around the fort, Ben could see or hear nothing. Sandy, still growling, walked a few steps away from his young master then stood deathly still, the noise from his throat no longer a deep hum but loud and interspersed with violent barking. Kai still didn't look up from his work, for the time being Ben was alone standing behind Sandy who no longer looked like the fun-loving, gentle animal that had licked Ruby's face but rather a violent protector, waiting for an enemy to strike.

What was happening? Were there really jumbies here? Frantic thoughts were flashing through Ben's twelve-year-old mind.

With razor-sharp teeth showing white under his curling lips, Sandy moved slowly forward, placing each foot cautiously, as if in slow motion. Then he leapt. Within the shadows of the trees, a dark figure moved. Kai had obviously seen the dog jump and looking at his stance, dropped his sketch book and ran to Ben.

Regaining some of his sensibilities, Ben called out, "Hey, who's in there?"

This seemed to be Sandy's signal to leave the boys and go and finish the job. The dog charged into the undergrowth, and within seconds there was a male voice yelling from above them.

"Call him off, man!"

This sounded more human than ghost, and Ben, who had been holding his breath, exhaled with relief that some distorted ghoul, known in Kamaria as a jumbie, was not going to come stomping towards them.

"Get that dog away!"

Gingerly walking toward the source of the noise, the boys could see Sandy standing with his back paws on the ground and his front paws stretching up a palm. Above the dog's frantically barking head was a skinny man wearing obnly a pair of cut-off shorts, gripping the narrow trunk with his feet, waving his hands at the animal.

"Who are you?" Ben yelled, feeling, at least for the moment, like he had the upper hand.

"Man, who you is?"

"Sandy. Come." Ordered Ben.

The beach dog looked back at the boy then up at the man in the tree but didn't budge. After Ben's repeated, insistent commands, Sandy reluctantly backed off the tree. He sat proud and tall between the two youths and intently watched the man, seemingly waiting for the slightest indication of a harmful move towards his new family as if to show that any slight excuse would be enough to take a chunk out of the guy's leg.

Kai was laughing at the stranger, pointing at him as he reversed down the coconut tree. The man was lean and so very dark that Ben was fascinated by the way he looked. He stood in front of them, eyeing the dog that was standing again with his hackles raised.

"I'm Ben; this is Kai. We were just exploring the fort."

"Nelson," the man said. He had long dreadlocks, and each individual muscle and tendon stood out under his glistening skin.

With much persuasion, Sandy relaxed his hackles and with a great deal of suspicion, sniffed at the stranger as he walked past him. Still not convinced, however, he placed himself between the boys and the Rasta.

"What are you doing up here then?" Asked Ben.

"Me go bush sometimes. Me live out here, hunt on the mountain and fish in the sea. What's up with that kid?"

"Kai is deaf and dumb. He can't hear you."

Kai was making weird noises jumping around pretending to climb trees. Ben had a sneaky suspicion he was taking the mickey out of the guy. He wasn't convinced that this was a very clever attitude. This Nelson dude still looked very strong and more than slightly weird to Ben.

Wondering what he had been hunting, but deciding not to ask, Ben said, "Well, we should probably get going, my Mum will be wondering where I am." Feeling a bit wet saying that but also thinking it would be a good idea to let the Rasta know someone else was around to come to his rescue if need be, Ben picked up his backpack and nudged Kai hard in the ribs.

Sandy, still keeping his body between his beloved Ben and the hunter, jumped to his feet sensing that they were out of here.

"There's still stuff around here from the English that defended this place. They had guns and cannons, ya hear."

Ben, intrigued by this, said, "Like what stuff?"

"Look on the far side. There's a cannon."

"Really? That so cool! Where?"

"Come."

The Rasta walked away from them, and Ben (disappointing his dog, who still behaved that this human was not to be trusted) followed. Kai, seeing the general movement up towards the top of the clearing, tagged along. Nelson scrambled up a steep incline and pulled away some dead fronds and piles of rotting ground cover to reveal an intact, single cannon. Jumping up so that he was on top of this leveled off piece of land overlooking the main fort area, Ben touched the huge gun. The metal was cold, and yet everything surrounding it was soft and warm. Even now the weapon meant business.

Kai, grinning again, sat astride the cannon, pretending to load balls into the black hole in the open muzzle. Using the built-in flash, Ben took some shots of the cannon and Kai.

"Me found musket balls before. There was a siege up here, and men fought. The English ran off the Spanish and then the privateers held the harbour for their own ships."

Not knowing anything about Rastas generally, Ben was surprised that Nelson knew so much about the history of the fort.

"It's an amazing place. Don't other people want to come up here?"

"No man, most people think it's protected by jumbies, so they leave it be."

"Mr. Hamilton said that, and his sons and nephew were too scared to come with us. Well, except Kai."

Nelson looked knowingly at Kai. "That boy, he has spirits in him. He don't need to be bothered by jumbies."

Puzzled by this comment, Ben asked, "What do you mean by that?"

"He was born like that right? He a special one. Spirits look out for kids like him. He knows things you don't, right?"

"Well I guess so. He can draw and swim well, and he seems to love nature and animals and stuff."

"See, he gifted, but because of that, the spirits took away his voice and his ears."

"You might be right about that," Ben said. "We've gotta go. Thanks for showing us the cannon."

"I'm heading back down the hill, too."

Waving at Kai to follow, Ben set off, glancing back over his shoulder for one final look at the fort. Maybe he would bring his dad up here; he'd love the cannon. What he would give to show Tony around. That would be sick. They could properly explore and discover some treasure, maybe.

Sandy kept shooting Nelson filthy looks every time he got too close to the boys, he seemed to be hoping he would get a chance to scare him off for good.

When they were almost at sea level, Ben crouched to remove his trainers, planning on throwing himself into the cool blue water as soon as he reached it. He noticed that Nelson was still hovering behind them and then he remembered something Mr. Hamilton had said—it was Rastas that took supplies out to the Frenchman.

"Hey, Nelson," he shouted over his shoulder, "What do you know about Scorpion Island?"

CHAPTER 14

A BIRTHDAY SURPRISE

Becoming thirteen is incredibly important to all kids, and Ben was no different. His parents were acutely aware that if they had been in England, their now teenaged son would have had a cool birthday party with his friends, probably at the yacht club. Instead, they tried to make as much of a fuss over him as their current surroundings would allow.

Two weeks on Kamaria, and Benjamin Johnston was very chuffed to finally be thirteen. He missed his English friends desperately that day. MSN messages and emails flew back and forth between the Caribbean and the South of England as Charlie and Tony laughed and joked with him and made a remarkable attempt at celebrating in cyberspace. Charlie teased Ben saying that he was only a year younger than her now. In reality, there were about eight months in it. She told him about her exploits on the Laser 4.7, the dinghy she was training with now at the club. He was envious but countered with his adventures in Sunset Cove. As expected, Tony liked the fort story best, especially the bit about Sandy chasing the man up the tree.

That Sunday afternoon, as a surprise to Ben, a small group gathered at his beach home to celebrate. The party consisted mostly of his father's colleagues and their families all, unfortunately, with younger children. Much to the birthday boy's amazement, however, his mum had apparently walked up the beach, introduced herself to Mr. Hamilton and invited him and his boys along, too. They turned up later than the rest of the party, which his dad told him was normal procedure in Kamaria where people were proud to live on "island time." Ben felt quietly pleased that he had made friends so quickly. Isaac was hanging out with him, and Shamoi spent his time consuming whatever Penny offered him. Jehiah was a bit more aloof, standing in the shade looking awkward while Kai was halfway up a tree examining a bug. Mr. Hamilton had become deeply engrossed in conversation with Frank. Ben couldn't decide whether this was a good thing or not.

For reaching thirteen, Ben received some cash, a mask, snorkel and fins and a nautical map of the local area. The closest islands and cays around Kamaria were all shown. Also illustrated were the depths of the waters surrounding the bays and inlets that couldn't be seen from the roads. Sitting up in bed that evening, Ben carefully studied the chart. Scorpion Island had a bay on the far side protected by reef, just like Mr. Hamilton had explained.

When Ben had asked Nelson the Rasta about Scorpion Island, he hadn't said much, just talked about occasionally delivering supplies to a "mad white man" on Long Bay. He explained that a local captain who kept a fishing boat in New Town harbour did the run and only when they'd had a lean harvest with their own lobster pots.

As his eyes got heavier, Ben memorized the route across from Sunset Cove to the tiny island. He fell asleep dreaming of meeting the buccaneer and discovering hidden loot.

The next morning, he couldn't wait to get to the beach to try out his snorkel gear. Pulling the huge fins on, making him look like something out of *Happy Feet*, he walked a few ridiculous steps before realising that they were best donned last, once you were in the sea.

The equipment seemed cumbersome on the beach, but once he lowered his face below the surface, he couldn't stop himself from screeching down the snorkel tube in his mouth. The blurred pastel shades and movements that he had been watching from above for the past two weeks miraculously came into sharp focus through the glass mask. The sight was so vivid it was almost shocking. Everywhere he looked was alive with marine creatures. As he floated over submerged rocks, brightly tinted fish—some miniscule and others pretty big—got on with their day in a complete, new world.

Ben wasn't prepared to see so much so close to his face. He slowly swam, hanging above cities of swaying purple fans, boulders painted with sharp corals sparing none of the colours from a rainbow. Anemones with thousands of delicate reaching arms caressed the tiny fish that hovered in their clutches while brittle black spines belonging to sea urchins stood arrogantly on the reef.

Looking ahead rather than directly below, his visibility extended into deeper water where midway between the seabed and the rippling surface silhouetted shapes swam. These fish were larger. Many had deep, v-shaped tails; some were black with intricate designs on their heads; some were covered in vibrant, bold splashes of colour; all moved regally through the depths.

A school of brilliant blue fish swam below him, each identical and each ignoring the boy that was still grunting down his snorkel with delight and discovery. They looked to Ben like they were showing off, the way they cruised as a team. He followed them and reached out his hand. They didn't look back but coolly increased their swimming speed to avoid the intruder. Realising that this species looked very much like Dory from the movie *Finding Nemo*, he smiled under his mask, feeling the tickle of leaking water around his nose as the seal broke for a moment.

Lifting his head above the surface for the first time in what felt like a short lifetime, he pulled the mask away from his face, draining the salty contents, then leisurely treading water, looked back at the beach. He had drifted further from the shore than he'd intended while totally engrossed in this dazzling marine world.

Heading back towards the beach and his beach house, he returned his face under the water and simultaneously splashed and screeched, spitting out the breathing tube in the process. To the boy's left, suspended a meter below the surface, was a very large, slender fish. To make matters worse, the giant was smiling at the thrashing snorkeler, showing off a perfect line of needle-like teeth. Ben kicked out with his fins and powered to the beach, all thoughts of passively studying the reef were gone in an instant. When he reached the shallows, he risked a look over his shoulder for the first time. Out of breath and feeling a little silly, Ben flopped on his back and let the sun dry his stomach.

"That was some mean-looking fish," he muttered to himself. He hadn't, in fact, seen the monster follow him or even move from its hovering position. One look at those smiling teeth and the ugly face was enough for Ben not to need a second one. He made a mental note to stay closer to the beach for a while, just to be on the safe side.

At his birthday party the day before, one of his dad's colleagues had told him, "There is nothing in the sea that can harm you more than a minor jelly fish sting or standing on the spines of a sea urchin." Ben wondered if David, his dad's coworker, had forgotten about this particular Caribbean sea monster or if its lack of good looks was the worst of its traits.

Noticing a wide shadow passing under him, Ben rolled over and peered through his face mask again. The fascination of everything coming into focus just like adjusting the lens of a camera was mind blowing. With his face so close, even the vast seabed became individual grains of sand. The shadow flashed past the edge of his vision. As he turned in the direction of the movement—still a bit jumpy—he saw, gliding like a hovercraft, just centimeters from the sand, a sting ray, lazily flapping the edges of his wings, creating a cloud of dust around him.

Ben could see the entire ray in detail: its comical eyes so close together on the upper body, holes that he assumed must be gills either side of his eyes and a skinny tail at least the length of his body that ended in a tip like a cartoon devil, complete with a spike on the top. Sting rays had gotten a lot of bad press a couple of years ago. Now that one was within touching distance, Ben figured it would be best to resist the urge to reach out to this particular fish. This underwater creature was so beautiful and yet so weird at the same time. Lying prone on the glassy surface of the sea, Ben watched the ray slide away. A few minutes later as he idly messed with a small crab, he heard his mum call him in for lunch.

After some food and a search online for tropical reef fish, Ben was bursting to go snorkeling again. He walked up the beach with Sandy in tow. That morning, the dog had stood in the shallows doing his own version of fish watching while his human friend splashed about grunting into his snorkel.

Isaac was at his uncle's, and he and Kai said they'd come in the water with Ben. Isaac explained where the best snorkeling was to be found, following the rocky edge of the cove beyond the shack. The three youths sat in the gently lapping sea and spat in their masks before pulling them on their heads. Ben had already decided this technique was totally gross, but it did make sure that the glass lens didn't fog up. Kai was leader of the pack—he cut through the water without a single splash, his fins remaining just below the surface. Ben followed, immediately feeling more secure swimming in close quarters with his friends. His imagination seemed to get far less carried away knowing Isaac was behind him.

Exploring the marine world with Kai was even more fascinating than earlier when he was alone. Kai knew where to look and which stones to move, uncovering a funny looking starfish or a type of crab that looked more like a long legged spider, and he even pointed out an octopus crouching in its lair. How cool was that? Kai also seemed to be able to dive down under the water with such ease. Ben tried it a few times, trying to get down to octopus eye-level. Kai demonstrated squeezing his nose and blowing to clear his ears as he descended. Isaac smirked and informed Ben that he looked like a total nerd, thrashing his fin-clad feet in fresh air for ages before he managed to get them under the water. Once he did get under, he found it hard to stay there, and although he had been warned not to touch the coral, he had reached out to steady himself so he could see the creature and felt a burning scratch on his finger.

Ben kept practicing until he felt a little more adept at using his snorkeling gear. He still had problems at the surface as he came up for air. He noticed that Kai didn't lift his head up at all; rather, he simply blew the water out of his tube and continued on. Ben found breathing out before you breathed in, when your lungs were screaming for oxygen, was not as easy as it looked. Mostly, he coughed out the mouthpiece, drawing attention to himself, before starting all over again.

It seemed that Isaac was not as adventurous in the water as his cousin. He had hung back just within his depth whilst the other two continued on, confident enough to explore their surroundings. Engrossed in a coral head that housed a whole myriad of tiny fish buzzing around and potting a huge, spiny lobster hiding in a crevice, Ben felt a bump on his shoulder. Squealing and spinning around, expecting to see the monster from earlier (that, according to the internet, was a barracuda, fairly harmless although there were some conflicting opinions), he instead got a face full of dog.

"Sandy, what are you doing here? You nearly gave me a heart attack!" The dog tried to climb on Ben, his sharp claws digging in.

"Get off me!" Sandy did and proceeded to swim in tight circles around him and Kai. Watching his legs pump away underwater was hilarious. He didn't seem to be stressed and wasn't going to be sent away, so Ben, nudging him each time he got too close to his face, just got on with his snorkeling. The boys discovered they could tease Sandy, if they dived under the water and held their breath for as long as they could, the dog lost sight of them and obviously figuring out that they were under there somewhere, he panicked and thrashed around until the boys popped up again, laughing at him.

Later that day, Ben's parents chilled while their children bathed the salt and sand away.

"It seems the kids have been talking online, hence the email from Charlotte's father."

"So, they are willing to fly her out here then?" Penny was trying to catch up with the news her husband had brought home with him this evening. They were sitting on the deck enjoying the rapidly setting sun.

"Yeah, she has the rest of the summer spare, and I think goes back to school just a few days before Ben."

"Frank, she's a girl."

"Well, I realise that."

"Where will she sleep?"

"That's the only problem. I was hoping Tony would be able to make some of the summer. If he does that's easy; he can bunk in with Ben, but I'm not sure about Charlie."

"It is a shame. They do seem to get along, and I quite like her. Is there anyone else she can stay with at work?"

"I could maybe ask Jonathan. He has two little girls, but if she does that, the logistics will be ridiculous— getting her over the hill and back every day."

Penny considered the problem as she sipped from her wine glass. "Maybe we could put some kind of partition up at the back of the living room. We don't spend any time in there; we're on the deck all the time. Can you borrow a bed from somewhere?"

"Yeah, I'm sure I can get something. Kids on holiday don't care what they sleep on, right?"

The sun was gone. It happened amazingly fast. Ben could actually see it move in the last couple of minutes as it disappeared behind Scorpion Island. Now the sky was a vast, dramatic, abstract painting with black edges around pink clouds, drifting on a violently blue background. Neither Frank nor Penny had gotten used to the display. They sat most evenings around this time in wonderment, catching up with each other's days' news, before Penny served dinner, and the bugs began to bite.

Tonight, the barbeque was lit in the yard just in front of where they sat. Smoke seemed to help to keep the noseeums at bay; they tended to nibble at sunset. Penny had taken to using a spray-on, personal bug repellent on herself and Ruby. The men in the family said it smelt bad and preferred to use plastic tennis rackets loaded with batteries. These were great toys. When they pressed a button, the metal strings became electrocharged, and if you managed to hit a mosquito, it cracked and fizzed as the insect was fried. Frank and Ben had hours of fun keeping score of kills.

"Do you think Tony's family will want him to fly over, too?" Penny asked as she stood to check on the charcoal.

"I don't know. They've gone a little quiet. They had talked about sending Tony to Edgington College with Ben, but I'm not sure that they have the finances to make it happen. I haven't said anything to Ben about either of his friends coming to stay because it's far from sorted out, and I don't think we should risk disappointing him."

Opening the screen into the kitchen, Penny replied, "Well if Tony comes, he can sleep in Ben's room—if Charlotte shows up, perhaps we should ask Jonathon to put her up. I can pick her up and take her back to their place when I drive in and out of town with you each day."

After dinner that evening, Ben received a nudge on Live Messenger from Charlie. He was delighted to hear that her dad was actually contemplating flying her out to Kamaria. He also noted that his heart rate suddenly increased and was glad he was in his room alone as he could feel his neck and face colour up as he read the instant message. After chatting with her about snorkeling with Sandy, he went to find his dad. "Charlie said she is allowed to come and visit us, Dad!'

"Yes. I had a conversation with her father today, and I told him that if you both were keen, then it was okay with your mum and me."

Penny interrupted, "We will have to arrange for her to sleep somewhere first, though."

"Um, yeah. I guess. Where?"

"Well, there are a couple of options. Let's just see how it pans out, okay?"

"Sure, Mum. It's so cool that Charlie's coming. She'll love it here."

CHAPTER 15
VISITORS

Although Sunset Cove was usually empty of beachgoers during the week, at the weekends, families came over the hill from town and splashed in the shallows. Some had floating toys and boards that the kids played with while the adults tended to stay up in the shady tree line at the edge of the sand. Ben never actually saw anyone swim. They mostly threw themselves under the water or stood in depths up to their chests but didn't do more than that.

One afternoon he was giving Ruby a swimming lesson—she could now kick happily with her orange arm bands on. In fact, she moved pretty fast and had caught Ben out a couple of times—he'd had to really work for a few metres to grab her. While they splashed about, he watched two businessmen and a Kamarian woman all dressed in office clothes and shoes standing in a huddle on the beach. Looking completely out of place and very hot, the strange group were deep in conversation close to Mr. Hamilton's shack, occasionally referring to clipboards and a large, wind-up tape measure.

This picture didn't look quite right to Ben—not just the long trousers and collared shirts but something else niggled at him. He felt annoyed that they were there, but he couldn't explain why. They moved out of their huddle and walked awkwardly to a vehicle parked at the bottom of the road from town. At this point, Ben recognised one of the men. He was the guy who had flown in the tiny plane with him and his family the day they had arrived on Kamaria. Maybe the other two were part of the welcoming party that had been enjoying the fizzy champagne; he couldn't be sure. He decided that he didn't like any of them.

That same afternoon, Nelson reappeared. Ben and Ruby were walking by the coconut trees looking for sticks to throw in the sea for Sandy. The dog, bounding back up the beach with one he'd retrieved for Ruby, spat it out halfway back to where the children were waiting and began growling. Spinning around, looking in the direction the dog's taught body was pointing, Ben eventually spotted the Rasta crouching on his haunches in the shade. Shouting at Sandy to stop it, Ben waved at the man.

"I'm sorry about Sandy, he doesn't normally do that with people."

"It's okay. He only doing his job," the man replied. "Who's this then?'

"This is Ruby, my little sister."

With Sandy's hackles only halfway flat, the threesome moved in Nelson's direction. The Rasta was doing something with a knife and a coconut shell. When they got close enough, Ben could see that Nelson had whittled holes out of the shell and tied a piece of line to the top of it. The holes made the coconut look like a face.

"Here. For you, little lady." Nelson offered the creation to Ruby who grabbed it and promptly threw it in Sandy's direction.

"Ruby! It's not a ball." Ben was embarrassed by his sister and ran over to where the coconut lay. Sandy glared at it, also very unimpressed. Nelson laughed and explained that it was a bird feeder. You hung it from a tree, filled it with sugar water and the birds would come.

"What kind of birds do you think will like it?" Ben asked.

"Bananaquits love sweet things and maybe hummingbirds, too. You'll see when you hang it."

"Thanks, Nelson. Ruby, say thank you." Ben's sister chose to go all shy and hung onto her brother's legs.

"Be sure to change the sugar water every day, or it turn bitter, and the birds won't come."

"Okay. Will do." Before walking away, he couldn't resist asking if Nelson had heard anything from Scorpion Island lately.

Grinning, the man cocked his head and looked at Ben. "What you want with that place?"

"I would just like to go there and meet the Frenchman and see his reef."

"They are going over from town tomorrow to buy some lobster from him. I gave them my pears to sell."

"Oh, wow. Do you think they would take me with them?"

Nelson laughed again. "You have anything to sell the mad man?"

"No, I just...Well, I just want to go for the ride."

"I'll ask if they want to take a white boy, but he won't let you near him. He talks to no one—just does his business, and that's it."

"I don't care if he doesn't talk to me. Will you ask your friends if I can go? Please?"

"Sure, maybe I go, too. They won't take you without me. I catch a ride to town with Beck and will come back here tomorrow with the boat if they say yes."

"Great. What time?"

"When they ready to go, man."

"I'll watch for you then." The Rasta walked slowly towards Mr. Hamilton's shack.

Hardly able to contain his excitement, Ben grabbed Ruby and the coconut feeder and ran up the beach, stopping short of his house as the realization of the practicalities of explaining all this began to sink in. How would he get permission from

Eye of **the Storm**

his parents to jump on a boat with a bunch of strange men? Maybe he should take his time and play with Ruby some more while he planned his approach to his mum and then, ultimately, his father when he returned from work.

"Hi, Mum. Look what Nelson made for you." Ben didn't feel it was necessary to actually point out that he gave it to Ruby. Besides, his little sister wasn't interested in it, anyway. Any little tactic that helped to get his mum in a good mood was worth it.

"Who's Nelson, for heaven's sake?"

"The man I met at the fort. Remember I told you about him?"

"Right. The Rasta man. You said Sandy didn't like him."

"Yeah, but he's really cool. He made this. Isn't it great?"

Holding it up by the string, she looked bewildered. "What is it?"

"It's a bird feeder, of course." Wearing his most angelic smile, he explained to his mother, "You hang it up on a tree and fill it with sugar water then the birds come and drink from it."

"That's very nice. Why don't you find a spot for it outside, and I'll boil a kettle and dissolve some sugar."

Ben did as he was asked, hanging it in a tree just to the right of the hammock on the deck, hoping that millions of pretty birds would flock to the holey coconut and make his mum's day, therefore preventing her from caring where he went tomorrow.

After fixing Ruby's favourite, plastic Fisher Price dump truck, Ben decided to risk introducing the idea of him going to Scorpion the following day. "Mum," he said. "Nelson asked me if I would like to go with him and his friends for a boat ride tomorrow."

"Does he have a boat, then?"

"Um, no…I think it's his friend's."

"What kind of boat and where are they going?"

"Well, they keep it in New Harbour, but they said they would pick me up from here on the way."

"On the way to where?"

"Well, I'm not totally sure, but he did mention the island just over there."

"They are going to another island?"

"It's right there." He pointed out of the open doorway in the general direction of the mystical island.

"You mean 'Scorpion Island'? I don't like that name at all."

Ben had to silently agree. It didn't help his cause much. Why couldn't it be called "Happy Island" or something that all mums would love? "They are just going to pick up some lobster, then come straight back again. Please, Mum? There's no problem."

"I haven't seen anyone wearing lifejackets since we've been here. Do they even have any?"

Ben couldn't disagree with that either, but he wasn't going to admit to it. "I am sure they do Mum. I'll wear one all the time."

"I'm not at all sure about this. You will have to talk to your father."

"Okay, whatever." Ben was disappointed but not surprised that he hadn't immediately gotten the thumbs up from his mum. He would wait until after his dad's second cold beer before he attempted to push the final decision in his favour.

A couple of hours later, when Frank was home from town with his first cold beer in his hand, Ben went and joined him on their front deck. Desperate to broach the subject of the boat trip but not wishing to seem too eager, Ben chatted about other stuff. "I saw some strangers on the beach this afternoon. One of them, I'm sure, was that guy who was with us in the little plane."

"I've met him a couple times since our flight. He is an investor, and our office is doing some business with him."

"That's cool." As he said that, Ben wondered if maybe it wasn't so cool, but he let it drop for the moment. The next subject was much more important.

"Dad, did Mum mention about me going on a fishing boat tomorrow?" Everything crossed, including his toes, he braced himself for what was to come next.

"Yes, she did say something about a Rasta and a trip to Scorpion Island, of all places."

"It's Nelson. He's really cool, and they are going to buy some lobsters from the man there and then come back and drop me off. He even made Mum the bird feeder. Look, it's a coconut shell."

"I had gathered that. Doesn't look like the birds have worked it out, though."

"It's nearly dark. I guess they like to eat in the mornings," he said. "So, can I go?"

"I would like to meet this Nelson person first before I make a decision."

Groaning, Ben knew that the Rasta wasn't going to be around before his dad left for work, so how was that going to happen? "But Dad, they won't be here that early."

"There are a couple of local fishing boats that moor on the ferry dock. Its probably one of those. If it is, I will talk to them when I get into town then call you after I've met them. If its not one of those, then you can't go."

Ben was lost for an argument around that one. He knew in his heart that this was the best he could expect and so just prayed for the rest of the evening that the boat was indeed parked on the dock in town and that Nelson had even asked the others about him going before his dad showed up. Otherwise, they would naturally deny all knowledge of some 13-year-old boy tagging along, and that really wouldn't help.

CHAPTER 16
SCORPION ISLAND

With his cell phone burning a hole in his pocket, Ben paced back and forth from the house to the beach straining his eyes for a boat approaching the cove, willing his phone to ring with news of his dad's "comforting chat with such responsible chaps."

It was nearly ten o'clock before his mobile finally rang. "I found the boat. They were loading fruit and vegetables in it, and I have met Nelson. I'm not sure the other men knew what I was talking about, but they did show me that they had lifejackets onboard, and you will wear one all the time, right?"

"Absolutely. Of course. Thanks, Dad!" Hopping from foot to foot he promised to be sensible (yet again) then hung up and ran into the house. "I can go, Mum. Dad said it's okay."

The diesel-engined fishing boat came rolling around the left-hand corner of Sunset Cove a half hour before noon. It approached the beach, but as it had a deep hull, Ben had to wade out to it. Throwing his backpack aboard, he swam the rest of the way, and Nelson hauled him over the side. Waving at his concerned-looking mum and Sandy who sat to attention next to Ruby, Ben then turned to say hello to the two other men on the boat. Neither said much. The captain only grunted something that Ben couldn't understand, so he retreated to the back, feeling a little less conspicuous sitting on an upturned bucket close to Nelson.

It turned out that Nelson had not gotten around to saying anything about Ben joining them by the time Frank Johnston showed up in his office clothes. Nelson had let the crew believe that the white man was a boat inspector—that's why they were so keen to show him their lifejackets! He then told them, after Frank had left, that the inspector's son wanted a ride to Scorpion and that if they did that, it would keep the official off their backs. Looking around the untidy boat, as the old engine rattled and droned, straining under its workload and smelling the reeking, ancient yellow lifejacket, Ben was very glad that he wasn't really an inspector's son, as he would have to recommend condemning the craft.

The sea was just a little bumpy. The occasional wave broke on the bow, but generally it was a dry trip. The captain drove them straight across from Sunset to the south side of Scorpion Island then headed right and took a course which led the boat between the island and a tiny cay. Ben could see breaking white water about two boat lengths on either side of them and remembered seeing a shallow reef marked on the chart that almost joined the two pieces of land together under the water. The fishing boat remained in the dark blue areas, avoiding unquestionable destruction on the harsh rock that lay in wait for less informed seamen.

As they turned the corner and could see the windward side of this lonely island, a huge, perfectly semi-circular bay opened up ahead. Simply called Long Bay on Ben's chart, it was lined with tall palms as if they had been measured out and planted by a human hand. The birds dived, and in several areas, the sea boiled with feeding fish, rolling on the surface. The swell was lazily crashing onto a reef that seemed to surround the entire bay. This protective arm converted the energy of the waves rumbling in from the Atlantic Ocean into a transparent pool of still water in which the sun's rays provided dramatic lighting, revealing some of the magic happening below.

It was so beautiful; even Sunset Cove didn't look like this. In the left hand corner, nestled a small building with two other wooden structures behind. A fire burned in a clearing nearby.

The captain was slowly approaching the reef, aiming his eight-metre fishing boat directly at the deadly breakwater. Ben wanted to scream for him to stop, and his face must have given away his anxiety as Nelson nudged him and said, "Wait and watch!"

The boat slowly motored over the reef. Twice the helm was spun hard across, making the boat lean into the violent turns. After seeing massive coral heads so close he could have touched them, Ben closed his eyes. Then they were through. The boy let go of the breath he had been holding in a gigantic sigh of relief, followed by a gasp as he looked over the side of the vessel. He was not yet used to the marvels of the underwater life in Sunset Cove, but even without a mask and snorkel, he could see that this pristine, secret place was far more mind-blowing.

The mate went forward to the anchor lying on the deck and studied the seabed for a good place to drop it. When he raised his hand, the captain responded by stopping the boat's propeller and, seeing sand below, the anchor was lowered, followed by chain—clanking on the edge of the hull. Nelson pointed at the beach.

"There he is. You wait onboard. He won't want you near." Squinting into the sun, Ben saw the figure of a tall man striding towards the shallows. He wanted to protest about being left on the boat, but he was so stunned by the surroundings and also this presence standing looking at them, he said nothing.

All three men checked the boat's holding and then moved the boxes of fruit forward, ready to unload. The captain jumped over the side into waist-deep water. He waded ashore and nodded to the Frenchman. They spoke for only seconds and then

Eye of **the Storm**

the exchanges began. Fruit was offloaded before a plastic crate was thrown onboard, containing angrily shuffling spiny lobsters.

Ben couldn't do anything but watch the scene. He could see goats. The fat ones tethered; others roaming free in the shade of the trees behind the dwelling. Chickens just like on Kamaria scratched the scrubby ground around drying skins hung from a line strung between two palms behind the fire. The settlement seemed organized and tidy, if a little primitive.

"What's that?" A strong, male voice shouted. Ben jumped and turned in the direction of the question.

"He's nothing, man. Just some white kid."

"Nothing? What do you mean, nothing? What's he doing here? You know my rules—no spectators."

"Its cool, man. We leaving with him right now."

"It's too late. He's here isn't he? Why did you bring him?"

Nelson spoke.,"He's a good kid. He was interested in the reef."

A taunting, sarcastic laugh came from the tall man. "Of course, he must be so interested in my reef!" He turned, staring directly at Ben. "Come here, boy."

Ben shivered; he couldn't move.

"You, boy, come!"

For the second time that day, Ben was frightened. "Me? I'm sorry, I didn't mean to disturb you, sir."

"Well you did, didn't you, boy? Now you are here, you shall come ashore."

Nelson looked at him smiling kindly. "He's okay. We're here. Do as he says. His bark is worse than his bite."

Ben slowly walked to the front of the fishing boat and slid into the still water. Hesitating, not sure whether to hide behind Nelson, he lifted his chin and waded clear of the sea. "Hi, my name is Ben."

The man stood so still in front of Ben he could have been a statue. He was white, but tan enough to pass as a West Indian. The stranger looked older than Ben's dad but very fit and wiry. He wore shorts that came to his knees, a loose white shirt and his long hair was tied back in a ponytail. His face was deeply lined and a gold shackle hung from one ear. For a fleeting moment, Ben imagined this man on the *Black Pearl*, fighting with a sword in one hand and musket in the other.

"I am known as the Frenchman around here, but I should introduce myself properly. Monsieur Michel de Grammont at your service. Why are you here?"

"I'm staying in Sunset Cove with my family for the summer, and Scorpion Island just looks so fascinating, and my Dad got me a chart, and I was wondering what the reef looked like, and um, well, Mr. Hamilton told me about where you lived, and…" Ben was so nervous, he gave up trying to make any sense and just stared at his bare toes in the wet sand.

"Beck! That old man still alive? I'm sure Beck told you some wild stories about me."

"No, sir. He just said that you are related to, well, I think he said a buccaneer."

The Frenchman laughed in a way that sounded kind of cold. "I get it now. You wanted see a real life pirate, eh, boy?"

Ben was wishing he was back on Sunset Cove with Sandy and Ruby.

"So tell me. Do I look like you imagined, or perhaps this is more like it?"

The man turned and walked away towards his wooden chalet. Ben stayed where he was, glancing at Nelson and the others to make sure they were still there. The two boatmen were back aboard the fishing boat, stretched out on the shady side of the deck, drinking from bottles of beer. Nelson was on the beach crouching on his haunches again, watching the conversation between the boy and the Frenchman.

"Come here, boy." The Frenchman was yelling at him again.

Ben, strengthened by a little anger for being treated this way, started up the beach. Curiosity was still getting the better of the thirteen-year-old. What was it his mum always said? "Curiosity killed the cat." Ben hoped the same fate was not ahead of him. Approaching the home of this man, he looked back, subconsciously planning an escape route in case this crazy guy came at him with a sword.

The threshold that Ben crossed as he entered the home was a piece of driftwood, worn smooth and white with time and saltwater. The room was dim, and Ben's eyes frantically tried to adjust to the lack of light after stepping out of the midday sun. Open shutters hooked back outside served as windows—there was no glass. Ben saw a space where a single man lived, surrounded by old and strange looking artifacts. There were objects and pictures hanging from the walls, and the longer he stood and looked, the more he saw stashed in the simple residence.

"Here, does that look more like your pirate?" Monsieur de Grammont was pointing at a portrait hanging on the wall.

Ben examined a painting, obviously hundreds of years old, of a man dressed in a maroon cloak with a white shirt underneath a matching maroon sash around his waist. His legs were clad in loose, black, three-quarter-length trousers. His shoes were open leather sandals (not black boots!) and a strap lay diagonally across his shoulder and chest. A musket was stuck out of a brown belt on the buccaneer's hips. His right hand was hidden beneath the cloak; his left held a long rifle resting on his shoulder. The handsome face was clean shaven, apart from a thin moustache. His hair was long, underneath a wide brimmed hat.

"Who is that?" Ben asked.

"That is Michel de Grammont."

Eye of **the Storm**

"Oh, I thought you—"

"He is my ancestor, the buccaneer. I was named for him."

"How old is the painting?"

"If you mean when was he alive, he was born in 1645 in France. He died here in 1699."

"Wow. He died here on Scorpion Island?"

"No. Kamaria. He lived there for thirteen years after the hurricane of 1686 when he was separated from his fleet and was assumed lost at sea." Ben tried to take in how long ago this was. As if reading his mind, Michel said, "Three hundred and twelve years ago."

"That's so cool. Did he raid lots of ships?"

"He was famous for taking four thousand hostages for ransom from Vera Cruz in Mexico. He and his compatriots operated out of a place called Saint Domingue—it's now called Haiti—look it up online."

Ben was taken aback by the reference to the internet. He had assumed this guy was a hermit that had shunned the modern world. "Yeah, okay. I will. I'm sorry for disturbing you, sir. I should probably get back to the boat."

"How old are you boy?"

"Thirteen—last week."

Ben watched as the man's face seemed to glaze over and his lips lifted slightly into a half smile as he looked straight past the boy. "So, what do you do apart from bother people?"

"Um, well I've been learning how to snorkel, but I really like to sail." This came out without him thinking about it.

"Sail? You mean you can actually sail?"

Self-consciously, Ben replied, "Yes, I can."

Walking away from Ben again, Michel strode out of the chalet then hesitated in the heat of the Caribbean afternoon. "You have come here disturbing my peace, and already I have given you too much of my time. Now you say you are a sailor. What do you sail?"

"Well Toppers actually and recently Lasers." As soon as he said this, Ben knew that this man would not know what he was talking about. Even to him, the names of the plastic boats seemed alien in this environment.

"I assume they're dinghies?"

"Yes, sir," Ben said, yet again surprised that this loner knew what he meant.

"Well, when you want to learn about something other than toy boats, let me know."

Hurt by this comment, but deciding that he ought to give up whilst he still could, Ben simply replied, "Okay."

Nelson stood and stretched as Ben approached, and the pair waded out to the waiting boat. Michel de Grammont stood and watched them prepare to leave.

As the anchor was hauled clear of the water, the Frenchman yelled in his clear, harsh voice, "Watch the smoke, Ben."

Although he had witnessed it done successfully once—less than an hour ago—returning to the open sea through Dog Leg Reef was no less scary. Ben wondered if he had heard the Frenchman correctly. He was sure that he had said "Watch the smoke," but Ben had no idea what that meant. Waiting until they were through the reef (as it seemed totally inappropriate to speak to anyone whilst the captain and mate were concentrating on not going aground), Ben asked Nelson what the guy had meant.

Smiling, showing Ben that regular visits to the dentist weren't a priority in a Rasta's way of life, Nelson explained that the fire was lit to show the approaching boat the direction of the wind. Being so close to the land, the breeze was fluky, and the smoke would demonstrate any shifts as they navigated the dogleg. Even a boat with an engine rather than sails was affected by the wind, and the captain needed an accurate indication of direction and strength so he could make small changes to the way he drove in and out. On the way home, Ben thought about this, understanding that with the wind on the side of the boat and no margin for error in the narrow channel, the captain needed all the information he could get. The fire was obvious—so simple and so clever.

Having about forty minutes to sit and think as the boat chugged its way back to Sunset Cove, Ben tried to remember every moment of his experience on Scorpion. He had been scared, shouted at and treated as an unwelcome guest. He had also in just a few short minutes met the descendant of a famous French buccaneer, learned about the original, seventeenth century Michel de Grammont, and had the weirdest conversation with a dude that a couple times had given him the distinct impression that he wanted to tell Ben (or at least someone) much more than he had. Did he want to repeat the encounter? You bet.

CHAPTER 17
GIRLS

It was sorted. Charlie was, at that precise moment, flying over the Atlantic on a charter flight that flew the same route that the Johnston family had taken. A short pond hop, and she would be arriving at Kamaria's totally understated airport at quarter past seven that evening.

Ben had these weird butterflies in his stomach and was convinced by late afternoon that his watch had to be going backwards. It was taking so long to get through the day. If only they could use a portkey like the wizards in *Harry Potter*. Eventually, the time came to go into town, pick his dad up and then drive to the airport at the end of the island. Waiting as the tiny plane came in to land and then catching glimpses of Charlie looking very anxious as the immigration (and then customs) officer looked down at her, was turning Ben into a nervous wreck. She was only a friend for heaven's sake, so why did he keep catching his parents looking at him sideways with knowing expressions on their faces?

When she walked through into the disappearing sunlight, Charlie was great. Normal. She didn't make a fuss, just said, "Hey, Ben," like she'd seen him at the club only yesterday and then was very polite and chatty to his mum and dad which took the pressure of him for a while. By the time they were back at Sunset, he felt chilled again and just keen to catch up with her, in the same way he had done each Saturday earlier in the year. It had been decided that they would go with the blowup bed behind a makeshift screen in the corner of the living room and see how she got on. Certainly, it would have been a shame to split up the friends as soon as she arrived. As it turned out, the plan worked fine, and there wasn't any need to find Charlie alternative accommodation.

The next day, the two teenagers ran into the sea laughing and cracking jokes at each other. Frank had borrowed another set of snorkel gear, knowing that the first thing Ben would want to show off was the marine life. They both spent so long in the water, their skin was wrinkled like raisins. They finally had to give in when the sun turned the sky red. Sandy fell in love with Charlie immediately, following her around like some besotted adolescent. Ben was almost tempted to get jealous of the infatuated dog but decided that would be really lame.

They talked for hours, catching up with stuff in England and also Ben's exploits on Kamaria, especially, of course, Scorpion Island. Between them, pouring over his chart, they hatched a plan to persuade Isaac to get permission to use his uncle's dory and return to Long Bay. Ben knew that it would have to be on a flat day when there was no swell, to be safe in the small boat, and also he had to talk to the captain of the fishing boat to learn the secret of the way in through Dog Leg Reef. He was too ashamed to admit to Charlie that his eyes had been shut most of the time the previous week.

The first problem went amazing smoothly. Mr. Hamilton didn't seem to have the same over-the-top worries as his parents and ended up being more concerned about them taking Kai along, so he could check his fish pots on the way there. The second problem demanded a trip to town.

This was done around the illusion that Charlie wanted to check out the shops. It seemed harmless enough to Penny, so she dropped them by the hotel on the way to her husband's office and told them that she would be back in half an hour. To her, that meant ample time to check out the almost nonexistent shops. Ben had to hope that he was lucky enough to catch the captain by the dock. If not, they would have to hatch up plan B.

The seaman was there. Unfortunately, he looked like he had slept on the smelly boat and was not in a happy-go-lucky kind of mood when they woke him up. After a very painful conversation, when all Charlie could manage to do was stare, the old fisherman finally remembered him and began to explain the method of approach.

Ben walked away thanking him for his time, but only having understood a couple of sentences out of fifty. Something about a black rock and crossing the reef when he was aiming at the third coconut tree from the left and could line it up with the right side of the house. Great. That was going to make all the difference.

Waiting for Ben's mum to pick them up, Charlie announced out of the blue, "It's a transit."

"What?"

"A transit," Charlie repeated.

"What's a transit?"

"You line up two or more fixed objects that you can see from your position on the boat. If they don't line up any more then you're not where you were before."

Trying to absorb this information that Charlie had recited, worryingly reminiscent of his maths teacher, Ben repeated her words, "You line up two objects that you can see, and if they don't line up, you're not where you are?"

Taking pity on her confused friend she suggested, "Let's do it now. Look over there towards the hill, and pick two things that can't move, like the side of a house and a telegraph pole or something—they just have to line up together."

"Okay. What about that truck and a coconut tree behind it?"

"Well yeah, I guess, but if you were doing it for real, the truck is no good because someone might drive it away. But never mind. Now take a step sideways."

Ben, feeling rather ridiculous staring at a truck and a tree with one eye closed, took a step.

"Hey! Not on me, airhead!"

"Sorry. So now what am I supposed to do?"

Sighing with growing frustration, Charlie said, "Can you still see your transit?"

Ben Squinted again. "No, I can't. The tree has gone."

"Well, actually," Charlie said, sounding more and more like his math's teacher, as she continued, "the tree is still there. It's just that because you moved your position, the two fixed objects no longer line up within your view."

"I see. Of course. I think—"

"In other words, if you drive the boat towards the reef and you are not lining up the third palm tree from the left with the right side of the house, you will miss the channel and go aground."

Ben kind of got this, but the general idea of using things on the land to avoid sharp things in the water didn't exactly fill him with confidence.

Spotting Penny driving the pickup towards them on the dusty road, they crossed over and leapt in the open back when she stopped. The journey back to Sunset Cove, out of earshot of Ben's mum, was long enough to plan more details. They decided to ask Isaac and Kai to come with them in the dory as soon as the wind eased and no Atlantic swell was forecast.

Before they grabbed their snorkel gear to cool off, Charlie and Ben checked an online weather site. They selected the local geographical area and displays appeared with five-day predictions of wind, rainfall and wave height for both sides of Kamaria. A satellite image of the Caribbean showed several coloured flourishes depicting meteorological systems. This was, after all, hurricane season, and it seemed to the pair that their window of opportunity should be sooner rather than later.

After having swum with the undersea world for a while, with Sandy bumping back and forth between them, not willing to stay on the beach out of their way, Ben showed Charlie the ruined sugar mill and explained how they made rum from the cane carried down on the donkey's backs. When she began to get all concerned about the poor donkeys, he gave up and climbed on top of a pile of stones that used to be a chimney, so Charlie could take pictures of him with his mum's camera.

Larking around, they headed to the far end of the cove and Mr. Hamilton's shack. Ben had been concerned that Shamoi and Jehiah would want to be in on the trip to Scorpion, and although he didn't mind including them, he was conscious of the extra weight in the small powerboat and also the Frenchman being angry at the amount of "spectators" he brought along. He needn't have worried, though, as Beck's two older sons were working over the hill on a construction site. Isaac was pleased to see Ben and shy around Charlie. He dragged Ben away from the girl in the bikini top and very short surf shorts, congratulating him on his "fine girl." Ben's face went bright red as he tried to explain that she was just a girl friend not a girlfriend, but that just made Isaac worse.

"So you wanna go tomorrow? We have to gas her up."

"No, let's plan to go the next day. The forecast said that the sea should be pretty flat."

"Okay, man. You bring the cooler." Ben figured that was the least he could do in the circumstances, so took food and drink orders from Isaac and Kai. At least this way there would be something other than orange Fanta to drink.

That evening and the following day passed with more swimming and hot sun. Charlie, like Ben in his first few days, got burned on her shoulders and nose. They had decided not to give the Johnstons too much time to think about the fact that the two teenagers were planning to go out in Isaac's boat, so didn't drop in the idea until the night before. With a surprising feeling of guilt, Ben had left out their planned destination in his request for permission and vaguely talked in circles about Mr. Hamilton's fish pots and Kai needing a hand. In the end, with the usual, boring, safety issues repeated from both parents, the adults gave in and said yes. Mostly, Ben thought, to get off the subject.

Excited, and in Ben's case, very nervous about the boat trip, they lay on his bed, chart spread under his and Charlie's elbows, both their heads held up by their fists. Occasionally a faint tickling sensation rushed through Ben's shoulder as the girl accidentally brushed against him as they discovered, according to the publishers of this navigational aid, that there was no way through Dog Leg Reef.

CHAPTER 18
SHARKS!

The forecast was spot on—not a cloud in the sky, almost no breeze at all, and the Atlantic Ocean was like a mirror. With Isaac driving, the outboard motor steadily buzzed as the dory cut through the calm sea. The young companions were on their own now, no adults, and any restrictions would be of their own making. That was why Ben loved to sail, it was the feeling of being in charge of your own vessel. There was no other way to do that. The closest alternative was to wait until you were sixteen and drive a motorbike. Today was the ultimate. They really were in charge of their own destiny.

A little knowledge can be a heavy responsibility on young shoulders, and Ben was getting pangs of this now as he repeatedly checked off a mental list of items that he had made Isaac put onboard. He knew they had more than enough fuel, an old rusty air horn had been found under a pile of rubbish, Kai's fishing gear had a knife in it, and Ben's mum had gladly provided a little plastic box containing some basic first aid things. The drinks and snacks in the ice box were enough to last them the rest of the week, if necessary, and with a cell phone and tiny digital camera in his backpack, they had to be fine. Charlie had seen Kai look longingly at his tatty sketchbook and pencils on the way out of the shack that morning, so she'd picked them up and shoved them in, too.

The only ballast in the powerboat that he was still unsure about was the four-legged one with the extra long tail. Ordering Sandy to sit still for the fiftieth time was making him regret giving in to the dog's whining as they were leaving. Listening to Charlie, who had been making cooing noises as if the dog was going to die on the beach if it was left alone for a few hours, had been fatal. She had wound Ben round her little finger, so today he'd conceded and called the dog onboard. He liked that Sandy was part of the adventure but worried about how the Frenchman would react to him and, more to the point, how Sandy would react to the bizarre man.

Isaac made a pit stop on the way to a polystyrene float marking a fish pot. Kai hauled on the rope and slowly brought a woven mesh and stick box close enough to the surface to be able to see any trapped inhabitants. Apparently, by the way he grunted and let go, dinner was not there. Ben was quietly pleased as he really wasn't into dead fish sharing the nice, clean ice box along with his lunch.

Driving on between the high cliffs of Scorpion on their left and Black Cay and its solitary, battered palm tree to the right, Ben began to get butterflies in his stomach about turning the corner and facing Long Bay. The dude had no idea they were going to turn up, and they were far from confident about getting through the deadly reef in one piece. If they did make it, what then? Just drop the hook and nonchalantly stride ashore? Ben was curious about the rest of the bay and wondered if it would look better if they approached from further down, but he had no way of navigating in anywhere other than facing the third palm from the left.

It was too late to change his mind now, anyway. They were all staring at Long Bay. The usually quiet Isaac said, "Wow".

It looked different from Ben's original trip. The sea was so flat, there were no breaking waves on the reef, creating the illusion that it had disappeared.

"Okay, man. You drive. You the expert." Isaac flicked the engine into neutral and moved from his seat next to the throttle arm.

Glancing at Charlie, whose eyes were glued to the wooden chalet in the corner of the beach, Ben changed places.

"One, two, three. There, Ben. That's the tree!"

Ben pulled the lever towards him, and the outboard pushed the boat forward again.

"Wait. You have to go over in that direction first before you'll be able to line it up with the house."

"Oh, yeah, right. I forgot."

Shaking her head and flicking Kai in the face with the end of her ponytail (which he didn't seem to object to at all), Charlie sighed, "The transit remember?"

"Yeah, yeah. Look, you tell me when you see it from the bow, and I'll drive, okay?" Ben said then mumbled to himself, "How does she expect me to do everything at once?"

"We're on it, now. That's the transit."

Aiming into the beach, Ben started to sweat. How would he spot the dogleg turn? He wished this had not been his idea. What if he trashed Mr. Hamilton's boat? Isaac looked worried, and Kai was gaping at the coral all around him. Frantically trying to recall when the fishing boat had changed course so violently the previous week, he switched the engine back into neutral.

Looking up at the beach beyond the nightmare, he saw smoke. Even in the nanoseconds he had to think about anything else other than where the next razor edged rock was going to spring from, he was sure that the fire had not been burning when they had begun their approach. The smoke was wispy and rising straight. Not a breath of wind moved it from the most direct route, up into the sky. That meant he had a little time to sit in neutral without drifting off course.

"Isaac, stand up and look ahead. Can you see a way through?" The boy did as he was asked.

Sandy took this movement as the signal to abandon ship. In a flash of brown fur, he leapt to the front of the boat and performed a perfect belly flop, generating a splash that Ben was sure had resonated off the cliff faces of Scorpion Island. "Thanks, Sandy. Add that to my worries. If you don't get cut to ribbons on the way in and bleed to death, you'll probably get shot by a mad pirate when you hit the shore."

Charlie cut in, "Ben, remember the black rock the captain told us about?"

"What about it? They all look pretty black to me."

"I think he meant under the water, not on the land. Look there, just ahead."

It stood out like a sore thumb, if you happened to know what you were looking for. Unlike the sharp, colourful, coral heads, this huge bolder was jet black and silky smooth.

"Yes. It has to be where the fishing boat turned right." Ben motored carefully forward, and just before the rock was lost under the front of the boat, he pulled the helm of the engine hard over.

After regaining his balance, Isaac shouted, "Hey, man, tell me if you gonna do that trick again."

"Sorry, but I had to—"

Isaac interrupted, "Wait. It's a little deeper here."

"Okay, now look out for another turn that takes us back to the beach." Tearing his eyes away from the sides of the boat, still anticipating the final bump as they went aground, Ben searched for the smoke signal. It was still straight.

"Where's Sandy, Charlie?" Convinced that he was going to see him stranded somewhere walking on the sea urchins, he couldn't bear to look himself.

"He's standing in the shallows doing his chasing-the-fish act."

"Thank God. That dog is a nutter."

Kai had been quiet up to this point, but now his sharp eyes had spotted the last turn into the beach. He pointed frantically to their left and made a noise to let them know he'd found it.

"There's sand that way," Charlie said.

"Okay, hold tight." Ben swung the throttle arm back, and the dory did her last ninety-degree turn putting them through the reef.

By the time Ben and Charlie's heart rates had returned to normal, and the adrenaline had emptied from their veins, Kai had placed the anchor in ten feet of pristine water. Looking around for Sandy, Ben's gaze settled on Monsieur de Grammont standing—feet apart with arms crossed—with the dog sat coyly by the tall man's side. Ben's concerns were forgotten as he watched an almost invisible movement of the Frenchman's hand as it dropped to gently stroke the animal's head. At least he liked dogs.

Isaac and Kai were already pulling on snorkel gear. As they threw themselves over the side of the dory, Ben felt like a trespasser. "Charlie, I think I should go and say hi to the Frenchman. Will you come?"

"Sure, let's go"

It annoyed Ben just a bit that she didn't seem in any way bothered by this guy. Still, maybe she would when he started ranting and raving at them.

As they waded ashore, the man began to clap his hands. It was a slow clap and Ben knew he was being ridiculed again. He wondered what the guy would have done had they gotten stuck out there. Ben suspected that he would not have been too quick to throw himself in to help the stricken children.

"Hello Mr. Grammont. Um, this is Charlie. I hope you don't mind, but you did say to come back if I wanted."

Laughing at them coldly, the Frenchman replied, "Yes I did, didn't I? Although you seem to have brought half of Kamaria with you."

Gesturing behind him he explained, "That is Kai and Isaac. They are family of Mr. Hamilton. It's his boat."

"I know the boat. So that must be the deaf boy. I remember him when he was a baby. His family thought that he had spirits in him."

"Yeah, that's Kai. He's amazing—a really good artist and swims like a fish."

"Usually, when you lose one sense, the others become very sensitive," mused the man, mostly to himself.

"This is Sandy. He is really well behaved and won't bother you."

This time the Frenchman laughed with some genuine feeling. "Boy, I have more time for most dogs than I will ever have people." Not entirely sure which way to take this last comment, Ben figured it was just good that the eccentric man hadn't tried to run them off the island, yet.

"Well I have things to attend to. I take it you have food and drink with you?"

"Yes, sir. Charlie and I were hoping to snorkel and maybe go down to the other end of the bay."

"Whatever you want, boy. You'll see young sharks in the pool down there. They have been trapped since the last spring tide."

"Sharks?" Charlie had said nothing until that moment, and both Grammont and Ben turned and stared as if they had forgotten she was there.

"Yes, mademoiselle, but they are very small and harmless to a human."

"Cool," Ben said. "Let's go check them out. I'll get the boys." He then turned and jogged up the beach so he could attract Kai's attention, knowing he was going to love the sharks.

"So tell me. Charlie seems like an inappropriate name for a young lady."

"Well my name is Charlotte, but everyone calls me Charlie." Looking up into the man's eyes for the first time, the fourteen year old sensed sadness so deep, she involuntarily took a step backwards.

Quietly the man said, "I knew someone called Charlotte once, but her nickname was Lottie."

"Yeah, my grandmother calls me that. I like Charlie better."

"Well, it's far too hot to stand around here. You run along with your friend. I have things to do."

She began to walk away but then turned back and spoke, "Ben told me that you sailed."

Grammont scoffed, "In a past life. I don't any more."

"Why is that, sir?"

"I have no need."

"But it's fun to sail, even if you don't have a purpose," she insisted.

The cold laugh returned. "So I take it you can sail toy boats, too?"

"Yes, I can. But they aren't toy boats. The best sailors in the world learn in dinghies." Then, as an afterthought to show a little respect, she added, "Sir."

"I'm sure they do, Charlotte. I'm sure they do."

Charlie caught up with the three boys, and they all made their way towards the west side of the bay.

"Lookee there!" Isaac pointed at something in the water and stopped abruptly.

"What?"

"Baby shark. See him?" Everyone strained to catch a sight of the black-tipped shark cruising along the reef line looking for a way out. The shark was about a metre long and very much a shark, with its flat, square head and dorsal fin displaying the juvenile beginnings of a black point.

Ben stood and watched the creature until it was out of sight then turned away from the water, idly looking at the undergrowth that met the sand near the tree line, just like in Sunset Cove. Something caught his eye—a blue tarpaulin. The manmade thing looked out of place here. He stood right next to whatever the tarpaulin was hiding now. It was a boat. It had to be, but unlike one or two wrecked powerboats he'd seen deserted on Kamaria, this was a different shape. Lifting up an edge of blue material he crouched and gazed beneath, knowing immediately what it was—it had to be—the sloop that Mr. Hamilton had said belonged to the Frenchman. It was her, left abandoned. It had to be.

"Charlie, come here." Ben pushed the bush away with his back as he slid between the covered hull and the trees that had grown around it. It reminded him of a fairytale from one of Ruby's storybooks about a wicked witch who had locked somebody in a tower with illustrations showing how the forest had grown up, hiding the hostage from the rest of the world. Peeling the covers away from the sloop, he glimpsed small pieces at a time. The protective wrap was still tied on well. He fought his way to the other end and was able to make a bigger gap, letting fresh air in over the high stern of the wooden sail boat.

"What's up?" Charlie had caught up and was looking at the dirty tarpaulin.

Excitement rising in his voice, he exclaimed "This is it!"

"This is what?"

"This has to be the sloop that he sailed with his wife. Mr. Hamilton said that they took her to New Town when his wife was pregnant. She was really ill and died there."

"What about the baby?"

"The baby, too."

"That's so romantic. No wonder he lives alone out here. He's pining for his lost love."

"What on earth is romantic about someone dying?"

Charlie rolled her eyes in explanation.

They were both leaning over the stern, their heads hidden from the sun, feet hanging in the air, trying to make out more of what was underneath. The moment was broken by a high-pitched scream that brought Isaac running. Charlie threw herself away from the hulk, batting at her hair.

Ben's face was panicky. "What's wrong? What is it?"

"Something was crawling in my hair. It fell down there somewhere." Charlie was still dancing in circles shaking her head. Isaac arrived and looked down to where she had indicated.

"Hey, it's a scorpion."

Charlie screamed again.

"Calm down," Ben said then spotted the tiny creature as it made its escape into the trees with its tail carried high, threatening the sting at anything that dared come too close.

"You lucky. They hurt," Isaac announced, throwing stones at the ground just in case.

"Gee, thanks." Sarcasm replaced horror in Charlie's voice.

Without cutting lines on the tarp covering the boat, it was hard to see much more than they already had. There was a long, hand-carved, pale wooden tiller in place, and once he'd pulled back weeds and bush surrounding it, Ben could touch the rudder on the outside of the hull. His bare arms and legs were scratched by the "prickle plant," as Isaac called it, but, too thrilled to let this slow him down, he kicked around in more undergrowth until he uncovered a long spar which had to be the mast. It looked like it was made from a single tree trunk—all one piece. As he exposed more of the

Eye of **the Storm**

long pole, two stainless steel collars glinted in the sun. These were drilled and fitted with shackles and the attached rigging wire had been carefully coiled. This boat hadn't been simply abandoned. Thought and care had gone into packing her away.

"Hey guys, come over here." Charlie was at the bow holding up a piece of loose tarpaulin.

"Look, here's her name. It's *Hardi*." They could see the word carved into a plank below the sloping front, the letters hand painted in red.

"I wonder why he named a boat that."

"I think it's a lovely name."

"Who this boat for?" Isaac demanded.

"It's the Frenchman's. It has to be. Your uncle said he used to sail to Kamaria in a sailboat like this."

"Where the engine is?"

"It doesn't look like she has one."

"What good is that, man?"

Ben just shook his head. There was no point in trying to explain to anyone around here why you didn't necessarily need an engine. Isaac was carefully placing one foot in front of the other, walking along the edge of the boat.

"She about twenty five feet."

After the mental conversion of imperial to metric, Ben looked at Charlie as she opened her mouth to protest and explained. "That's about eight and a half metres."

Realising he hadn't seen Kai for a while, Ben scanned the area. "Isaac, where's Kai?"

"Scribbling again."

Charlie wandered over to where the boy sat on a round rock. She smiled, gesturing to him in an attempt to ask if he minded her looking at his work. He offered the sketch book to her. Taking it, she sank to the sand next to him with her hand over her mouth in astonishment.

The page of white paper had been transformed with a soft pencil into a likeness of the *Hardi*, fully rigged with two billowing sails as the sloop charged over surf-topped waves in front of a back drop of Long Bay. In Kai's sketch, two people were aboard her. With just a few inspired pencil strokes, he had made Charlie and Ben the crew. With a grin and tears in her eyes, she kissed the deaf boy on the cheek and returned the sketchbook to his talented hands.

"So you found it then."

They all jumped in their skins except Kai who still had a dazed look on his face from the kiss. Ben spun around to find the Frenchman, hands on hips, watching them with a black look on his face. Sandy bowled up to him and for a split second the expression changed to compassion as the dog distracted Grammont's gaze.

Raising his head to glare at Ben he asked, "So, what is your expert opinion, boy?"

"I hope you don't mind. We haven't disturbed the cover, just looked underneath. Um, I…she looks great, sir."

Charlie, sensing Ben's nervousness, asked, as brightly as she could, "Why is she called *Hardi*, sir?"

Smirking at them, he just said, "Look it up on your internet. That's where all the answers are now, I understand." The sarcasm was evident, but Ben still made a mental note to do that, just to spite the weirdo.

"Why don't you sail her anymore, sir?"

"I told you. I have no cause to."

"Don't you ever leave Scorpion Island?" Charlie's natural nosiness was spilling out now.

"No. I have everything I need here. Nelson and his friends deliver items I cannot grow or hunt myself."

Determined to not be outdone by Charlie's brave questions, Ben couldn't control himself any longer. "Sir, could we sail her?" There, he'd said it, what was the worse that could happen now? The guy would throw them off the beach maybe?

"You?" He moved his hard gaze from one teenager to the next. "You're just children!"

"Yes, but we can sail, and Isaac and Kai are good boatmen; they would learn fast." The Frenchman seemed to be looking past them, just like he had the previous week. Eventually his focus returned to Ben.

"She needs to be rigged and her mast hoisted and stepped. You can't do that alone, boy."

"But with your help we could!" Ben could feel the stern man's desire to see his sailboat afloat again seeping through.

"I cannot sail this boat again." It was a simple statement but said with such regret that Ben fell silent.

Thinking for a while, he offered. "If you help us get her ready, we can sail her for you."

For the first time, there was a glimmer of humanity in the haggard face. "Charlotte, do you want to be a part of this madness?"

"Yes, sir. Very much so!"

"I think you are all crazy, but why not? We will do it. Don't think you have earned my respect yet; it will take hard work to get her seaworthy once more." For the first time, he laid his hand on the covered gunwale but then pulled it away as if an electric charge had shocked him. Striding up the beach he looked over his shoulder and called back, "Well, get the tarp off, then."

That afternoon they removed the tarpaulin, and, much to Charlie's disgust, three more scorpions and a handful of spiders and lizards escaped from the sloop. The wooden boom was made from another piece of tree and longer than either of

Eye of **the Storm**

the young English sailors had seen before. The mast step was a far forward, and the elaborately carved stem held the metal fitting for a jib sail. There were lines and ropes in a canvas bag but no sails to be seen. Isaac did his Kamarian trick of falling asleep under a shady tree, but Kai was in raptures over the contents of the hull. He stood at the back holding the tiller with one hand, with his other dramatically sheltering his eyes, pretending to be some great sea captain sailing into the sunset.

Conscious of having to navigate over the reef again, Ben suggested they begin to make their way back to the anchored dory. They had not seen the Frenchman since their strained conversation, so he thought he should call at the small house and update him on their progress. Ben stood in the open door, searching the gloom for signs of life.

Then without preamble, a voice said, "The bag to your left, it has sails in it. The main must be laced around the boom and tied to the wooden rings on the mast. The jib raised on the halyard."

"We've got everything ready to lift the mast. I'm not sure when we can get back, though, there was some bad weather forecasted for later this week."

"Whatever you choose. If you don't return, she will rot where she is."

There was no answer to this, so Ben retreated. As he did, Charlie pushed her way past him.

"Sir, I thought you may like this. Kai drew it this afternoon." Charlie handed over a piece of grubby paper from the sketch book that had been carried over in Ben's backpack.

Offhandedly, the Frenchman reached for the paper and glanced at the picture. He breathed in suddenly, "How did he know?"

"I'm sorry what do you mean?" She asked.

"How on earth did he know that she looked just like that?"

"He's a special person, I think, sir."

"Thank you, Charlotte, and thank the boy for me."

Gobsmacked, as this was the first time Ben had ever heard the man be in any way polite to anyone, Ben could have hugged Charlie for thinking of this. With that thought making him all flustered, he stumbled outside, mumbling about "getting a move on as it was getting late."

They retraced their steps over the reef with the fire still lit and the smoke showing that the wind was blowing gently offshore. On the way home, Kai drove and the remaining three friends chatted about how and when they would return to Scorpion to raise the mast on *Hardi*. Sandy slept in the bottom of the boat, oblivious to the plans that were being made.

CHAPTER 19
TROPICAL WAVES

Not being able to focus on much else other than rigging *Hardi*, the two friends schemed together and digested as much online information as they could about this kind of sailboat. The first thing Ben had done the night they'd returned to Sunset Cove, after thanking Mr. Hamilton for the use of his dory, was to Google the original Monsieur de Grammont. A couple of sites confirmed that he truly was a buccaneer in the seventeenth century, and his claim to fame seemed to be as the Frenchman had boasted at their first meeting—taking thousands of people hostage along the coast of Mexico, eventually exchanging them for "shed loads" of cash. There wasn't much else to discover, except one very interesting fact—the name of his flagship was none other than the *Hardi*!

The weather site that Charlie had relied upon to predict conditions for their boat trip appeared to have gotten its facts right yet again. The blob they had seen on the satellite picture was now hanging over the island. The wind was still very light, but clouds hung low over the tops of the surrounding mountains, and the torrential rain that had begun to fall at daybreak completely obscured Scorpion Island as if a spectral paintbrush had whitewashed it and its neighbour, Black Cay, off the horizon.

Growing tired of staring at the small computer screen, Charlie and Ben decided to brave the rain and get some fresh air. Ruby was playing up her mum. She too seemed frustrated with being inside the tiny beach house and without the traditional bad weather option of watching her favourite cartoons on TV, so the two-year-old was stomping around, whining and bugging them all. Agreeing to take her with them for a walk, the teenagers dressed her in a yellow rain jacket and hat and opened the front door. Sandy was on the deck looking totally miserable, curled up in a tight ball with his nose pushed up under his tail. As they stepped into the downpour, the dog lifted his head and stared at them as if they must be out of their minds.

"I guess he's not coming for a walk then," laughed Charlie.

Swinging Ruby between them as she held their hands, they made their way under the limited shelter of the palm trees to the place where Ben, a couple of weeks before, had started to climb towards the fort. The sound of rushing water came from within the dark canopy of dense trees.

"Hey, that must be the ghut."

"Whats a ghut?"

"Remember? I told you that's what Kai and I followed up the hill to find the ruins of the old fort. It was dry then, but it's a kind of gulley that leads the rain water off the mountain. Now I can see how. Let's take a closer look." Reluctantly, she followed him into the shadows. The noise got louder, and there, not far ahead, was a fast-flowing, miniature waterfall, tumbling over slimy green rocks.

"That's pretty."

Ben agreed. "It's amazing how much water is coming down the mountain. That's just since this morning." Sitting for a while, watching Ruby mess around on the edge of the fresh water flood, Ben realised that it was a nice change for the sun to be hidden behind thick clouds and his skin not to be red hot. A bit more like home. Charlie must have felt the same as she was chatting about the yacht club.

Only half listening, as he waited for the inevitable moment when his little sister would topple off a slippery stone, head first into the ghut (that was, before their very eyes steadily spreading towards the open beach eventually to mingle with the ocean), Ben's ears suddenly pricked up as he heard the name "James."

James was one of the junior clique at the club. Last year, Ben had admired him, as he was fifteen and a good sailor, but this year he couldn't understand that admiration because the kid was just a loud mouth. Charlie's next statement sent the strangest feelings shooting through Ben that made him stand up and then wonder why he had, so he promptly sat down again. His stomach immediately filled with bouncing butterflies, and for a chilly day, Ben was experiencing a weird, overheating sensation.

Charlie had just calmly announced that James had asked her to go out with him the week before she had flown to Kamaria.

"That nerd?" Was all Ben could think of to say.

"Well for your information, I said no."

"Whatever."

He knew he was not handling this very well. If he continued to make out that he didn't care either way, he suspected that would not be what she wanted to hear, but the alternative was to say something profound and with his stomach now in his mouth, his tongue didn't have any room to move let alone form sensible words.

"Just thought you should know, anyway."

Even to Ben's untrained ear on romantic scenarios, she sounded pretty annoyed at his lack of reaction.

Ruby to the rescue. Just as Ben was about to die of the embarrassing silence, Ruby fell from her perch with a yelp into the cool water. So relieved to able to legitimately get out of the uncomfortable atmosphere surrounding them both, he was

Eye of **the Storm**

a little over the top about the fuss he made of Ruby, who once she knew she hadn't done too much damage to her knees, began splashing around in the clean mountain water. Charlie laughed with her and the moment was gone—for now.

On their return from Scorpion Island the previous evening, there had been the predicament of what to tell (or not to tell) Ben's parents about the happenings of the day. Eventually, after running on blindly about empty fish pots for a few minutes, Ben came clean and admitted they had ended up at Long Bay on the north side of Scorpion, making it sound like it had been an accident and they'd just kind of decided at the last minute, "as they were so close they may as well."

Neither adult said too much, but they were certainly listening. It was Charlie who finally owned up about hoping to return again soon to work on the sloop. She had thought it may ease the pressure off Ben by making out that it was she who was pushing to go back. Penny didn't like the idea, but even she couldn't come up with anything other than the old favourite excuses to back up her fears.

Frank was partially swayed by the very mature way Charlie was predicting and understanding the weather patterns, quoting all sorts of phrases that he wasn't entirely sure of himself, preventing him from pursuing the subject. In the end, the Johnstons resigned themselves to the inescapable fact that the four youngsters would return when the conditions allowed.

Secretly, this was exactly what Frank had been hoping for when he had taken the post out here. Compared with the necessary boundaries that were placed around his son growing up in what he and his colleagues called "the real world," this island still offered relatively safe environments for a teenager to explore unrestricted.

Frank had loved to camp as a boy, and he and his two brothers had been allowed to go off for weekends into the woodlands behind the next village where a river provided fishing and canoeing adventures for them and their mates. Building fires and climbing trees was such an important part of his childhood, and when he looked back, even with the freedom they had been given by their parents, they had never done anything too controversial. The odd cow got chased, and he remembered one incident when they had gotten kicked out of an orchard by an irate farmer (he also had memories of the pain in his stomach that evening due to the amount of unripe fruit he had consumed). He wanted Ben to make the most of his summer here, and if that meant Frank giving his blessing to cross a channel to another island where they could restore an old sailing boat, then so be it.

The rain was relentless, and by late afternoon, water was pouring past the beach house that, with the exception of areas of the deck and a soft spot over Ruby's bed, thankfully was impressively dry. Frank had called Penny at three o'clock that afternoon and asked her to come and get him early as the roads were becoming treacherous, and some were already littered with rocks washed from the hills. It was now obvious why all the vehicles on Kamaria were four-wheel drive.

Ben had volunteered to keep his mum company on the trip into town whilst Charlie stayed with Ruby. Penny tentatively drove the pickup up the hill from Sunset Cove towards the clouds. It was like driving the wrong way up a river. Moving water passed under the tires, and every now and again, the back wheels spun, making an awful screaming noise before they found something solid to grip again. Reaching the clouds reminded them of foggy days in England, but Penny was far less bothered about the lack of visibility than the amount of water flooding past her wheels. Mother and son sat in the truck on the brow of the hill looking down. They couldn't see New Town—just cloud. They were now about to drive *with* the flow down the course of a flash flood.

Wouldn't that be worse? Penny worried, but kept those thoughts to herself. "Oh well, here goes!" She shifted into the lowest gear and pointed the vehicle down the hill.

They got down in one piece, having to dodge a small landslide consisting of a tree and lots of dirt spread three quarters of the way across the road. Both were relieved to see Frank waiting outside the office building, and Penny was more than happy to relinquish her position as driver as she moved over and sat squashed between her husband and son. Twenty minutes later, they pulled up next to the beach house in Sunset Cove and sprinted to the deck, all three piling through the door into the dry kitchen.

The open door was Sandy's opportunity to slink in behind Penny, who ran in last. In the rush of being home and safe, no one noticed the damp animal curled up behind a wicker chair. In fact, it wasn't until Ben went to feed his dog that he noticed that he was no longer on the deck. With the smell of Pedigree wafting around, Sandy couldn't resist revealing his hiding place, and everyone laughed as he appeared looking thoroughly guilty.

"Ben feed him outside and then let him back in tonight. The poor dear cant be expected to sleep out in this ridiculous weather!"

Trying very hard to keep a straight face at his mum's concern, Ben did just that, and Sandy did just that, too, quietly taking up position behind his chair for the evening, somehow understanding that he shouldn't push his luck and make his presence too obvious.

The family and friends in the beach house at Sunset Cove had witnessed a "tropical wave." Charlie's weather site explained that during the Caribbean summer months, spinning low pressure systems shoot off the West African coast, some growing dangerous as they cross the Atlantic Ocean. The bottom end of the scale in which these weather patterns are measured is the "wave," then comes a "tropical

Eye of the Storm

depression," if it continues to build, it is given a Christian name and called a storm. At the top end of this scale are hurricanes. A category number is allotted to the impressive monster of a system, depending on the strength of its associated winds.

Ben understood the Beaufort scale which was how wind was calibrated in the UK, and this was sort of a similar idea. However, being in the path of a hurricane with winds above seventy-five miles an hour wasn't something he hoped to experience in this rickety old house.

Atlantic storms of any kind apparently also brought with them ground swell to any unsuspecting, exposed coastline. Early the next morning, after a restless night listening to rain hammering on the tin roof, Ben could hear a new sound. Peering out of his slatted window, he no longer saw a gently lapping edge to the turquoise sea as it kissed the sand. Instead, rolling breakers crashed onto the beach, moving the high water line significantly closer to the house, before sucking sand backwards as it rushed away, repeating this process like an opening and closing mouth. One thing was for sure, they weren't going to Scorpion Island today. Body surfing turned out to be the activity of the moment, and Ruby went without her swimming lesson.

CHAPTER 20
"PROGRESS"

The swell on Kamaria's north side stayed up for two more days, gradually dropping away, leaving in its wake debris littering Sunset's beach. Coconut husks, dead branches, a surprising amount of broken sea fans, driftwood and plastic bottles carried in from elsewhere made the place look astonishingly untidy as the friends walked toward Mr. Hamilton's shack, hoping to talk to Isaac about heading back to Scorpion.

Approaching the shack at the end of the bay, Ben saw strangers standing by the front door. Clad in town clothes, these were the same three people he and Ruby had seen with tape measures a week ago. Hesitating, thinking that they should wait until the visitors had left, both he and Charlie could see Mr. Hamilton standing in the shade of his partially open door. Watching out of earshot of the four-way conversation, Ben could see that Mr. Hamilton was not happy. He was waving his arms around a lot, just like he had at Sandy the first time he'd chased him off his property. Ben half expected to see him brandishing his machete any minute. Then the volume of the old, Kamarian man's voice was raised enough for the two young onlookers to hear him.

"I tell you people, I won't sell this land!"

A broad American accent replied more calmly, but still loud enough to be heard. "Sir, this is simply a courtesy offer as I am afraid with the land we have already pinpointed in Sunset Cove, your small lot will be surrounded by essential development, crucial for the future of this island. With this highly generous offer we are making for you and your family, a new home on the top of the hill or in town with all mod-cons will be well within your grasp."

Mr. Hamilton didn't hesitate, "Me not interested in moving. This my grandfather's land, and it stay in my family!"

"Sir, I am afraid life moves on, and tourism is an important part of the investment your government is making in this country. Our company will provide Kamaria with a five-star resort facility, attracting the world's most discerning visitors to your home. Don't you wish to share this beautiful place with the rest of the world, sir?"

Yet again, there was no indecision. "No!"

The door was slammed, and the American and his two sidekicks (who had been staring at their feet throughout this exchange) took a step back in amazement as if this was the first time anyone had ever had the nerve to close a door in their faces.

"That sounds serious," Charlie said to Ben. "Did you hear what that guy said?"

"Yeah, and if I was Mr. Hamilton, I would have wanted to do the same thing."

"Why? They are probably offering to pay well over what the land is worth just to get rid of the old codger. He's a lucky guy. He could build a lovely home for him and his sons somewhere else."

Ben glared at Charlie. "Don't you see that's his whole point? He doesn't want to. Mr. Hamilton doesn't have a TV or a telephone. He doesn't know about computers and iPods, and he has never seen a high-rise hotel. What more can he possibly need than to stay right here on his land?"

Charlie cocked her head and looked at her good friend. "Coming from 'Ben the Techy' who hated the idea of, I quote, 'spending the summer wasting his time in a boring dump,' that's quite a turnaround."

"Yeah, well I don't like the sound of these city dudes bringing hordes of tourists here. It would ruin Sunset Cove. Don't you think so?"

Charlie took her time to reply, "I guess so, but you can't stop progress, Ben."

"We'll see about that."

Ben strode past the unlikely beachgoers with his nose in the air, as they tried not to fill their shoes with sand walking back to a hired car. He wanted to talk to Mr. Hamilton and make sure he was okay. As he lifted his fist to knock on the door he stopped his hand in midair, he could hear Mr. Hamilton's eldest son Jehiah inside and a heated debate going on.

"Let me see that paper."

"You don't need to study that, they ain't getting our land, boy."

"They want to pay how much? We have to take this. It's crazy not to!"

Beck was shouting at the top of his lungs now, "We… We… I will decide, this ain't none of your business, boy. This my land 'til I dead."

"When you gone, what do Shamoi and me do, eh? It'll be too late. The land will be worthless."

Ben thought better of interrupting this family chat and turned and walked back to Charlie. She looked at him enquiringly, but he just said he didn't want to disturb the old man yet.

The thirteen-year-old felt like he had the world on his shoulders for the rest of the day. He wanted to talk to his dad. That evening, he did. "Dad, we overheard a conversation today about developing Sunset Cove into a five-star tourist resort."

"Really? I've heard similar talk at the office. Why the concern?"

"That American dude is trying to buy Mr. Hamilton's land and kick him out."

"I didn't realise they were going that far down the beach. But you know they will pay him a lot of money for his land, so maybe it's a good thing for him and his sons."

"He doesn't think so."

"Well, old people often resist change, and in a place like this, it's bound to happen sooner or later. That's progress."

"Not you as well," Ben exclaimed, getting up and stomping back inside.

"Hey, wait a minute. What do you mean?" His father stuck his arm in Ben's path.

"Nothing."

"It doesn't sound like you think its nothing."

Ben stared at the wooden deck below his feet. "It's just that, do you think everywhere should be like 'the real world'? You know, with technology and loads of people and cars and cities and pollution everywhere?" Stunned into silence for several moments, Frank Johnston's heart jumped with love for his son who was growing up before his eyes.

"Actually, now you have asked me to consider this question, no. I very much do not think that, Ben."

Pressing on with his unrehearsed speech, Ben said, "So in that case, we have to do something to stop this dude ruining Sunset Cove and taking away Mr. Hamilton's home."

"I don't think that's possible. His company is already poised to buy acres of waterfront, and I would guess they will have gone up the hill quite a bit, too."

Now looking beseechingly at his father, Ben insisted, "But they will trash the beach and kill the reef and, what do you mean up the hill?"

"It's a pretty impressive proposal they have put together. To fit it all in, they would have to build back up into the mountain."

"They can't do that; they would destroy the fort and the old sugar mill."

Holding his patience, Frank continued, "Perhaps they will restore them."

Somehow Ben suspected that the last thing the developers were worried about saving were a bunch of decaying ruins. He lay in bed that night, staring at the stained ceiling, making plans.

CHAPTER 21
HARDI

Back on the pale sands of Long Bay, it was obvious that Scorpion's north shore had taken a beating too. The tide had reached *Hardi*'s bow, pushing fallen palm fronds underneath the hull where she lay on the edge of the beach. The young team had more or less figured out what the mast should look like once it was raised, so they began checking the wire stays to make sure they weren't frayed and each had the fittings ready to attach to the boat. Each time Ben looked for something, he found it, confirming that the Frenchman had taken care when he decided he no longer wished to sail her, not discarding items that you certainly couldn't buy from the Kamarian supermarket.

One aspect that bothered Ben was the keel, or lack of it. From what he could see, the underneath of the hull was flush, imagining sailing the sloop in and out of Long Bay, he could only think that this was a very sensible design. However, if she had no keel and no centerboard, what stopped her from going sideways or falling over?

"Ballast!" The Frenchman had appeared from nowhere while the four where laying out the mast and clearing the debris left by the swell. As if reading Ben's mind, he explained, "The old sailors used stones arranged in the bilge to balance their sloops. It's a simple, clever system. You can alter the weight of the ballast stone that you carry depending on what cargo you have or even in which direction you want to sail. If you walk up to the far end of the bay, you'll find plenty of smooth rocks the size of your head that will suit her."

"Hey, that's cool. So you can have a shallow draft but still stop her from heeling."

"The down side is if you don't stack them just right, they will roll around the bottom of the boat. This, I am sure even you can imagine could be disastrous."

Charlie chipped in, "If all the rocks end up on the leeward side, then—"

Nodding his head at her, Grammont agreed before she had finished her sentence, "Exactly, mademoiselle!"

The sloop's owner walked around the boat, slipping into his own brooding world again, before abruptly turning in the direction of his home. As he strode away he called over his shoulder, "Collect the stones, and I will be ready to step her mast."

"Um, sir, how many stones do we need?" Ben asked his back.

"You work it out, boy."

"Thanks for the advice," Ben muttered under his breath.

"If we all walk down there and just pick up two or three, that's not going to amount to much weight, so we had better get started cause I reckon its going to take several trips," Charlie advised.

Isaac stormed off up the beach without a word. Ben figured he wasn't excited about the most recent task they'd been assigned. At this point, it was so hot that none of them felt like diving into a new task, so they dove into the sea instead. Ben and Charlie, followed immediately by Kai, charged into the water and floated face up, gradually allowing their body temperatures to return to normal.

Ben was squinting at the mountain behind Long Bay when he saw a strange sight. Wading towards them, waist deep in sea water, was Isaac leading the dory behind him like a faithful goat.

"What on earth is he doing now?"

Laughing out load, Charlie guessed straight away. "It's a rock transporter."

"Brilliant idea. Why didn't I think of that?"

Isaac yelled at them, "Hey, let's go get these crazy rocks, man."

They loaded the dory with smooth, dark rocks then easily towed the boat, the engine tilted, back up the bay to the waiting sloop. Unloading, Ben was careful to make sure no one put a stone on the sand. He made them spread the ballast out on a piece of tarpaulin for the Frenchman to inspect. Taking the dory back to her anchor and retrieving their lunch, they all sat in the shade of a huge palm and watched Monsieur de Grammont's livestock wander around.

"You kids ready to do this?" The man towered over them as they sat finishing their sandwiches.

"Yes, sir. We're ready!"

"I'll see you up there, then." They all looked at each other and then back at the striding figure on his way to the *Hardi* and jumped up, tossing the remains of lunch into the dory. Not sure whether to sprint and catch him, they ended up following at a respectable distance, due to the fact that he wasn't the sort of dude you made small talk with.

What followed that afternoon developed into a three-tier system where Grammont dished out the orders, Charlie served as 'middle management' and the three boys provided young, strong backs lifting and hauling the rocks to the boat. The Frenchman directed like he had done this job many times before and with no patience for young ignorance. Ben struggled to keep up with him, but was so fascinated by what they were doing, he committed every new word or technique to memory, determined not to let himself or the others down.

By late afternoon, the mast was up and secured and *Hardi* looked like a sailing boat again.

"That's it for today. You must return to Kamaria."

"Yeah, we do have to get going. I promised my mum we wouldn't be late."

"The sloop is ready to drag into the shallows and allow her planks to take-up. Bring old fenders from Beck's yard next time; we'll need them to roll her over the sand. There is a full moon in two days, so the tide will be at its highest at three o'clock that afternoon. That is when we will launch her."

"Okay. I think we can be here, I'll ask my—"

"Yes, yes. I know. You'll ask your mother."

His impatience getting the better of him, Grammont waved the teenagers away, he'd had enough of them. The Frenchman craved his isolation back. This was the most time he had spent in human company since… Involuntarily, he glanced up the hill to a glade of sea grape trees.

That's where his gaze remained as Charlie returned for her forgotten flip-flops. Without speaking, she followed his stare to some trees a short climb behind *Hardi*. The trees were shading a small area of cropped grass. Funny she hadn't noticed it before, but there seemed to be stones in the centre of the pretty grove. The mysterious man was lost in his thoughts, and even with her curiosity egging her on to ask what it was, she didn't dare break the spell. She turned, and carrying her shoes, jogged back to the boys.

"Charlie, do you remember when our council at home tried to take over the club dinghy park for more pay-and-display car park?" They had arrived back on Kamaria in time to take Ruby for a swim while Penny drove to town for supplies and her husband. Ben was seriously tired, but if he was to persist at clearing off for the day on a regular basis, he needed to score as many points as he could with his parents. He sat in the shallows and let the water bury him in wet, shifting sand. Charlie played with armband-clad Ruby who always insisted on throwing the ball as far away as she possibly could from the person that was supposed to catch it.

"Yeah, why?"

"Well they didn't, did they? I mean they got stopped 'cause we had nowhere else to store the boats and loads of people 'climbed out of their trees' about it."

"They got a petition up, and all the club members and people who walked their dogs in the park signed it."

"Exactly."

"What does this have to do with anything?" Charlie was tired, too.

"What if someone on Kamaria wrote a petition and the whole island signed it? Wouldn't someone have to stop those developers carving up Sunset Cove then?"

"Oh, I see. I dunno." Thinking aloud, she continued, "Hey, you could do it online. You'd get millions of signatures then."

"Great idea, but we should probably start with the people that actually live here."

"What if some people do want this resort thing here? Then what?"

"I just think they should at least be told about it. There's a newspaper that they print in town, and I looked the other day for something written about what is going to happen in Sunset, but there was nothing. I reckon they are making sure no one knows until it's too late."

"I think the petition would have to be done by an adult. No one's gonna take us seriously."

"What if we got my dad to write it and Mr. Hamilton to put his name to it? Then me, you, Isaac and Kai could take it round the island. With Nelson to help, it should be easy, and Isaac's dad has a truck; he could drive us."

"Let's see what your dad says tonight."

"The upside to any development like this is employment and money-making opportunities for the local people. I think you will find that many Kamarians will be looking for jobs within the resort as well as spin offs like taxis and boat charter businesses that will cater to the visitors." Ben had asked Frank about the petition after he'd opened his second cold beer.

"But there are plenty of other places on the island where they could build this resort and still protect Sunset's reef and beach and the ruins that everyone's going to step on. Let the taxi drivers bring the tourists to the cove for the day and take them away again as soon as possible."

Frank laughed kindly at Ben, still struggling to keep up with his son's naive but concerned imagination. He couldn't help but agree with him. Fundamentally, he was right and there was no doubt that no matter what noises the suits that had been hanging around town were making about conservation, once the bulldozers stumbled in, those empty promises would go straight out the window. Frank knew that Kamaria's establishment was not yet equipped to keep a multibillion-dollar corporation under control once they were established, and he could see no real harm in allowing the two young activists to at least try to create some awareness with their petition. The best it could hope to do was make the bosses at DreamWorld, Inc. sit up and take a little notice.

Deciding that it would not be politically correct to draft out a petition on behalf of Beck Hamilton on his office computer, he sat with Ben's laptop after the children had fallen asleep and typed.

We the undersigned, as residents of Kamaria and its surrounding islands wish to express our wholehearted opposition to the development of the land of Sunset Cove, as outlined in the proposals recently issued by DreamWorld, Incorporated.

We believe that because of its ecological and environmental significance, this land should remain in public ownership, accessible to all as open space, in order to protect it for the enjoyment of current and future generations of residents and visitors alike.

Signed,

Mr. Beck Hamilton

When Ben checked his emails the following day, he found the words on his desktop. "Dad, this is awesome! Thanks. I'll take it to Mr. Hamilton this morning."

"Ben, listen. You have to understand that this is a type of legal document. Please don't ask people to sign it and then lose it, will you?"

"No, of course not."

"You are going to find some people will not want to sign and will disagree. You must not be disrespectful in any way to them. Do you understand?"

"Yes, Dad. Of course."

"Type some dotted lines underneath the statement so the signatures stay tidy then print it off. Good luck!"

Eye of **the Storm**

CHAPTER 22
AFFAIRS OF THE HEART

Explaining to Mr. Hamilton about the petition took some doing, because, ultimately, Charlie and Ben had to admit that they had heard the scene between the old man and the developers. Eventually, after a lot of teeth sucking and his nephew Isaac turning up and joining in on the side of his friends, Beck Hamilton clumsily signed above his name. The three youngsters signed below his and were heading out the door to ask for a ride into town from Ben's mum, when Shamoi and Jehiah burst in. The tiny shack was suddenly extremely crowded.

"Hey, what's up?" Shamoi asked.

"We were just talking to your dad about the resort that they are trying to build here. We may have found a way to stop them from ruining the place."

Jehiah pushed his fatter brother out of the way. "What you mean stop them? You kids ain't stopping nothing."

"Don't you want to keep your grandfather's land?" Charlie was confused.

Ben realised that he'd omitted to tell Charlie about the argument he had overheard between Mr. Hamilton and his eldest son.

"These kids reckon they will get us to sign a bit of paper and the Americans will go away and stop bothering us."

Shamoi chipped in, "I want them to build. They say there'll be four different restaurants in Sunset Cove. That's what I call progress."

United just for a moment, in despair at Shamoi's priorities, everyone threw things at the boy and his ever-hungry stomach and then ignored him.

"Go back to where you come from and stop interfering with our business, boy. We don't want your paper." Jehiah was not looking happy, and Ben was very uncomfortable. Mr. Hamilton just shrugged. Asked to choose between his eldest son and some kid he barely knew, he threw his hands in the air and told them all to get out of his house.

"Now what do we do? If Jehiah is against the petition and he wants his dad to sell their land then maybe we shouldn't interfere," Charlie said.

Ben was about to reply, but Isaac got there first. "My dad is Jehiah's dad's brother. He say that this land is not just for Jehiah, Shamoi and Kai, but me, too. I want to build me a house like the one you in and fish with a big boat. Kai, he want to show people the birds and trees and tings. We don't want our home to be taken by outsiders. Our family will look after Sunset Cove, and those tourists, they can come visit for the day."

Both Charlie and Ben were stunned into silence by what was the most they had ever heard come out of Isaac's mouth at one time. If there was any doubt in Ben's mind about going ahead, it was dismissed now. If Isaac wanted to fight for his home, then the least he could do was to help him as much as he could while he was here.

They walked back to the Johnston's beach house and talked on the deck while his mum got ready to go to town. Kai turned up and took the petition from Ben. Unaware of Kai's reading ability, Ben was not sure how much he'd understand. Kai handed it back and wandered away, peering under rocks while the others plotted. One of the logistical problems was the time it would take to get to everyone.

Penny had dropped them off by the ferry dock, and they stopped a few people to try out various approaches with an assortment of reactions. Some walked away, most listened, many refused to sign. Charlie quickly realised that it wasn't necessarily because they disagreed; rather, they didn't understand what the children were trying to get across and seemed a bit suspicious of outsider opinions. She decided that a rehearsal was needed, together with a larger audience.

When Penny pulled up with the pickup after shopping, they had seven signatures. She was impressed, but the kids weren't. They drowned their sorrows in ice cold Cokes and an hour of snorkeling.

Sunning their backs in the late afternoon sun and feeling the warm sand beneath them, Ben and Charlie were alone on the beach.

"So, you pleased you didn't stay in England and go out with James?" Ben all but spat out the last word.

Sensing a loaded question, Charlie tried not to smile. Finally, he was going to say something nice to her, maybe. "Yeah it's so cool out here, and my tan is coming along nicely, don't you think so?"

Ben glanced at the shoulder closest to him, going redder by the minute and wondering why he had been idiotic enough to bring up this subject. "Yeah, you're really brown."

She rolled over, closer to him, looking like she was expecting him to do something. Oh God, should he do it? Should he kiss her?

Too late, she did it. She kissed him! Kind of quick on the lips, but it was definitely a kiss.

Eye of **the Storm**

"Thanks" was all that Ben could think to say.

"You're not supposed to say 'Thanks.' You're supposed to kiss me back."

"Oh, right." He pursed his lips and went for it. Hers were hot and soft. His insides flipped, and he quickly pulled away and lay on his back as now he really was lost for something to say. Apparently, it was the right move as she laid her head on his chest and stared at the sky, talking about clouds or something.

Everything had changed in those few moments. Ben's mind didn't function anymore. He tried to plan the petition signing or tomorrow's trip to Scorpion and the launching of *Hardi*, but he couldn't concentrate on any of these important issues, just the fact that she was stretched out on the sand with her hair tickling his chest. His leg was beginning to go to sleep because of its angle, but he just couldn't find it in him to move, not wanting her to think that he was uncomfortable. He was desperate not to be the one who disturbed the atmosphere first.

He didn't have to, Sandy did. A wet nose shoved in between them was enough to kill the magic and send both of them rolling away, laughing at the dog's attempt at getting some attention. A jealous four-legged friend was a relentless opponent. He jumped on them, licked them and hurled sand everywhere from his prancing paws.

Charlie jumped to her feet and asked, "Shall we go and get your little sister? Your mum probably wants a break."

"Sure."

The rest of the afternoon was a lot less tense. They played with Ruby whilst all the time they were finding excuses to touch each other. Sand fights, water fights all ended up with Ben's arm snaking around her waist or over her shoulders.

That night after dinner, the two lovebirds planned every detail of their sail across to Scorpion, down to the type of sandwiches they'd make, anything to avoid saying goodnight. Charlie did it in the end. She kissed Ben and left the room for her makeshift sleeping space.

On the deck, Ben's parents were deep in hushed conversation. "Well, what did you expect to happen?"

"I thought they were just friends!"

"Yeah, one's a blonde, skinny, fourteen-year-old with a ponytail and the other is a thirteen (going on thirty) year-old boy!"

"Alright, I get it, but what do we do now?"

"Nothing. They're just kids." Frank was secretly chuffed that his son had found himself a smart, pretty girlfriend.

"But what if they get carried away?"

"I think we're okay for the time being. If I were you, I would be more worried about how long it will be before they fall out. Heaven help us then."

Kai and Isaac were waiting by the dory the next morning. Ben gathered that their unusual efficiency was mostly due to Mr. Hamilton not wanting any of them around him. It was windy, and when they approached Dog Leg Reef, the smoke was leaning hard over to the right. On the second half of the dog's leg, Ben was nervous about getting pushed onto coral heads before he could make the beach. He kept wondering how it was going to be done when under sail.

The Frenchmen was already by the sloop. After they'd anchored their dory, the team walked towards *Hardi*, delighting in the sight of her. She stood proud, her rigging glinting in the morning light. The eccentric owner was raking away rocks and tree debris, making an uncluttered path for them to drag her down to the sea. Kai and Isaac had five fenders between them, slung over their shoulders; but none of the group was entirely sure why.

"She will go in bow first as she lays now. I've cut bamboo poles for four of us to lever her. The remaining person moves the fenders as she rolls forwards."

Ben couldn't help wondering where the "Good morning, everyone" was but dismissed the obnoxiously curt attitude as he tried to take in the first set of orders. The bamboo poles where about five-metres high. The Frenchman laid two on either side of the hull. The next commands were coming. "Ben, you are on the port side with me and the cousins starboard. Charlotte, you will be ready with the fenders as we lift."

"Okay. I think I understand." The other three looked at Ben for help, so he interpreted for them. "Isaac, take Kai and go round that side and pick up a pole each. Charlie, get the fenders ready to shove under the bow as we lever her up."

The bamboo poles were strong but flexible, and with everyone eventually coordinated, the bow of the boat was levered up off the sand as Charlie thrust a sausage-shaped, air filled fender under the bow. Each time they did this, Charlie was able to gradually place fenders further down the length of the sloop, until the last one was just over halfway back. The Frenchman then had the boys position their bamboo poles under the stern, and swinging their feet off the ground like pole-vaulters, *Hardi* slowly slid along the rolling fenders. As soon as the first one popped clear at the back, Charlie ran forward and replaced it beneath the bow, stopping the heavy boat from digging a hole into the soft sand.

An hour later, the sloop's bow was touching the gentle wave that was slithering in and out. The team collapsed in the sea, sweating and exhausted from the effort of moving the sailboat along the burning beach.

Grammont sat with his back resting against the wooden hull, obscured from the youngster's view. He had to admit that these teenagers had done everything they had promised to do so far, and despite himself, he found he was warming to their juvenile enthusiasm. Looking back up towards the Sea Grape Grove, he whispered to a ghost.

"Lottie, I have broken a promise I made to you. Your beloved *Hardi* will sail again, although I can only bring myself to watch her from the beach. I hope you approve of these young people. I can't help thinking that if you were still here with me, we would have a son who would sail and swim and be eager for knowledge just like this one. I miss you so much, but I believe that you would want your boat to feel the wind and the seas once more. Watch over her and these young adventurers for me."

Charlie had seen the man alone and felt sad for him. She believed that there was good in everyone, and even this solitary guy had his okay points. After all, he was about to let a bunch of kids sail his boat away.

"Lottie, I mean Charlotte, you startled me."

"I'm sorry, sir, the boys are getting on my nerves. I came out to see if you were all right."

"Yes, yes fine. Why shouldn't I be?"

"Who is Lottie, sir?"

"What does that have to do with you? You'd do well to mind your own business." Angry with himself for reacting like that to this perfectly pleasant girl but unable to apologise either, the Frenchman got to his feet and yelled at the others to come and help with the job at hand.

They had quite a way to go before *Hardi* floated in the shallows, and by lunchtime they were all so tired they fell asleep in the shade of the coconut trees, their stomachs full of sandwiches and chocolate bars. In spite of Isaac's sarcastic comments, Charlie cuddled against Ben's shoulder as she closed her eyes. Michel Grammont retired to his home and glanced at a bottle of rum he kept for the most desolate times, but moving past it, he instead poured cold water from his generator-powered, rusty fridge.

An bit later, the children were still under the palms. The sight of the boy with his arm around the girl made a surprised smile creep across Michel's lips. However, no one was awake to see the tenderness underneath his practiced, sour, public image. Not bothering to rouse them, he returned to the sloop and examined the submerged planks at the bottom of the hull. They would swell and seal themselves, becoming water tight after so many dry years ashore.

The team stirred themselves into life and with renewed energy raced down the sand, eager to see what was to happen next. Grammont was apparently not concerned about the sea water inside the boat; he told Ben that the ballast stones would need to wait until the wooden planks had swollen again. The next job was to find her anchor. This was lying in about twelve feet of water behind the reef, directly out from where they stood.

"Brilliant, a job in the water. That sounds cool." Charlie retrieved snorkel gear from the dory as the rest listened to the Frenchman's instructions.

"The anchor has heavy chain attached to it. Check that the shackle is tight and there is wire locking it off. Make sure the links are not coiled or twisted. The rope down there will be rotten by now, so you will have to cut it free, then take this shackle and fix the new warp to the chain. Got it?"

Looking at Isaac for support, Ben said, "Yep, got it!"

Michel handed Ben a knife and a pair of pliers. To Isaac he gave a coil of heavy rope; the boy drooped under the weight of it. The end of the warp had a thin line and an orange float spliced to it.

"The float will support the rope while you swim, so just drop it to the bottom and drag it," he said then left. Just like that, they were on their own again.

Donning their snorkel gear, they chatted about who was going to do what. Ben had noticed since the day before that Kai had seemed even quieter than normal. Even now he didn't join in, just letting them struggle into the water with their tools and equipment. They found the old anchor quickly. Judging by the fish that had made it their home, it had not moved for a long time. The chain was buried in the loose sand and took a bit of tracing back to the old rope that had to be cut away. Although Ben and Charlie were happy now with their masks and snorkels, they struggled to get to the sea bed and have time left to do anything useful before they had to kick to the surface, gasping for air. The job that had sounded fun was proving to be an exhausting challenge. As usual, Isaac found every excuse to stay in about 6 feet of water. He actually was not a swimmer and only confident where he could stand up. This left Kai.

It was weird and annoying that Kai was not volunteering his skills but was swimming away from them, lost in his fish-watching activities. Charlie and Ben were taking turns hacking the old rope away from the chain. One did a bit then passed the knife on the surface where the other was treading water.

At this rate, Charlie thought, they would be here until tomorrow just getting the old one off, let alone shackling a new warp on.

Under the water, the hardest thing was keeping her body down there. As soon as she reached the rope and grabbed it, her legs felt like they were being sucked up, and she was left hanging vertically. So much energy was expelled holding on to the chain to stop herself from shooting up backwards that any cutting was a pretty pathetic effort before she had to return to the surface again. Determined to give it one more go, she took a gulp of air and duck dived. Kicking down to the end of the chain, she put her face extra close to the sea bed and forced her legs horizontal. This worked for

Eye of **the Storm**

a moment, and she reached out to start cutting. Keeping low helped, and she got in a couple of worthwhile hacks at the fraying rope with the serrated edge of the knife. Running low on oxygen, she let go. Her body and legs started to float up to the blue sky above, but her head didn't.

Instant panic filled Charlie's brain. She pushed off the sandy bottom, dropping the knife. Her neck was trapped. In an instant that felt like weeks, she knew what was wrong. The necklace with the gold cross her Nan had given her when she was a baby (which she had worn permanently since), had fallen into a chain link and twisted. Incredibly, it was strong enough to hold her as she fought to free herself.

Lungs burning and head screaming with the lack of oxygen, she thrashed and kicked. Her face mask filled with bitter, salt water. As she was about to surrender to the urge to breath in the deadly ocean, she felt a hand. Kai had seen her danger. Without returning to the surface for air, he swam to her, retrieved the knife, and with one strike, cut the chain from Charlie's throat. He forced her upwards, kicking hard. Bursting out of the water, Charlie coughed and heaved as Kai held her. Ben was only just registering that there was a problem seconds before the two erupted from the depths.

"What's going on? What happened?"

Not able to communicate properly yet, she hung onto Kai, spitting out water, her mask high on her head. "I got stuck. I couldn't get free. Kai saved me…my necklace…"

"What about your necklace?"

She let go of Kai and was floating easier now, the panic slowly subsiding. "It got trapped in the anchor chain. It held me there until Kai showed up and cut it. Ben, he saved me from drowning."

Lots of emotions filled Ben all at once. Guilt for not noticing the emergency sooner, relief that Charlie was okay and a kind of jealousy, that it was Kai who had rescued her, and now he was her hero. "Where is he?"

They spun around in the water, seeing only Isaac who was oblivious to the action closer to shore. Ben pulled his mask back over his eyes and looked below them. Kai was back at the end of the chain shackling the new rope with the pliers. Ben hadn't even noticed that he'd dropped the tool in all the fuss. Finishing the job, Kai swam lazily up and reached out his hand to Charlie. She looked at him and opened her hand. He dropped the broken, gold necklace into her palm with a shy smile on his face. She reached both arms around his neck and kissed his cheek.

CHAPTER 23
SUNNY

The incident under the water at Scorpion Island caused ripples throughout their day. They had decided not to bother enlightening the Frenchman on what had happened at the end of his anchor chain, thinking he probably would change his mind about them sailing his sloop. Ben was gutted that he had not reacted quicker and come to his girlfriend's rescue. He was equally gutted that Kai had won the day, proving how inadequate Ben's skills and reaction time were when it came to the crunch.

Charlie recovered quickly, shrugging it off until she lay down that night. Nightmares and cold sweats woke her up in the early hours. She had decided to limit the story when she recounted it to Ben's parents, just mentioning to Penny that her gold chain had snapped in the water and luckily Kai had found it for her.

Penny was giving her son very weird looks the next day. For the first time ever, she invited herself and Ruby along when Charlie and Ben left for a swim after breakfast. Ben suspected it had something to do with him and Charlie being more than just mates, but he dreaded his mum bringing up the subject.

The previous afternoon, they'd left Long Bay with *Hardi* swinging around her new mooring, looking very pleased with herself. The weather was holding, so Ben and Charlie gently separated themselves from Penny's overprotective grip and headed for Mr. Hamilton's place.

Isaac and Kai weren't there, and the old man was still not talking to anyone. They played with Sandy for a while, hoping the boys would show up, and after half the morning had gone by, they did. Kai acted both proud and shy as soon as he spotted Charlie. Ben was annoyed and ignored him, talking to Isaac, asking if he had enough gas for the return trip. "Yeah, man. We just have to lay some new pots for my uncle and then he's cool."

By the time they left, they didn't bother to pack lunch, just grabbed some water from home and aimed the dory for Scorpion Island.

"So, are we gonna sail that boat today, man?"

"Don't think so. We have to put the stones in her and then sort the sails out, and that'll take all afternoon, I reckon." Sandy had jumped aboard today, so as was now usual, when they approached the Frenchman's bay, the dog leapt over the side, swimming directly for shore as the dory had to be carefully navigated around the coral heads.

The dog went straight for Grammont's home, sniffing around the open door looking for the man. The domestic goats and chickens sounded the alarm as Sandy bounded up, but there were no signs of human life. By the time the friends had anchored the dory, Sandy was on his way down the beach towards the space where the sloop had sat for so many years. They followed him and as they walked saw movement on *Hardi*.

Standing ankle deep in front of where the boat rested easily on her orange float, Ben waved at the Frenchman as he hauled the jib up the forestay. Just a little agitated that he hadn't been there to help get the sails ready, he sat down on the sand and waited for the guy to indicate if he was welcome to join him.

A few moments later a voice yelled, "Come!"

Nothing like small talk, thought Ben, but he waded into the water and swam half a dozen strokes to the boat. Hauling himself aboard, he could see that the owner had tidied up and had added some bits and pieces. There was a tiny cuddy in the centre of *Hardi*, now the hatch was pulled back revealing a narrow bunk slung from either side of the hull. A long oar lay in clamps fixed to the port side, and an aluminum boat hook was clipped to starboard. The main was still in the sail bag along with covers to keep the sails tidy and protected when not in use.

"Pass me the small sail cover." Not bothering to turn around as he spoke, the Frenchman dropped the smaller front sail on a series of bronze rings that slid up and down the forestay (one of five wires that held the mast in place). Ben found the blue canvas cover and passed it forwards. It was designed to zip around the bundled sail as it lay on the bow of the boat.

"Right, now for the main, give me a hand to bend it on the boom first." This was a new phrase to Ben, but he quickly figured out he had to lace a long white line, threading it in and out of the eyes in the sail—passing it around the wooden spar each time. Stainless steel clips were sewn into the front edge of the huge sail. These twisted and then held into matching clips on the hoops that were waiting on the treelike mast. Man and boy silently worked, shoulder to shoulder, until they reached the top corner of the mainsail. The heavy material was lying in their laps and at their feet. Michel tied the halyard to the reinforced head of the main and gave the other end of the line to Ben.

"Go on then, pull it up, boy." Nervous that there was finally to be a sail hoisted, Ben pulled. Not much happened.

Scoffing at Ben's effort, Grammont said, "That won't work, and there are no winches on her, so you'll have to use your shoulders and body weight." Ben stood up on the deck directly below the mast and hauled, reaching up high for the line then bending his knees. The sail began to slide up the mast. By the time it was fully raised, Ben was sweating hard. He was determined not to let his breathlessness show, but silently vowed to award this job to the stronger Isaac or Kai in the future.

Grammont hauled another line until the boom was hanging much higher than its normal sailing position, folding the main into itself. He told Ben this was called scandalizing the rig, taking the power from the sail while the boat was on a mooring.

Charlie had been sitting on the beach watching the activity aboard, and when the sail was up she clapped her hands causing Sandy—sure that something exciting must be happening somewhere—to run rings around her. Seeing the island dog, Michel whistled at him, and like magic, Sandy threw himself into the sea and paddled to the sloop. Amazed at the dog's response, Ben grabbed the scruff of his neck and dragged him over the side, jumping away from the inevitable shaking of wet coat.

"It seems he's happy to sail," the Frenchmen said, mostly to himself as he rubbed the dog's ears.

For the next half an hour, the four teenagers, briefed by Michel Grammont (shadowed by Sandy), went through the sailing sloop, learning from her designer and builder what each line and fitting was for. The two brothers where fascinated by the sculling oar which slotted onto the top of the transom, reaching back four meters into the water behind them, allowing the handler to propel *Hardi* by twisting and circling the inboard end. The hardest thing was maneuvering it in and out of its rack on the side of the boat; Kai managed to swipe both Charlie and Isaac on the way.

Ben understood the controls and principles of how they worked but had butterflies bashing around in his stomach as he practiced in his mind how they would hoist sails, leave the mooring and worse of all, navigate through the reef. Although always fluky, the wind normally blew offshore on Long Bay, and that he thought, was a good thing—on the way out.

The Frenchman had left *Hardi*'s crew onboard and swam back to the beach, seemingly uncomfortable at their excited behaviour. Charlie noticed him glance up to the sea grape grove before he walked back to his cabin.

"What's the weather like tomorrow, Charlie?"

"Good, I think. We can check online tonight, but I'm sure it said ten to fifteen knots and no swell."

"Perfect." Ben covered the lowered mainsail and set up the wooden crutches that Grammont had explained held the heavy boom off the deck. *Hardi* looked ready to go although she was still riding high in the water as she had no ballast stone yet. They planned to row up to the beach and allow her to sit on the sand while they passed the rocks over the side and arranged them, ready for the Frenchman's inspection in the morning.

"Do you know, it's a shame to have to go home as we have to be back here so early tomorrow. Wouldn't it be fun to camp here?" Charlie asked.

That sinking feeling of sleeping apart from his parents hadn't raised its ugly head for weeks now. He'd had no reason to dwell on it and had been too busy to contemplate the fate waiting for him at the end of the summer.

"Yeah, I guess, but we don't have a tent."

"My cousin does," chimed Isaac brightly.

Remembering all the old, rehearsed excuses, Ben threw in, "And my parents won't let us and besides, how will we eat and stuff?

"Ben it's called camping. You pack up food and clothes and a sleeping bag and get to spend the night outside, away from your parents."

"I know what it is. I'm not stupid. I just don't think its practical here, and besides my Mum won't let us."

Charlie was looking staggered at the lack of interest in her idea of escaping for a whole night. "Yeah, Yeah, you said that already. Listening to your excuses, anyone would think you were scared of camping out."

"Look, we can't stay here, so we'd better get ready to drive back to Sunset. Come on, let's get back to the beach, alright?" Ben dove off the sloop and swam under the water until his lungs were empty. He surfaced and angrily waded up the beach, swearing at Sandy for bugging him on the way.

Isaac, Kai and Charlie all looked at each other in disbelief at this little tantrum. "What's with him, man?"

"I'm not sure, to be honest, but I don't think he's into camping." Charlie and Isaac giggled, and Kai smiled at them.

As Ben was now ahead of the others, he reached the cabin first and thought he should let the Frenchman know their plan for the next day. Stepping onto the driftwood threshold made him feel small and slightly nervous of what lay within. His eyes took their time adjusting to the dreary light which would give anyone inside the advantage of surprise. "Mr. Grammont, are you there?"

"Hello." A new voice shocked Ben who had been under the impression that Mr. Grammont lived alone.

"Hello," Ben said back.

"Hello, are you there?"

Who was this person, and why were they copying him? He could see the room now. The portrait of the original buccaneer, Michel Grammont, was staring back at him. Then someone began to whistle a weird tune, if it was a tune at all. Movement caught Ben's eye, and he jumped. Peering at him around the doorframe, standing on a piece of wood, was a green parrot.

"It was you talking to me," Ben said, partially delighted to see a talking bird in real life and also rapidly feeling like a dork for talking to himself. Looking over his shoulder for Grammont, he edged closer to the bird and said hello again.

"Hello!" The parrot scampered up and down the piece of wood, lifting and ruffling his feathers. Having no idea whether this was a good or bad reaction, Ben kept still and watched. It wasn't tied or in a cage, and it certainly looked like his wings worked, so he assumed that the parrot wanted to be there.

The parrot was lime green with flashes of brilliant red topped off with a bright yellow crown. His beak was curled to a sharp point, and his six toes each ended in long, dagger-like claws. Tempted to put his hand out to the bird but not sure what would happen if he did, Ben tried to think of something to say. Not having ever held a conversation with a parrot before, he was surprisingly tongue tied.

"What's your name, then?"

"Hello!"

"What's your name?"

"Hello!"

This obviously wasn't getting either of them very far then another voice answered Ben's question. "Her name is Sunny." Ben swung around to see Grammont standing behind him, hands on hips, his shirt still draped over one shoulder after his swim from the boat.

"I was just looking for you to let you know we would try and get back early tomorrow to load the stones, and then the parrot spoke to me and, um…" Ben always ended up talking nonsense around this guy. He hated himself for it, but the Frenchman just made him nervous and then when he opened his mouth to speak, gibberish came out!

"I was milking the goats."

"Oh." There didn't seem to be anymore to say on that subject. "Does she bite? I mean, can you touch her?"

"Yes she likes to sit on my shoulder, and she loved…" Grammont seemed to catch himself and change his mind about what he was about to say. "Well anyway if she wants to with that beak, she can tear your ear open or put a hole in your finger, so it's up to you." By now the others were crowding around the door.

"Cool parrot. Does it talk?"

As if in answer to Charlie's question, the bird flapped its wings and said "Hello!"

"Can I hold it?"

"It's not an 'it'. It's a she, and her name is Sunny" Grammont had retreated to the far side of the dim room leaving Ben to repeat what he had just explained.

Charlie moved her hand towards the parrot that was now motionless on her perch, watching the girl with her head cocked to one side, using a single eye to track the path of Charlie's hand. A low grunt came from the throat of Sunny as she lurched at the stranger's fingers coming too close. Charlie pulled away just in time to miss the flesh ripping beak, grabbing at her hand.

"I guess that was pretty clear. She doesn't like you then." Ben was laughing and hoping that he was going to win this little competition for the bird's confidence.

"Not surprising with all you boys hanging around her, scaring her with your ugly faces."

"I bet she lets me touch her." Ben reached gingerly in the direction of the parrot as she again studied the approaching hand. She seemed to let him get closer and his hopes were rising, before she grabbed his first finger and bit down hard.

"Ouch! That hurts!" The parrot let go only to squawk loudly at Ben.

"I did warn you, boy. She is very picky. Go and wash that with some fresh water."

Ben cradled his right finger against is chest. His t-shirt showed a spreading circle of dark red. Pushing past a grinning Isaac, he went to the water tank outside. The parrot's beak had put a deep v-shaped hole in the side of his finger, and it was throbbing. Feeling angry that the stupid bird hadn't chosen him as a friend, he turned to look back at the cabin door as Kai stepped carefully out with Sunny on his shoulder.

"Typical! I should have known the thing would like you. What is it about you and animals anyway?" Realising too late that he was mouthing off to a deaf boy, Ben shut up. The parrot was nuzzling Kai's neck making funny cooing noises in his ear.

"I think Sunny is in love." Charlie announced.

"Well that's a relief. Perhaps he'll stop mooning all over you now."

"Don't be like that. It's a good thing he can't hear you." Ben had the distinct feeling that Kai had quite easily gotten the gist of the conversation.

"I'm getting out of this dump. I'm hungry." Ben stomped off to the dory, climbed aboard and started the engine, waiting for the others.

As he drove away, he could hear Sunny yelling from her perch, "Hello, Hello!" He felt ashamed at his attitude towards Kai as he realised that the deaf boy had no idea the parrot was desperately calling after him.

Ben lay on his bed that night worrying while his hand throbbed. He and Charlie had gone over and over all the various maneuvers they would have to do to get in and out of Long Bay and then what they did when they cleared Dog Leg Reef. Ben felt it important for all of them to have designated jobs and know what they had to do before they began pulling up sails. He had made a list of positions and jobs in the boat that could be assigned to each of them. He was most worried about Kai as he was quick and strong, but not being able to hear was going to make life tricky if he was not looking at them. The three of them could probably manage the boat, so Ben decided to keep Kai close to him.

Eye of **the Storm**

Knowing that, just like in a airplane, the take offs and landings were the most likely times for a disaster, Ben needed to have a plan well rehearsed in his mind of how to leave and return to the mooring. There were several options of what sail, in which order they pulled the sails up and how each of these scenarios could help or hinder them navigating the coral heads. It then all depended on what the wind was actually doing the next day, so he just needed to think about something else until then. A big part of him wished that the miserable Frenchman would take charge for the first trip, and he wondered about asking him to consider this in the morning.

The other pressure on such young shoulders was the petition. He hadn't had time to do anymore canvassing for the cause and felt guilty about that. Mr. Hamilton had not spoken to them all week, so he wasn't sure if he should be carrying on with it, anyway. After the next day's test sail was done, he would get Charlie and Isaac to help him figure out a way of at least filling the papers with some names. When he thought about the development, it made him angry inside. He was feeling stress for the first time in his life. Up until now, decisions had been made by his parents or teachers or sailing instructors, but here on Kamaria, he was doing things and being handed responsibilities that wouldn't happen at home. In the "real world," he was just a kid; here, he could make a difference. What with that and his first proper girlfriend, he was beginning to wonder if boarding school may be safer after all.

CHAPTER 24
THE MAIDEN SAIL

The trip over to Scorpion that morning was uneventful but strained. Everyone was tense about their first sail together. Before this could happen, though, the ballast had to be placed in the bilges and covered with the floorboards. They swam out to the waiting *Hardi* and Isaac used the long oar to scull her to the beach. Once a human chain was organized, it wasn't too bad transferring the stones to the boat. Ben stayed aboard receiving each one and placing it neatly, trying to spread the weight evenly along the full length of the hull.

Grammont, accompanied by Sandy who had greeted him halfway, strode down the beach just as they were finishing. He stopped short before reaching them, examining *Hardi*'s waterline now that the ballast was onboard. Ben prayed he wouldn't ask for more rocks—the sun was already getting unbearably hot.

"Move some weight aft," commanded the owner.

Muttering to himself, Ben shifted some rocks to the back of the boat.

"Stand still, boy!"

Wondering how he could be expected to move rocks and stand still, Ben stood up and looked at Grammont. "She looks good enough from here. You'll need to see what happens as the stones settle. Have you secured the floorboards as I showed you?"

"Yes, sir." As he spoke, Ben twisted the last turnbuckle holding the board beneath his feet.

"Right, well I have work to do. I trust you can get on with it yourself now, boy?"

"Yes, sir, but, actually, I was wondering whether you'd like to come with us just for the first sail?"

Without hesitation, the Frenchman answered angrily, "No. I told you I would not do that. What's wrong? You told me you could sail her."

"Yes, sir. I am sure we'll be fine, but, well, I can't decide the best way to leave the mooring. Is she better having both sails up, or just the jib, or just the main, or well… what did you used to do?"

The man stood for a long moment without speaking. Ben watched him as he seemed to be wrestling with an answer. Ben knew it was a perfectly sensible question. After all, each boat is different, and it made sense that he would ask the owner of the boat the best way to sail her, but Grammont's pause made Ben think that he'd said something else to irritate the man.

"The sloop answers well with just a main up. She falls off the mooring easily without having to back the jib, but if you have to tack under main alone, you need boat speed. She is very likely to stall otherwise. As long as you have the wind behind you like today, either sail will get her out through the reef. The jib is less powerful and no problem if a shift makes you gybe. However, pulling the main up underway can be hard work. She likes to sail, not stand still. Coming back in, if it's a beat, you need either both sails or neither. In light air, pull everything down and use the oar."

Ben took it all in. Charlie, who was listening too, kept nodding her head. Ben hoped that wasn't just for show, he really needed her to understand what the Frenchman was getting at.

"Thanks. That makes sense. I think we'll try going through the gap with jib alone and have the main ready to haul up when we are clear of the bay."

The Frenchman simply nodded once and left them.

They had discovered that there was another way through the deadly reef that protected Long Bay. It was no coincidence that Hardi's mooring had been laid at that particular spot. A straighter channel than the one they used daily in the dory was hidden directly beyond the anchor. Ben had Kai staring over the side, standing by to check that he was steering the correct course. Isaac was on the mooring line ready to throw it clear, and Charlie was on jib sheets. They'd prepared the main, and once in open water, Isaac and Kai could haul it up while he held the boat into the wind.

With his stomach in his mouth, Ben called to the crew (that could hear him), checking one more time that they were ready. "Okay, Isaac, let go!" The jib flapped as Hardi fell slowly backwards and then Charlie forced the port sheet across making the sail catch the breeze and drag the bow around. They were turning!

Barely breathing, teeth clenched, heart thumping hard in his chest, Ben stared rigidly ahead as they slowly progressed over the clear, shallow water. Kai was making his usual noises. Now and then they grew louder until the tiller was adjusted to aim at deeper water. At one point, if he could have left his position for just a second, Ben would have clouted the boy around the head as he mistook his signals and almost steered them into razor-sharp coral because Kai had suddenly begun gesticulating and making ridiculous noises whilst pointing madly at the water to the right of the boat. Luckily, Charlie's sharp eyes spotted an innocent turtle poking his head up to check out the strange sight above the waves, and she also spotted the coral he was about to hit. During all this stress, Isaac dangled from a wire shroud one foot in midair, hanging over the side of the boat looking a lot like a trapeze artist in a circus act. Charlie, however, was still, watching her sail with a very slow smile creeping over her face.

Eye of **the Storm**

The reef came to an end at a wall that dropped to the seabed twenty metres below and then rapidly increased to forty metres (according to the chart). Ben breathed out, looking behind him for the first time since they slipped their mooring. They were clear and safe, for now.

"We did it!" Charlie shrieked.

"Yeah, we did. Now the main. Let's get her sailing properly."

They worked to their plan, and without any problems, (just a lot of sweating and grunting from the boys), *Hardi* fell off the wind, and the two white sails eagerly filled.

When Charlie had finally dared look back at the island, she'd seen the Frenchman in the sea grape clearing, gazing out to sea to where his sloop was clambering over the gentle swell.

The four young sailors were beginning to relax and enjoy the ride. Isaac had slung a fishing line over the rear of the boat and lay on the side deck with a foot on the reel, his eyes closed to the bright sunlight. Charlie sat next to Ben, her ponytail flying in the breeze as she occasionally ducked her head under the huge main sail, checking for approaching boats. They had seen none since they left Long Bay. They were totally alone on this part of the tropical Atlantic, and Ben was unable to believe the feeling of complete freedom. His tanned face was covered by a grin so wide it threatened to reach his ears. The fourth member of *Hardi*'s crew was sat astride the bow, his legs hanging over the front of the boat, his feet getting buried in white water as the sloop dived into the troughs between the metre-high swell.

They sailed along the northern edge of Scorpion, discovering white beaches and small bays, every one looking like it had lain untouched for hundreds of years. Ben vowed silently to come back in *Hardi* to explore them all, noting the entrances and reefs and wondering how easy it would be to anchor his charge.

A scream rudely shook all plans from his mind as he jumped like he'd been shot at. Looking all over the boat not knowing what awful disaster he would see, Ben's gaze rested on Charlie who had sprung to the side of the deck and was yelling. "Look there, did you see?"

"What are you screaming about? I thought we'd hit something!"

"No, look over there!"

"Look at what over where?"

Isaac sat up from his lazy doze and was scanning the water for signs of what Charlie had seen. "Dolphins!" he yelled, "on the bow."

"They're swimming with us," Charlie said

Ben stood up and watched in disbelief as a family of dolphins played in his bow wave. He'd seen nature programmes portraying this before, but they did not prepare him for the awesome sight and the incredible privilege that he felt, knowing that these beautiful and agile mammals had chosen to swim with their sloop. It seemed to be a family, all roughly the same size, but every now and then they would glimpse the youngest member of the group, a baby dolphin that appeared to be invisibly stitched to his mother's underside. Every move she made he mirrored, as if he knew in advance what she was about to do. Kai was standing on the very tip of the bow, hanging off the forestay with one hand while the other waved and pointed at his new friends. As quickly as they had appeared, the dolphins were gone. The disappointed children searched the water, straining their eyes to catch a glimpse of a surfacing fin. Almost at the point of giving up, Ben looked back at the far end of his tiller and yelled at the others as all four acrobats curled their glistening, grey backs clear of the waves and kicked their tails at the sloop.

"They're playing with us. I'm sure of it!" Ben wished desperately that he could share this moment with his parents, and then he remembered the camera in his backpack. "Charlie, quick, get the camera. It's down below."

She dived inside the tiny cabin and thrust around inside Ben's bag for the digital camera. Feeling it in her hands, she grabbed it and jumped back on deck.

"Here, you do it. I'll helm."

Ben took the camera and gave the tiller to Charlie, and he was soon rewarded by another appearance, alongside them this time. He aimed his camera at the graceful creatures. They dived beneath the hull of the sailing boat one last time then, without a backward glance, took off at lightening speed towards the empty horizon.

If he never sailed *Hardi* again, Ben knew that he would be content to remember something so special and impossible to describe to his friends and family. Carefully tucking the camera back in his pack, he prayed the images would do justice to the experience of a lifetime.

The friends sat in their positions, stunned into silence as they thought about what had just happened. Kai was so quiet that Ben had to check he hadn't gone overboard after the dolphins. When Ben did look carefully at the impressionable deaf boy, he was shocked to see tears in his eyes. Understanding these were tears of delight as well as sadness, he didn't say anything to the others, sensing a private and maybe mutual respect between Kai and the special mammals.

They had been sailing for about an hour when everyone agreed it was time to turn back and attempt the final part of today's challenge—safely returning *Hardi* to her mooring. Adjusting the sails to achieve a closer line to the wind, the lively sloop lifted up on her side, digging in to the waves as she carved a course back to Long Bay. The crew were splashed with cool seawater and reveled in the refreshing feeling as they chatted about what they had done and seen. So far, Ben's plans had worked out fine, but he knew that the last maneuver of the day would be the hardest. As they came in sight of Long Bay, his stomach once again began to churn.

Eye of **the Storm**

"Okay, let's go over this again. I think we should try to sail in with both sails up. The wind is pretty strong for Isaac to row against, and once we drop the sails, if he can't manage it, we're dead!"

"I agree, but when we get close to the mooring, we are going to have to haul everything down real fast, otherwise, we'll be on the beach." Charlie was feeling the pressure, too. Ben knew she was aware of what could go wrong as they tacked so close to the unforgiving reef.

They both looked at Isaac who shrugged and said, "Hey, man. You the boss." That was not what Ben wanted to hear, but at least it meant he could get away with ordering around Isaac if necessary, who was, after all, his senior.

Approaching the reef in line with the orange buoy they had left behind earlier that morning, all were alert and aware of their jobs, holding onto lines and halyards ready to release or tie up. As they entered the narrow opening, a lone laughing gull glided effortlessly on the lift created by *Hardi's* bow. Before Ben considered the scary issues of how he would have to turn in this small space at least once, he took a moment to smile to himself as he though perhaps the gull was Humphrey. Once he refocused his concentration on the boat, he remembered that he had meant to experiment out in the deep water to see how long *Hardi* took to come to a stop. In all the excitement with the dolphins, he'd forgotten. Now he would have to guess as he aimed her at her buoy.

Overshooting the buoy just a little, the sloop arrived unscathed in the glasslike lagoon inside the reef. The young crew quickly dropped the sails and *Hardi* fell back onto the mooring of her on accord, allowing Isaac to retrieve it with his boat hook.

Charlie noticed that the Frenchman had not left his position in the clearing since watching them leave, but by the time the team had tidied the sloop and checked she was safely attached to her mooring, he had disappeared.

Traipsing back along the beach, Ben looked for Mr. Grammont and eventually found him tending to his goats. "Thanks, sir. She sailed brilliantly, and we saw dolphins." Ben waited for the man to respond.

Without turning to face the speaker, he replied curtly, "Did you check her mooring?"

"Yes, sir. It's fine."

"Good. I am busy, so I trust you can get along now?"

Despite Grammont's gruff attitude, Ben had this continual need to try and impress him. Disappointed yet again that after the four teenagers had actually done all they promised to do without any hitches, the dude still wasn't interested. He shelved his plan to pick Grammont's brains about anchoring, something he wasn't accustomed to doing on the fourteen-foot plastic Toppers that he sailed.

Ben caught up with Kai and Isaac who were readying the dory to head home to Sunset Cove. The three boys impatiently sat on the small powerboat waiting for a missing Charlie. "Finally. Thought you'd got lost."

"Sorry, I had to check something out."

"What?"

"I'll tell you later."

Intrigued but also tired, Ben shrugged and helped Kai pull the anchor over the side of the boat.

Eye of **the Storm**

CHAPTER 25
MICHEL & LOTTIE

Michel Grammont had spent the time the children were sailing sitting in the sea grape grove beside two graves. Each was bordered with smooth, pale stones taken from the ballast beach at the end of the bay. The headstones were similarly simple, but the graves were not the same size; one was a tiny imitation of the other.

Lottie and Michel had met on Kamaria. She was sailing through as part of the delivery crew on a yacht bound for Florida. The boat had anchored off New Town, seeking shelter from an approaching storm. Michel was passing the time of day with the local fishermen on the ferry dock when the crew had come ashore in their tender looking for supplies and a meal. Charlotte Christy, as she introduced herself later, asked him directions as she attempted to tame her wind-tangled, blonde hair. Michel was unusually shy when answering her. The three young men who had accompanied her left to find the local hotel, but she stayed, keen to hear about the island and its people.

The storm that had delayed the yacht delivery to Florida had lasted just long enough for Michel and Lottie to fall in love. She abandoned the delivery crew, and Michel took her to Scorpion Island where he had ideas of building a smallholding and home one day.

Michel was born on Kamaria. His family owned land on the island, and his father had returned to claim this along with his American bride in the 1940s. It turned out, much to his parents' disappointment, that the family land was mostly on deserted Scorpion Island. At twelve years old and an only child, Michel left the Caribbean with his family and attended school in the United States until he graduated. He then travelled alone to Northern France to train at a boat building college.

As a young man, he lived and worked on the outskirts of Paris where in his spare time, he began to dig into his ancestral past. Eventually, he learned more about his namesake, the famous buccaneer, reportedly lost at sea during a mighty hurricane in 1686.

The ruthless pirate's flagship, the *Hardi* had, in fact, floundered off Long Bay, Scorpion Island. All onboard had drowned that horrific night, except the captain who was washed injured and weak onto the beach. Uninhabited apart from wild boar, Scorpion became the buccaneer's home for weeks until he was strong enough to repair a salvaged long boat from the wreck and sail to Kamaria. He hoped to find a passage out of the "Godforsaken land," as he called it, but infection had left him crippled and unable to return to his previous cut-throat lifestyle. He had no choice but to settle in this remote part of the Caribbean until his premature death left children to continue the name, if not his line of business.

Lottie was American, and after a whirlwind, romantic stay with Michel on a tropical island that she quickly grew to adore, the time had come to return home. They both travelled to the US and were married in the presence of her family. An aspiring young writer, she published a successful novel then was rewarded a commission to write more. Lottie convinced Michel that they should return to Scorpion and build the home he had planned before they met. In the winter of 1985, they arrived with just two suitcases and a trunk of carpentry tools, longing to construct their dream home on the deserted island.

She wrote her books, spending her days sitting beneath the sea grape trees. After completing their modest cabin, he began to build her a surprise. Lottie's passion was sailing, and he had trained as a boat builder. Michel designed and constructed an island sloop which was kept covered and off limits to his wife until the project was finished. He wanted to call the sailboat *Charlotte*, but fascinated by her husband's history, Lottie insisted on naming her *Hardi*, painting the name onto the sloop's bows herself. They sailed her often, and she became their only form of transport once the engine on his old fishing boat failed for the last time.

After years of hoping, the devoted couple discovered that Lottie was pregnant. Michel, at this point wanted to move back to the States to provide every possible modern convenience and medical option for his wife and unborn child. Lottie refused to leave Scorpion Island, and after many arguments convinced Michel that they could move onto Kamaria when she was close to the end of her term, repeatedly telling him that the hospital there was good enough for Kamarians and would be good enough for them.

Her pregnancy was normal, and plans were made for Nelson to collect them both a week before she was due, this way they could settle into the hotel and be near the hospital when the time came. Tragically, Nelson never had the opportunity to perform this important boat trip as Lottie became ill one evening and Michel knew he had to get her to hospital immediately. Even through her pain, his stubborn wife assured him that she would be fine in her sloop and they could sail there faster than any summoned help would get to them.

As the sun drew low in the sky, he rigged *Hardi* and headed her out through the reef with his beloved Lottie huddled quietly next to him. The wind was light and against them as they sailed to New Town. Frantic for his wife and child's safety, Michel cursed the boat and the wind and God for not helping him move faster. Halfway there, he radioed for anyone with a powerboat to meet them, but by the time someone responded to his pleas for help, it was too late. Lottie was carried into the tiny hospital, and in the early hours of the following morning through complications of the premature birth, both mother and son had died.

Today, he had sat by his lost family, watching the boat that he had grown to hate for not looking after them, sail away from Long Bay once more, crewed by children that if his world had not been shattered, would have been joined by a son he was never allowed to love.

Eye of **the Storm**

CHAPTER 26
FESTIVAL!

Ben Johnston had been on Kamaria one month. He was halfway through his stay in the Caribbean now, and with his two new friends, Sandy the beach dog, his girlfriend and *Hardi*, he was deliriously happy. Tony had gone quiet on Messenger, mostly, Ben suspected, as the two friends were so far apart not just in miles, but also in the way their individual summers had panned out.

Kamaria's festival week was the beginning of August, and the descriptions of the traditional celebrations sounded colourful, to say the least. The annual event commemorated emancipation, which Ben learned was the abolishing of slavery at the end of the nineteenth century. These days, the week is set aside to lime, which Ben now understood meant "chill" or "hang out," or, in the case of the adults, to stay up drinking all night. The main event—the festival parade, was happening on Monday. This apparently began really early in the morning and continued on to the afternoon when the whole island congregated in New Town to listen to local musicians.

"That's it!" Ben said. "That's the time to hit them with the petition." Ben and Charlie were lazing around Mr. Hamilton's place catching some shade after another successful day exploring aboard *Hardi*. Isaac was explaining about festival and about all the food stalls that are set up around the ferry dock. "It's the perfect place. A captive audience."

"Yeah, and they'll be in a party mood," added Charlie.

"Exactly, we could have every person's signature by nightfall."

"My cousin in the fungi band that's playing. He could tell them with his microphone."

Ben smiled as he heard that Isaac had yet another cousin. Considering it was such a small place, it made sense that almost everyone that lived here was somehow related.

"Well that's a plan, then. We'll print a bunch of signature sheets and share them out between us and then maybe we can get these developers to back off once and for all."

The morning of the parade, the Johnston family and Charlie packed a cool box full of iced drinks, sandwiches and Ruby's lunch and climbed into the old pickup. The two friends rode in the back, but as they pulled away, Sandy seemed to notice that everyone was leaving him. Normally, he contented himself with sleeping under a coconut tree if not much was going on after breakfast, but today he ran behind the truck madly barking. Ben felt awful. He wanted to explain that they would be back tonight, and it wasn't much fun for a dog in a crowded town. Instead, he yelled at Sandy, telling him to go back and stay.

As the rattling vehicle built up some speed after the bend in the mountain road, they lost sight of Sandy and assumed that he would give up and return to the house. After all, he couldn't run all the way to town.

Main Street was almost completely enclosed from above with bunting and banners. Every telegraph pole and tree in town had something that fluttered in the breeze tied to it. Mr. Johnston found a parking space amongst what had to be every vehicle with a wheel on each corner that existed on Kamaria. Kamarians sat in groups under small tents or palm trees. Some old, wrinkled, men were thumping away at a low table set between them. As Ben and Charlie wandered closer, they saw that the banging came from a domino game in progress. Each time a player laid a piece, he hit the table with it. Weird, especially as the ancient, wooden table looked like it would give way under the strain any minute.

A line of trucks decorated with more bunting and flags were parked in the middle of the road in a sort of "follow the leader" style. This was the parade. Not sure whether it was finished or about to start or maybe somewhere in between, Charlie and Ben told Frank that they were off to locate Isaac and would be back later. "Okay, I'll leave the cooler in the back of the car, so you don't have to come looking for us when you want lunch," Ben's dad said. "Be careful how you speak to people about the petition, and try to stay out of trouble."

"We will. See you later." Grabbing the bag containing copies of the petition and tons of lined signature pages, Ben and Charlie turned to face the crowds, wondering how they would find Isaac.

Ben had now gotten to like the fact that everyone spoke to you if they caught your eye on the street or the beach. It was a pleasant feeling to be acknowledged. He had also learned that Kamarians tended to shout at each other and get into extremely heated discussions which, if Ben were in England, he'd expect to end in serious punch-up. But here they would finish the argument then laugh and get on with life.

They made their way towards the dock along from the rocks where Ben and Isaac had first met. Isaac was surrounded by his friends from the only high school on the island. More than slightly intimidated by this group of older boys, Ben eased his way towards Isaac and said hi to his friend. There were some sniggers and funny looks shot in his direction, then the boys spotted Charlie, and the sniggers stopped and the whistles began.

"What's up?" Isaac asked.

"Not much. You wanna try and get some signatures with us?"

"Yeah, man." Isaac got to his feet and began to walk away from his peers.

A voice followed him, "You leaving with them?"

"Yeah."

"What that is?" A tall boy pointed at the wad of paper that Ben was holding out to Isaac.

"Nothing."

The high school student, wearing a white vest stretched over a muscled chest made a grab for Isaac.

"Hey, man, get off me!"

The group parted in the middle as Isaac struggled to release himself from the older boy's grasp of his shirt. In the scuffle, the documents in Isaac's hand fluttered to the ground. Without thinking, both Ben and Charlie made a grab for them as the wind threatened to blow the lot into the sea. The local kids were laughing and cheering now as Isaac picked up the remainder of the loose papers.

"What's this say, then?"

"What, you can't read?" Was Isaac's angry reply to the kid who had managed to catch the front page of the petition. He was waving it around above his head as Isaac tried to retrieve it.

"Just hang on. Let me read the thing."

"It's not your business. Give it here." The boy leapt onto a discarded crate on the dock and pretended to conduct the audience with his hands.

"We the undersigned, as residents of Kamaria and its surrounding islands wish to express our wholehearted opposition to the development of the land of Sunset Cove, as outlined in the proposals recently issued by DreamWorld Incorporated."

Ben and Charlie could do nothing but watch, helpless and scared that this was going to get out of hand.

"We believe that, because of its ecological and environmental significance, this land should remain in public ownership, publicly accessible as open space, in order to protect it for the enjoyment of current and future generations of residents and visitors alike." This part of the statement obviously caused some reading comprehension issues from the mocking teenager. "Don't sound like something you wrote, Isaac!"

"It ain't, but it's important. Just give me the paper."

Most of the young crowd were jeering and winding up the two boys. Then someone else spoke from the back of the group. "That's a petition. What's going down at Sunset, Isaac?" Everyone turned to look at the owner of the voice.

"What it says, man," Isaac replied, "is that the outsiders are trying to take my uncle's land and build a resort on the hill. We no give family land to the Americans."

It appeared to Ben that the kid who had asked the question was the leader because when he spoke, the rest of the gang fell silent. "So this here is signed by your uncle Beck. That mean all your family want these guys out?"

"Well, mostly. My father and Uncle Beck want to keep his share for us kids to build houses, Jehiah just wants the cash, and Shamoi, well, he fat gut wants the restaurants!" Some chuckling broke out amongst the crowd of onlookers. They obviously knew Shamoi.

Pushing on with his questions, the leader asked, "So who these kids, Isaac?"

Ben and Charlie would have welcomed a large rock to crawl under as everyone twisted to stare at them. They both turned bright red.

"They family living in Sunset. They father a lawyer in town. He say the developers can't force my uncle to sell, so we need everyone to sign and then tell them to leave."

"I'll sign your paper," the leader said. "I have no time for visitors who think they have a right to walk all over our people." The boy took the petition and the pen Charlie rushed over to hand him and wrote his name under the few that were already in place. The thug that had ridiculed Isaac sucked his teeth and strode off, but the remaining members of the gang each took the rapidly creasing paper and signed their names on the dotted lines. All Ben could do was stand there with his mouth open.

What happened next was even more incredible. Isaac gave out the blank pages to the group that had stayed with the leader, whose name was Shak, and there were now over a dozen signature collectors, most of whom were Kamarians. This had to work. Realizing quickly that it was much better to let the Kamarian boys do the talking, Ben and Charlie stood to one side smiling and nodding and occasionally pointing out the value of the reef and the historical sites that would be disturbed or even destroyed by uncaring developers.

By lunchtime, all the pages were full. They hadn't printed enough, and Ben needed to find his dad to persuade him to unlock his office so they could print some more. Taking Isaac back to the pickup to share their lunch, they were all full of the morning's excitement. He explained that the kid that grabbed him was a challenger to Shak's reign as leader of the year group, but as they witnessed that morning, Shak was not only physically strong, he was intelligent, too, and always won the day.

The three sat on the tailgate of the pickup eating sandwiches with cans of ice cold Cokes resting between their legs. "So, where's Kai, Isaac?"

"Dunno. Around somewhere. He stays away from crowds. He probably up the hill with his drawing book." It turned out that their lunch spot was a perfect vantage point for the parade that seemed to be getting ready to move. Small girls with cheerleader costumes and pom poms in their hands lined up in front of the lead truck. At the other end, a low loader waited, carrying a full band, complete with equipment and massive speaker stacks. Right now all that could be heard from its sound system was a throbbing, bass beat, pounding from the cabinets.

When they finally began to move, the carnival goers were treated to wrapped candy thrown at them by the painted, dancing troops on the floats. It was difficult for the infectious high spirits not to rub off on anyone watching, and for a while, Ben and Charlie forgot about petitions and joined the tail end of the parade as it passed them, heading through the town. As they marched to the beat of the reggae music, Charlie spotted Penny and Frank standing on the side of the road ahead. She ran to Ruby, grabbed her hand and pulled her back into the growing line of celebrating Kamarians. Ruby took up her favourite position, dangling between her brother and his girlfriend, screeching with delight.

As the parade dispersed, the band was replaced by Isaac's cousin's fungi group who were a little more laid back. Fungi, pronounced to rhyme with bungee, was danceable, fun, Caribbean music that perfectly represented the happy lifestyle of the Kamarians.

Frank had opened up his office, got the copier going and provided Ben with another pile of blank forms. He told his son how impressed he was that they'd done so well, and Ben noticed that he seemed really surprised at their success.

Isaac's cousin in the fungi band stood by his word and announced to the audience after every few songs if they hadn't already done so, they should step up to the stage and sign the petition. Charlie and Ben flanked the band with pens borrowed from Frank's desk, helping each person that came forward to add their name to the growing list. As always with these things, once one or two had come forward, others followed out of curiosity and not wishing to miss out on anything. Ben had done all the explaining he could for the day and just smiled and pointed at where the person should write their name.

As the afternoon grew a little cooler, people began to prepare for the second most important event of festival—donkey racing! Ben had seen many "old boys" traveling up and down the mountain on their gloomy-looking donkeys. Their leather saddles often carried two five gallon buckets, one on each flank. Sometimes sugar cane or palm fronds were also strapped on. The donkeys always looked like they were about to keel over, and Ben could not imagine how on earth they were going to race them. This, however, was exactly what they did. Buckets were removed, and riders, appearing substantially younger than the ones that actually used the animals as a form of transport, attempted to line up four donkeys at the far end of Main Street. The obstinate animals were not having any of this and kicked their hind legs, dragging the handlers all over the place.

Eventually, one race got underway with the riders thrashing the donkeys towards a finish line chalked on the road, surrounded by cheering spectators. Judging by the fists full of dollars being waved in the air at that end of the street, there was some friendly betting going down. Three out of the four runners finished the race, with one being declared a winner. The fourth animal had abruptly stopped halfway down the street and was now digging his front hoofs in, while the frustrated guy on his back kicked, slapped and yelled at the stubborn donkey. Eventually the rider gave in, jumping down from the saddle, and dragged his mount the rest of the way.

A couple more races were managed, and the onlookers kept track of the fastest finishers as ribbons were pinned to their bridles. It was announced that the last race of the day was for young riders. Eight donkeys, most strongly objecting by now, were held by their owners as brave children came forward to claim a mount. It seemed that there were less donkey riders in the younger generation of Kamaria, as it took a while to find enough willing to race. Two donkeys remained with no riders on their backs. A smiling fat lady standing behind them shoved Charlie in the back and announced to anyone paying attention that these two kids would race.

"No way," Ben yelled. "I can't stay on one of those things. I'll fall off!"

More Kamarian adults, most who identified the pair as the "ones that were going to save Sunset Cove," pushed them forward. Desperately looking around for someone to get them out of this, the two "Sunset saviours" were half carried to the line of irritable donkeys.

"Looks like mine's the one with the ribbons," declared Charlie.

"Wait a minute. How come you get that one? The other one doesn't have any at all!"

"I'm a girl," she said.

"What difference does that make? I thought you didn't like discrimination against women."

"Only when it's not in my favour," she said.

It was too late to do anything now other than avoid the curling lips of his donkey who was trying hard to bite a chunk out of Ben's thigh with some disgustingly green teeth. He had this awful sinking feeling as he was helped into the saddle by the owner who, when he grinned at the quaking boy, proved that the dental condition ran in the family.

"Just kick him hard, boy!" Was all the information Ben was given. So, gripping the reins and the front of the saddle tightly enough to make his knuckles turn white, Ben looked for the dude with the flag that was about to start the race. Charlie appeared totally at home on her donkey, which stood calmly awaiting her command to run.

After what seemed like a lifetime, the starter dropped his flag, and the audience cheered for their favourite young rider. Ben's donkey thrust forward as it was smacked on the rear end by the owner. Coming very close to doing a backward somersault at this point, Ben put his head down and held on. It was the most uncomfortable ride he

Eye of **the Storm**

had ever imagined. He was thrown from side to side and bounced up and down on a totally unforgiving, boney back barely covered by the hardened saddle. As quickly as it had started, the donkey stopped dead in his tracks. Ben ended up staring into the eyes of the crazy animal as his momentum carried him forward over the long neck and onto the road in a crumpled heap. Meanwhile, the donkey sniffed at the road, appearing to have completely forgotten that he was supposed to be racing.

Embarrassed more that hurt, Ben unwrapped himself from the trailing reins and stood up as the crowd cheered at him. He looked ahead to see a rider with a blonde ponytail taking the flag at the end of the track. No one approached him and took control of the obnoxious mule, they just yelled to climb back on. Why on earth would he want to do that? But it seemed he had no choice. Throwing himself at the saddle, he hooked his leg over and hauled on the donkey's mane. Upright again, he kicked and pulled at the rope rein but nothing happened. This of course wasn't the first time his donkey had performed the trick today. It was the same one they had all laughed at in the first race of the afternoon. How had he managed to be unlucky enough to get lumbered with this useless beast?

For the second time today, Ben wanted the ground to open up and swallow him whole. It didn't; however, something equally as gobsmacking happened next. All of a sudden, from down the road where the race had begun, came a barking dog. It was running directly at the donkey, and Ben could feel already that this was something that the animal under him was definitely going to react to. As the dog came into range, Ben's donkey took off like it had been shot out of a gun. With him hanging on for dear life, they galloped past the finish line and proceeded to disappear from view as the now surprisingly energetic beast, forgot to stop. Whilst realizing that he had not been briefed as to how to halt a donkey, it also sank in that this was no random dog trying to round them up; it was Sandy!

The donkey kicked his back legs, narrowly missing Sandy's head as the beach dog snapped at the bucking hoofs.

"Sandy, stop that! You'll get hurt!' About to let go of the frantic donkey and risk being stamped on, Ben was relieved to see Charlie and Isaac running towards them calling Sandy. Reluctantly, the yapping dog backed off and Ben leapt down from the saddle. As soon as his feet hit the road, Sandy was on him, jumping up and licking his face, excited that he had saved his master from the savage brute that was carrying him away.

"Sandy! What the? How did you get here?"

Charlie was making a fuss of the dog now. His chest was heaving hard, and his long tongue dripped as he panted. "I think he needs water. Do you think he ran all the way over the hill?"

"I can't believe he could do that. It's so far, but how else did he get here?"

By this time, a little crowd had gathered, and the owner grumbling to no one in particular, reclaimed the donkey that was happily grazing on the short grass behind them.

"Great race, by the way," said Charlie.

"Yeah, right."

"Next time, I'll let you pick your donkey first!"

"There won't be a next time. I'll stick to sailing, thank you."

Sandy drank litres of water from the cooler and collapsed on the bed of the pickup, licking his paws that were raw from the trek to town. Soon after the climax to the donkey racing, the family decided that they had all had enough action for one day and headed back to Sunset Cove. They picked up Kai on the way, and he explained energetically with his hands that he had seen Sandy coming down the hill alone, earlier that afternoon. Obviously the dog really did want to go to the festival.

CHAPTER 27
A FAMILY SAIL

The festival celebrations provided three official public holidays on Kamaria which meant that the petition couldn't be submitted until the end of the week. Frank was quite pleased about this as he didn't really know how he was going to process it.

His firm was handling the American development corporation's account that had already provided the finances necessary to purchase plots in Sunset Cove. Professionally, the last thing he should be doing was rocking the boat with eighty pages of signatures from objecting Kamarians. Personally, however, he had to agree with the children. He could not imagine any real benefit to the island from a multimillion dollar conglomerate at ease with literally bulldozing its way into profit. He certainly couldn't let Ben down, so he would have to find a subtle way of presenting the petition to both the representatives of DreamWorld, Inc. and the Kamarian government.

Frank's days off work that week meant he had some time on his hands. The two lovebirds were used to having lots of space to themselves, but that all changed as Ben's Dad was in the house. They made a special effort to show him the sugar mill ruins and impressed him by explaining how the rum was distilled, but Ben wanted to head over to Long Bay on the Wednesday and sail *Hardi* to a bay tucked around the side of Scorpion that they had not checked out yet. He had this awful feeling that his dad would want to come with them. If he was honest with himself, it was only right that his father, who had cooperated so much with their adventures up until this point, should at least see the sloop that they talked so much about, but taking him to meet Grammont didn't sound much like fun.

When Frank hinted at coming along for the ride to Scorpion Island, Ben made excuses about the dory being unsafe with anymore bodies aboard, but then he had a brainwave of a compromise. Why didn't they sail her to Sunset Cove? It would actually be the longest sail they had attempted so far and wicked to bring her into the bay opposite his beach house. Ruby would love to climb all over the sloop, and his mum would be so proud. They could pick up his dad, take him for a sail and then drop him back off, returning to her mooring before dark.

The more he thought about it, the more he liked the idea. Isaac was up for it although grunting about the early start that Ben demanded, and Kai always wanted to sail, so he was easy. When they reached *Hardi*'s mooring with the dory the next morning, Ben thought he should explain his plan to Grammont. So, as the others got the sloop ready for her long sail, he swam ashore in search of the Frenchman.

They had stopped anchoring the dory at the other end of the beach, now they drove in the same cut that they sailed through. It was a vast improvement as they didn't have to drop an anchor each time and returning to the mooring in *Hardi* with a boat already attached to it gave Ben something bigger to aim at.

Ben found Grammont in his cabin reading. Sunny the parrot was perched on his shoulder which made it appear like she was reading, too.

Michel glanced up and simply said, "Morning."

"Good morning, sir. I wanted to tell you about our plans for today. I hope you don't mind, but I was hoping to sail *Hardi* to Sunset Cove so my family could see her."

Slowly, the Frenchman lowered the book he was studying. Sunny began to get spooked by the boy in the doorway and ran up and down Grammont's arm squawking and displaying his plumage in "terrorize" mode.

"You'll have to watch the passage between Scorpion and Black Cay."

"Yes, sir, we should be fine. Just a couple of tacks in the passage then we'll be in deep water."

"Sailing back here will take a while."

"Yes, sir. I was hoping to take my Dad for a quick sail before heading back. The forecast says we will have wind all day, so I am sure we can be back before dark."

The Frenchman fell quiet then said, "By my reckoning, you are pushing your luck to get all that done before nightfall."

Ben's heart began to sink as he got ready to hear the guy say no, although he couldn't help but secretly agree with him. If the wind did ease or they took longer than he thought in Sunset, they could get caught out.

"I think that you should plan to anchor the sloop in Sunset overnight and then sail her back the next day." Ben took a while to take this statement in. He was being told he could keep the boat overnight outside his home! Resisting the urge to punch the sky and yell, "Yes!" but not able to keep the huge grin off his face, he said as an alternative, "That would be great. We would make sure that she's safe. I've got the hang of anchoring her now, and there's lots of sand in about five metres of water right off the beach. Thanks, Mr. Grammont. My parents will be amazed."

"Just have her back here by three o'clock tomorrow then I know you are all safe." Then, seeming to catch himself, he added, "Well, what I mean is, I'll know the boat's in one piece."

Standing in a daze, still stunned at the permission he'd been granted, Ben realized his mouth must be open as an adventurous bug flew in it. Spitting the intruder out and coming back down to earth, he thanked the Frenchman and ran the length of the beach to where the others were getting *Hardi*'s sails set.

"Was up with you?" Isaac didn't approve of people moving that fast unless they were an athlete or something. Charlie's face dropped as she imagined that Grammont had put the mockers on the trip.

"Can you believe this? He said we can keep *Hardi* in Sunset Cove overnight."

Shaking his head, Isaac sat down on the deck again. It was way too early for all this fuss.

"That's fantastic. Just think, we'll be able to say goodnight to her."

Not entirely sure he was into wishing a boat "nighty-night," but understanding, nonetheless, what Charlie meant, he just laughed. "Yeah, it rocks."

When they were clear of Dog Leg Reef, they sailed right, instead of their customary left turn. Knowing there would be a lot of tacking back and forth in the narrow channel before they reached open water and the longer, upwind legs to Kamaria, Ben had Kai concentrate on how Charlie was handling the jib as it switched from one side of the boat to the other that way he could help by sharing the load on the long trip.

Ultimately, the difference between a sailboat and one powered by an engine is that no matter who you are and what shape the boat is, it cannot sail directly into the wind. Aiming at the wind is actually how you stop a sailing vessel. Therefore, if you need to go somewhere which happens to be in the same general direction as where the wind is coming from, you have to make do with tacking, or zigzagging back and forth across the wind, hoping to eventually end up at your chosen destination. This, if you are a powerboat driver like Isaac, is not so easy to comprehend.

Also, the closer you steer your boat to the wind, the more it tends to tip up. In small dinghies like Charlie and Ben were used to sailing, this was one of the occasions when, if one or more elements of the overall equation went slightly amiss, the boat capsized. This is not a problem in a Topper, but neither of the English sailors wished to experience anything close to this wet situation in a twenty-five foot, wooden sloop.

The exploring they had done in *Hardi* up until this point, had involved very little of this upwind stuff, and Ben was now especially conscious of the stones that he had carefully stacked below the floorboards not two weeks ago. So far, they hadn't moved.

Isaac's new job was to work the mainsheet. This is simply a mass of rope attached to the boom which was, in this case, a tree trunk perpendicular to the mast and suspended beneath the largest sail. When you pull on the rope or ease it out, the sail moves into or away from, the centre of the boat. Again, things change with this control if your target is upwind. The sail has to be dragged much deeper into the boat, so it takes more muscle, especially when it's a sail as powerful as the *Hardi*'s. Ben also thought that if he gave Isaac an important job to do, he may get the hang of what they were trying to accomplish instead of complaining about how many more times they needed to turn around.

"Man, this thing needs a motor."

"That's the whole point. It doesn't need a motor. Anyone can drive a powerboat in a straight line, but this takes skill. Look at it this way, it'll be plain sailing on the trip back."

Isaac didn't get the joke, forcing Ben to give up.

Sailing into Sunset gave Ben a lump in his throat, and he felt taller all of a sudden. Waiting in the shallows, was his whole family, all waving frantically, including Sandy who followed suit by wagging his tail. As he organised Kai, who was ready to dump the anchor over the side, Ben also noticed Mr. Hamilton and a stranger watching from the other end of the beach. It was a doddle to anchor and let *Hardi* hang back off the patch of sand. They dropped the jib and tidied it on the bow so Kai could see what he was doing, scandalizing the main the way Grammont had shown them.

Neither of Ben's parents were sailors. With the exception of a couple of cross-channel ferries and a ride out on a safety boat at the yacht club once, they were novices. Ben was too young to understand the emotions rushing through his dad's head at this moment. Frank saw his son taking responsibility, directing instructions to his peers and getting the very most he could out of his new surroundings. Everything he had wanted for Ben at the start of this summer had come true and lots more besides. Penny just cooed at them as they dived off the deck into the sparkling waters of Sunset Cove. Spotting her big brother, Ruby hurled herself into the sea with her clothes on and splashed around until Ben reached her and towed his sister out to his pride and joy.

They were all treated to a guided tour from Ben and Charlie whilst Isaac dozed in the shade and Kai, grinning from ear to ear, jumped around the visitors, making Ruby giggle hysterically. Sandy scratched at the hull, asking to be dragged aboard, and the sloop no longer felt so big at all.

Everyone wanted to go for a ride, so Charlie arranged them where they wouldn't get hurt or be in the way of the now slick sailing team. Raising the anchor, they cruised out of Sunset. Not wanting to frighten Ruby or his parents, Ben reached smoothly along the northern coast of Kamaria and then turned *Hardi* around and gently returned to their home.

Insisting that he ought to be useful, Frank went forward to where Kai was standing waiting patiently for the signal to once again lower the hook. This nearly ended in disaster as when Ben gave the okay to lower away, Frank decided to stand on a neat coil of rope that just so happened to be attached to the chain that was currently sliding over the side. Tripped up by the tightening process as the anchor took hold and the boat began to tug against the rope, Frank landed on flat on his back with a thump amongst the now tangled line, his foot wrapped around a loop and holding fast. The boat was taking up the slack against his ankle. Kai and Isaac nimbly took up the strain as Charlie unwrapped Ben's father's right foot from the mess. Ben could have died at this point. Parents! Who'd have them?

Once anchored, Ruby decided that her favourite thing to do was jump over the side of *Hardi* which she had already renamed "Didi," presumably because it was easier for her to pronounce. With arms bands attached, she threw herself into the sea, and then yelled at whoever was patient enough to respond and lift her back onboard, simply so she could immediately repeat the exercise.

Gradually, the passengers and crew dispersed, muttering about tea and jobs to do. This left Ben and Charlie, which was fine with them. It really felt like *Hardi* was all theirs, and for tonight, at least, they were going to dream that she was. Not wanting to break the spell, they stayed aboard listening to Charlie's iPod, sharing the earphones. The sun began to disappear behind Scorpion Island, and Ben wondered out loud what Michel Grammont was doing this evening. Charlie had a pretty good idea. She hadn't told Ben or the others about what she had seen in the sea grape tree clearing the day she'd disappeared.

"The day we sailed *Hardi* for the first time, did you see Monsieur Grammont on the hill watching us?"

"Yeah, I did. Why?"

"Well, I walked up to that spot on the way back, that was why I was late."

"What about it?" Ben was checking his transit for the tenth time to make sure the boat was not dragging, so he was only half listening.

"There are two graves up there."

"What? What do you mean graves?" She had his attention now. "Are they pirate graves, do you think?"

"No they're not that old. They're the graves of his wife and stillborn son. Do you remember the story Mr. Hamilton told you about his wife dying in childbirth?"

"Yeah. That's a bit weird sitting up there alone with dead people."

Exasperated and a little disappointed at her boyfriend's lack of tenderness, Charlie pushed on, "Her name was Charlotte."

"Weird."

"Yes, but that's not all, I looked at the dates. The child was a boy and they both died thirteen years ago, the same year you were born. He would have been thirteen if he had lived. The same age as you now."

This news silenced Ben and finally began to make him think. The miserable hermit had been looking at Ben for nearly a month now wondering if this was what his son would have said and done, probably imagining his son helming *Hardi* in Ben's place.

Both youngsters fell quiet, lost in their own thoughts. Feeling guilty about all the names he had called the guy under his breath, Ben wondered how this would change the relationship now that he was beginning to understand the reasons behind Grammont's pained expressions and awkwardness. It wasn't something that could be changed, but he promised himself to try even harder to live up to the Frenchman's tough standards.

CHAPTER 28

TROUBLE IN PARADISE

While Ben's eyes stayed focused on the end of the massive, wooden boom, the rest of his crew lounged around as the waves gently picked up *Hardi* from behind and rolled underneath her like a fat surfboard.

The young helmsman's concern was concentrated on not getting caught by shifty winds filtering off the side of Scorpion. He really didn't want any dodgy situations in the tight space by Black Cay. As it turned out, they gybed once, deliberately, without a problem. Beginning their approach into Long Bay, Ben and Charlie automatically looked towards the sea grape grove for signs of Grammont waiting in silent vigil for his tragic sailboat to return. There was no evidence of him on the hill, and it wasn't until they'd finished packing the sloop away that he appeared on the beach.

"Double check the holding and shackles on the ground tackle, Ben. I understand there is some weather coming our way."

Registering that the man had said his name and not the normal "Boy," Ben stuttered over his reply. "Okay, yeah, sure. We'll do that now."

Grammont walked off, and Ben turned to Charlie and Isaac. "Did we know there was some bad weather coming?"

"I did see some coloured areas this morning on the satellite picture. I'll look again when we get home."

Swimming on an anchor to check that it was doing its job was really not an unpleasant chore. Any excuse to go snorkeling appealed to Ben after a long sail with the sun doing its best to bleach anything it could touch, so he and Kai jumped over the side with their masks and fins in place while the other two watched. Charlie had lost some confidence following the incident a couple of weeks earlier, so she and Isaac made a perfect pair gushing with all sorts of excuses why they didn't want to get wet.

Kicking along the mooring line, Kai made funny noises down his snorkel to attract Ben's attention. Following the direction of the boy's outstretched arm, he spotted a baby turtle swimming just ahead of them. Wishing Charlie could see the cute creature, Ben dived, kicking hard in an attempt to catch up whilst the turtle lazily flapped his wide, dumpy legs, appearing totally unconcerned at the boy's curiosity. Just as Ben thought he could touch the hard, mottled shell, the young leatherback put a tiny bit more effort into his next stroke and shot out of reach again. Knowing he was somehow being teased by such a comical but graceful animal, he smiled under his mask and swam back to the anchor.

Two days later, a mass of oranges and reds swirled their way across the online weather chart displaying the Atlantic Ocean, heading in the general direction of the islands south of Kamaria. This was enough of a warning for Penny to buy more candles and an oil lamp that she hung from a hook in the ceiling of the beach house. The last tropical wave that came through had caused the power to be cut for hours, although to be fair, it didn't seem to take a storm for someone to shut down output from the electricity plant. In fact, Ben had already decided that the guy with his finger on the off button timed it deliberately to coincide with his shower or when the laptop needed charging.

If a bad storm came through Kamaria, there would be no power, hence no water, for maybe days. This was repeatedly lectured to the youngsters by Frank who was reliably informed of this by his contemporaries at the office. Ben got the impression that the handful of English families also stationed on the island secretly regarded the Johnston family as completely nuts to be so far away from town, especially during hurricane season. The thought of being cut off for days by a raging hurricane appealed to Ben in a warped kind of way, but he also knew that the damage to buildings and boats could be bad. Remembering the north swell that had been generated last time, it dawned on Ben that *Hardi* could be vulnerable where she lay in Long Bay.

Talk of tropical storms was given a breather when Frank returned from work that afternoon. "I presented your petition to one of the directors of DreamWorld, Inc. at lunchtime today," Frank said to his son and Charlie. "He's the one that you've seen around Sunset Cove talking to Mr. Hamilton. He accepted it and promised to look into the situation when the remainder of his board of directors arrives on island later this week."

Charlie seemed quite impressed by this. "That's great, so maybe they will change their minds after all."

Ben was quiet for a moment. "What do you think Dad?"

"All you can do is hope that the amount of signatures will make them think."

Actually, Frank was still reeling from an unpleasant situation involving his boss and two of his fellow lawyers, including his friend David Ridgeway who happened to be the direct contact with the DreamWorld account. Frank had not warned his colleagues about the petition, mostly as he was afraid they may have found a way to stop him from producing it at the end of a general update meeting scheduled that day. The director had quickly recovered from the fleeting flash of anger displayed across his face as he registered what he had been handed. It was replaced by his usual smarmy, false smile and all sorts of comforting noises that Frank knew meant absolutely nothing as the guy all but sprinted for the door.

Frank had been honest with his boss and David afterwards, explaining how the petition had come about, but they refused to see how he could have let it get past a "kid's game" and told him to "bury any more teenage rebellion before it became an issue that would cost the company tens of thousands of dollars."

Not in a position to protest further, and possibly already risking his status in the company, Frank had no choice but to bite his tongue and conceal his concerns over what he was now convinced was an unscrupulous deal with no real regard for the preservation or future of Kamaria and its people. Disillusioned, he left the office early and drove the long way home. It was such an unspoiled part of the world and indescribably beautiful. Frank stopped the truck on the brow of the hill, looking down on Sunset Cove: the mountains were framed by a dramatic, rolling cloud formation promising rain and perhaps more.

Weather forecasters were predicting a storm to form by early the following morning. This was officially defined by a system producing forty knots of wind plus, which was enough to make Ben worry even more about *Hardi*. A ground swell had already begun to crash onto the beach outside his bedroom window, and even Sandy was restless when Ben put him out on the deck on his blanket.

He and Charlie quietly talked in his room about what to do about the sloop. For a while, his mum had made them keep the door open in the evenings if they were on the computer or listening to music; he wasn't entirely sure what she thought they might get up to, but after a week of bursting in with the offer of hot chocolate or cold water, she seemed to get used to the idea of them being alone.

"Don't you think that the reef will protect her from the waves?" Charlie seemed less worried than her young boyfriend.

"I guess, but it won't stop the wind, and if she breaks free, she'll be on her side, either on the beach or the coral. We have to go there tomorrow and ask Grammont what to do. He's so angry all the time, I wouldn't trust him to do anything to make her safe. I bet he would leave her to get wrecked on the reef if he had his way."

"What about the swell in the channel? I'm not sure it would be safe to drive over to Scorpion if the waves get much bigger."

"If only the bloke had a telephone like normal people, we could at least call him."

Frustrated, Ben threw himself on the bed next to Charlie and the open laptop. "Let's see what it's like in the early morning then go find Kai, even if Isaac's not around. We can take the dory over and at least strip her sails off."

CHAPTER 29
THE STORM

Everyone had things on their mind that Thursday morning. Frank left in a mood, knowing he would have to do some "crawling" with the lawyers he had upset the day before. Ruby was irritable with an upset stomach; this caused Penny to have a headache whilst Charlie and Ben silently brooded, eyeing the sea and the sky and the internet, trying to gaze into the future like fortune tellers, desperate to predict the next few days.

The storm had a name now—Dolly. A hardly scary name, it seemed to Ben, but nonetheless, it was heading on a curving path towards their part of the Caribbean and already showing its effect on the sun's strength, now hidden in thick, low cloud. Looking behind them, both youngsters saw the tinges of a black sky hanging motionless at the top of the mountain. What was weird, though, was the lack of wind. It was so still, making the atmosphere feel charged and heavy.

"Okay, let's go get Mr. Hamilton's dory. He may be grateful if we offer to lift his pots for him on the way." Ben was stuffing his bag with snacks and a waterproof jacket his mum had made him pack when they left England.

"Are you sure about this? It says the seas will keep rising on this side of the island."

"How about we drive to the edge of Sunset and take a look?" Ben had no intention of not going to Scorpion, but knew he should try his best to appear sensible in his decision making.

Still looking doubtful, Charlie nodded and they left the house, chased, as always, by Sandy the dog.

"It's rough in the deep, boy. You watch the boat." Beck Hamilton was equally as dubious as Charlie about the whole thing, and even Kai made no move to get the gas ready. Ben tried to explain to Kai using diagrams in the sand and a quick round of charades why he wanted to go to Scorpion. When Kai finally got the message that it was to protect *Hardi*, he ran around gathering fuel cans and a ridiculously old-fashioned, orange foul weather jacket, complete with a hood that reminded Ben of the black and white images of old lifeboat men when they rowed to stricken vessels.

The old man wanted all his pots collected. This would take some time and effort. Conscious that the looming weather was working against them, the three friends hastily threw gear in the dory and hauled the anchor up. As they headed towards the outer protection of Sunset Cove, Ben was torn between caution and the physical ache inside him to do all he could, to make sure *Hardi* was safe.

A shrill whistle made them turn their heads. Isaac was standing on the beach waving frantically at them. "We don't have time to go back for him," Ben said.

"We have to. We can't just leave him behind. Besides, we need his help with the pots."

Hurling the throttle arm away from him, Ben spun the boat and aimed it back at Isaac. As they got close, Sandy made another attempt at climbing aboard but was shouted at by his master to stay put on the beach. The last thing they needed was a dog jumping around in the boat today.

"My uncle say we have to get he pots and come back."

"But if we can make it to Scorpion, we should, because *Hardi* needs us."

"Man, it's a boat!"

"I know, but still, we should try and make certain she doesn't get damaged. What does Mr. Hamilton say about the storm, Isaac?"

"He already pen goats in and he taken roof off the shack in the yard, cause the tin, it blow away with the wind."

Finding it impossible to picture Isaac's uncle studying the internet, or even a TV for that matter, Ben was curious enough to ask the local boy how he got his information on the storm.

"He say the birds, them back from the sea, so there must be a bad storm coming."

"The birds are always here. How does that change anything?"

"No, not them gulls, the frigates. They are flying over the land. They the ones he watch."

Frigate birds were giant, black seabirds with red throats, long narrow wings and a deep v-shaped tail. Now that Isaac mentioned it, half a dozen had been swooping low over the beach this morning. Normally, Ben only saw them when he was sailing, and they were high in the distance over open sea.

As they reached the edge of Sunset, the tense youngsters saw long, rolling, swell surging down the channel. The wind was still very light; this meant the waves were not topped with white peaks, yet. The dory, designed for flatter water, had a habit of using its blunt, low bow like a shovel, scooping up water and sending it running past their feet, soaking the gear on the floor before gathering at the back in a pool around the petrol tank. Charlie had a cut-up water bottle and was bailing regularly as Ben drove as best he could, trying to avoid digging the front into the troughs between the mounting waves.

They had picked up three fish pots, and the boat was seriously overcrowded. Now about halfway between Sunset and Scorpion's south shore, Ben ploughed on.

Eye of **the Storm**

They could see rain over Black Cay blurring out most of the tiny island. It was moving like a white blanket, threatening to cross their path. Charlie pulled out a jacket for her and Ben and they shrugged them on. No one spoke, just stared tight-mouthed at the next wave as the little dory surfed, nose-dived then surfed again.

When the rain hit them, the visibility dropped to little more than a hundred metres. Suddenly there was no Scorpion Island or Black Cay ahead just a white curtain, playing games with their sense of direction. Isaac, seeing Ben's confused expression, reached for the control arm.

"Let me drive, me know where to go, even in the dark!" Relieved to relinquish the responsibility without having to ask, Ben let go of the engine.

Astonishingly quick, they were drenched and cold. The squall hurled stinging wind and rain at them. The sea changed instantly, suddenly surrounding them with white-topped waves, some of them breaking as they charged past. The powerboat collected water faster than Charlie could bail.

"We have to go back. This is not good," she said. Charlie was huddled over, hair stuck to her face, her ponytail dripping down the back of her neck.

Ben ignored her plea. "We're closer to Scorpion than Kamaria now. It's better to keep going."

As it turned out, it was not the wind or rain in the squall that did the damage, but the reduced visibility, stopping them from seeing what was up ahead, veiling Ben's view of lethal ocean rollers, surging towards the far side of Scorpion, preventing him from having to admit that it was too late to save *Hardi*.

Their small fishing boat struggled as the fuming sea made fools of them all. The light vessel was being tossed about—the stern lifting precariously before being hurled down the steep slope of the next wave. The propeller screamed as it spun, fighting to keep its grip on the water.

"Man, we need to go back. The engine, she won't make it through this!" Isaac had to shout to be heard over the noise of the gathering storm. Ben grappled with his rising panic, trying to keep it under control, mesmerized by the white water crashing on the corner of Scorpion Island—each wave managing to climb higher than the last, spray bouncing around the seabirds that were forced to abandon their perches.

As his friend started to turn the thrashing boat back for home, he yelled over the relentless noise. "That way is upwind, Isaac. If we try and drive back through that squall, we'll be turned over for sure."

Charlie had frightened tears in her eyes, and looking at her made Ben want to cry, too. "Then what?" she asked. "Please do something!"

Kai was frantically bailing with the sadly inadequate plastic water bottle, his other hand pointing in the direction they had been going. Although unable to speak, the boy was demonstrating his determination to go on. Certainly they were closer to land now than they would be if they tried to turn back. Ben had to agree with him.

"He's right. Let's keep going. We'll find some place to get ashore to wait it out. If we go back, we'll risk capsizing." As the word "capsize" came out of Ben's mouth, he realised two things: they had no lifejackets on board, and, even worse, Isaac couldn't swim. How had he gotten so sloppy? Just over one month in the Caribbean and he had disregarded everything he'd ever been taught about being safe on the water.

Taking the helm back from Isaac, Ben increased the speed of the idling engine and headed further into the gap between the two pieces of harsh land, Scorpion Island and Black Cay, both bordered with unforgiving rock faces. He watched the narrow channel force the sea into a funnel-like space building taller, whiter, waves that climbed on top of each other to reach the other end. They were in the worst place possible right now, but if they could just make it through, it had to be a little calmer on the other side, didn't it?

Without warning, a rogue wave hit the four teenagers. A wall of blue water broke over the side of them. Kai was propelled head first across the small dory, and then there was a noise missing. The three others turned and stared at the silent motor, its throttle still in Ben's hand. Isaac leapt up and reached for the starting cord. He pulled and pulled, pumping the choke and the revs, but the outboard engine was waterlogged.

Charlie's face was grey with fear, her hair plastered to her cheeks. Kai continued to fiddle with the engine, but they all knew it was pointless.

Isaac turned to Ben, "So what now, eh? You the clever one, you got us here, now you get us drowned!"

"It's not my fault. You didn't have to come, anyway. You were the one that was calling us back, remember? Not wanting to be left on the beach."

The ridiculous argument pulled Charlie back to her senses.

"For heaven's sake, pack it in, you two. Fighting will not help. We are not going to drown! Let's calm down and decide what to do."

Both boys stared at the petite, blonde girl shouting at them and immediately fell silent.

The isolated squall subsided, and they found themselves in three-metre, churning waves. Ben fought to calm himself then spoke. "Okay, let's think a minute, we have a cell phone, but that's not really going to get us to safety. That, we are going to have to do ourselves. Isaac, take over the bailing, we have to keep this thing from sinking." Ben continued to think out loud. It was oddly reassuring. "Right, the wind and the waves are more or less behind us. We have two paddles, and we're going to have to use them. Isaac gave him a filthy look.

"We'll never get anywhere, will we?" Charlie looked beseechingly up at him.

"We don't have to. There's no way we could paddle against this, but we can go with it. We've been doing nothing for five minutes already, and we are getting pushed down towards the other side of Scorpion, but also I think a bit sideways, too. That means we're drifting closer to Black Cay, so we just have to keep ourselves off there. I reckon that's possible if we all take turns."

He passed a paddle to Kai and indicated that he should only use it on the right side of the boat. Ben did the same with his. To begin with, each time a wave picked them up they were twisted around and lost ground, but after a few minutes the boys found a rhythm which maintained their distance from the shallows of Black Cay.

It was hard going. Thirty minutes later, Ben wasn't sure if they had made any progress at all. He wondered about digging out his cell phone and calling his mum. No, bad idea. His dad, maybe, but there was no fast response rescue boat on Kamaria, and all he would achieve would be to frighten his parents silly. He guessed he would have to make the call sooner or later, but he thought it better to get to some form of land first.

Another half an hour, and the youths were all showing signs of exhaustion. They were level with the north side of Scorpion now, and the back of Black Cay was to their right. The uninhabited, bleak island was the closer of the two. Long Bay was further to paddle across the wind. This was the next decision they would have to make. Which way did they attempt to go? If they didn't make Long Bay, there was nothing else on the horizon for hundreds of miles. They could drift for days with a major storm on the way. If they reached Black Cay, could they get ashore? If so, then what? There was no food, shelter or help there.

Ben spelled it out to Charlie, in just the way he had thought it through. She was not interested in going anywhere near Black Cay. "We have to get to Long Bay. At least Monsieur Grammont can help us."

"I guess we can try. It's my turn to paddle with Kai, again. Here we go."

They edged closer to Scorpion's rocky shoreline which confirmed without a doubt that no boat or swimmer was going to safely land before the stretch of sand at Long Bay. Ben's shoulders and arms were hurting more than he could bear. His back muscles were screaming at him to stop paddling. Kai was tiring, too. He kept misplacing his paddle blade in the water and heaving on air, sending him crashing backwards onto Charlie. If they hadn't all been so scared, it would've been funny.

They were getting nowhere. If they didn't change course soon and head for Black Cay, the dory would be taken out into the Atlantic, and they would be lost. "It's no good," Ben said. "We're not getting any closer to Long Bay, and I'm sure we are getting pushed out to sea. We have to head to Black Cay. It's our last chance."

Charlie was too tired and scared to argue, so Ben pointed at the reef around Black Cay, and Kai understood immediately.

The paddling was easier with some of the wind's strength on their side. They made some headway towards a reef painted white with breaking surf. Ben strained his eyes, praying he would spot some less chaotic opening as they drew closer to the pebble-strewn beach waiting beyond the danger. The thought of crossing an unknown reef in these conditions was horrifying. Not the least of which, if they were to ever get off the island again, they needed the boat in one piece.

"Isaac, is there anywhere to get on to the island without so much coral?"

'No, man. Just reef."

"Great." Ben sighed.

"What's that over there? It looks shallow and there's less breakers."

"That's the flats, I took a white tourist there once. He wanted to catch bonefish."

"Bonefish? What are they?" Ben asked. "Never mind. Can you get the dory onto the beach from there?"

"Yeah, with a pole."

"A pole?" Considering the kid had already declared they were all going to drown, Ben couldn't believe how evasive Isaac was being.

"A pole," Isaac repeated. "To get the boat through with the engine up, if not you get stuck on the bottom."

"I see. We have the paddles. They can push us. It has to work!" Excited by a piece of positive news, Ben changed the course of the boat a little to the left, pointing it at the flats.

From a short distance away, the water that rushes over a coral reef somehow has a soft appearance—snowy white and foamy—giving an almost mellow impression. However, if you dare to get closer in a small boat, the menace is blatantly visible.

To their right now, less than two boat lengths away, were huge coral heads, hidden most of the time under furiously crashing surf that curled over and over as it raced across the razor sharp, living rock. If they got it wrong, that's where they would be sucked. Unable to stay upright, the dory would succumb to the waves, and the children would be thrown out with no form of floatation to give them even the slightest chance.

Dead ahead was a natural break in the reef, a raised area of flat rock resembling a table, covered with what looked like about half a metre of gurgling, clear water.

Further over to the left were sheer, bleak rocks forming the unapproachable north side of Black Cay.

"Lift the engine up Isaac, we're only gonna get one chance at this. The strongest paddlers need to get ready, one on either side of the boat. We are going to have to go as fast as we can to not get knocked sideways into that surf."

Isaac took both paddles and handed one to his cousin. "We will do this."

"Okay, Charlie, sit in the middle of the boat back here with me." She sat petrified where she was as if not hearing Ben, her eyes wide and terrified, glued to the reef so close to them. "Charlie, come back here!" Ben tugged at her sleeve and she gave way, collapsing into his chest. "Its going to be fine," he whispered to her then said, "Are you ready, guys?"

Feeling the tug of the underwater rip current, tempting the dory into the deadly surf, he yelled to the poised paddlers, "We have to do this now, Isaac!"

The boys dug their blades in and pulled. Working together, they built up some speed, aiming the vulnerable, cathedral-hulled boat at the shallow water. A wave hoisted them, carrying them forward much faster than they could propel themselves, but still tugging to the right. Isaac guided the dory back on track, using his paddle like a rudder. Although everything was happening so fast, Ben still managed to register an inward admiration at this maneuver.

The next wave launched them on top of the flats. Suddenly the water around them was a fraction of the confusion and depth of before. They were safe, for the moment.

"Chill, guys. Give us the paddles. We made it." The four marooned teenagers had massive grins on their faces, all panting hard, delighted to be out of the roaring ocean. It was quite surreal how the flats calmed the oncoming rollers. Carefully rowing around the shallowest parts they gazed at the shoreline, it's steep, narrow beach made up of rounded stones reminded Ben of the ones they had collected for *Hardi*'s bilge.

The bottom of the boat scraped on a rock, then another, and then they stopped. Without thinking, Charlie jumped out to push. She shrieked as she landed. Crispy, stubby coral broke under her feet.

"Watch for spiny urchins. They everywhere here!" Isaac said.

Resisting the urge to point out that Isaac could have mentioned these earlier, Ben ordered, "Charlie stand still!"

The coral under Charlie's feet, although sharp was very brittle. It collapsed when she put her weight on it, producing a crunchy sensation. When they stared hard under the surface, trying to make out the consistency of the bottom, they could see black, spined sea urchins everywhere.

The dory was currently stuck on a coral head and was only going to float off if at least some of them climbed out and pushed. "We'll just have to go really slowly. If we look where we're standing, it should be fine."

"I'm already out, so I guess I'll stay out." Charlie was balancing against the boat trying, to keep still when Kai nimbly hopped over the other side. If Ben was honest, he was hoping one of the boys would volunteer. Although he wore his trainers less and less now while he was on the beach or sailing, their feet had tough soles from a lifetime of living on a beach and rarely wearing shoes. He was always amazed when they ran over sharp stones or gravel.

Very, very, gradually Charlie and Kai maneuvered the dory, Isaac and Ben towards safety. The two boys still aboard acted as lookouts, pointing out black forms under the water so their guides wouldn't stand on them. As they grew closer to the stony beach, the texture beneath their feet became softer and slippery with sea grass. Four were wading now, towing the dory still laden with fish pots and gear. Dragging it clear of the swell, they all collapsed on the stones.

Having stared at the fast-moving grey clouds above his head for a few silent moments, Ben sat up, hugged his knees and squinted at Scorpion Island. From their vantage point, they could make out the corner of Long Bay and then the far side, including just the last couple of palms that lined the beach. They couldn't, however, see the Frenchman's home or *Hardi*'s mooring.

"I'm hungry," Isaac muttered, grumpily.

"You're going to call your parents now, right?" Charlie asked. "They'll be wondering where we are, and we need help before this storm gets worse."

He got up and stumbled to the boat in search of his bag. Groping for the bag in the bottom of the ravaged craft, he lifted it high and watched seawater pour from the bottom. Already dreading what he was going to find inside the backpack, he unzipped it and fumbled past random belongings until he found his mobile phone.

It was in a black case that was shaped to fit and featured a see-through plastic window so you could read the screen and press the buttons without removing the phone. One glance at the front showed a misted up window. Rubbing it with his finger didn't change anything, suggesting that the moisture was underneath the cover. Glancing back towards the others and finding three pairs of eyes all staring at him, he pulled the phone out of its sleeve. The liquid crystal screen was badly fogged up, and the keys were damp.

Pressing the shortcut to his dad's number did nothing to bring the electronic device to life. He dialed the number in full with equally no response. With all the frustrations suddenly bubbling up in his throat he kicked a stone and threw his arms in the air in disgust.

"The thing is dead. It's drenched."

"It can't be. We need it. It's our only way to talk to anyone." Standing up and running towards him, awkwardly on the huge pebbles, Charlie asked, "Are you sure?"

Ben always thought that people in movies asked really dumb questions at times like this. Did she honestly think that he could have mistaken a wet phone with a blank screen for one that was functioning? "Yes, of course I'm sure. Here, you check it out. It's soaked."

Charlie took it from him and pressed a few buttons, but it made no difference. They had no form of communication now. They were on their own.

Eye of **the Storm**

CHAPTER 30
THE BOX

"When do you think they'll start missing us?" Charlie asked.

The useless cell phone was lying next to him on a rock, drying in the weak sun. "It's one thirty now. Mum will miss us soon." Racking his brains to remember his exact wording as they left this morning, he didn't exactly recall clearly stating their destination, purpose of trip and estimated time of return. He was, in fact, deliberately evasive as everyone was on his case about the weather closing in. Miserable in his thoughts of being proved wrong, he tried to make an attempt at thinking straight.

Kai was mooching along the shoreline. The large, round stones had been pushed up steeply by the elements over time, so it was really quite hard to move about. Ben climbed to the back of the stones where the island rose directly up in front of him. Rock covered in harsh, low brush and some giant, nasty looking cacti blocked his path. Walking along the top of the stones a short way, he found a place that if you insisted on trying it, you could probably scramble up the cliff a way, but you'd need the balance of a goat to get far.

Isaac was down at the edge of the water unloading the fish pots, carrying them high enough that a normal tide would not reach them. Finishing this, he lifted the cover off the outboard and began tinkering.

Charlie was the only one still and not interested in her surroundings. All she could think about was spending the night in this barren place with nothing to eat, drink or shelter in. Trying to remember the tracking forecast of the storm, she thought that it had said by tomorrow morning, things could be pretty bad over Kamaria. She wished she had insisted that they should not attempt the crossing to Scorpion, but most of all, she wished she was at home with her family on the south coast of England, watching TV in the comfort of her sitting room.

Ben came up to her from behind, startling her. Angrily, she jumped up and muttered something at him.

"Charlie, what do you think we should do?"

"Brilliant. Now you value my opinion."

"Look, I'm sorry, okay? But we need to attract someone's attention, otherwise it will be dark before they realise we're here."

"How do we do that? We have a broken cell phone and no radio. All I can think of is smoke."

"I was thinking that, too, but I dropped out of scouts after the second time I went, so I don't know how you do that fire-making thing."

This brought a faint smile to Charlie's lips, despite her mood. "No, me neither. I hated the idea of wearing that Brownie uniform."

Ben relaxed a little and laughed with her. "Maybe Isaac knows."

Isaac shook his head, too. Kai was the last to be asked the million-dollar question. Once he understood, he grinned and stuck his hand in his shirt pocket. It came out clutching a box of matches!

"They will be drenched, surely," said Ben.

"Under that souwester jacket of his, he seems to have kept pretty dry, don't you think?" Charlie pointed at his t-shirt.

"True. Should we make a fire now, then?"

Isaac looked up at the black sky. "It going to rain a lot from now. We should climb higher and make a fire up there." Ben could see the logic of getting on higher ground, but couldn't imagine actually making the climb up the side of the cliff. "There are coconut trees there. We use them."

Not totally understanding the goal, but bowing to the boy's confidence at this point, he nodded in agreement. "Okay, but how do we get up there?"

Not speaking just tipping his head in the direction of the place Ben had already looked at, he walked off.

"Charlie, I'm not sure we are all going to make this. Maybe you should stay here and wait."

"No way are you leaving me here alone, Ben Johnston. Besides, I can climb just as good as a boy any day." Thinking that this was going to be another embarrassing moment when his blonde girlfriend would be able to do something better than he could, he inwardly cringed.

The four teenagers, who were beginning to dry out now from the horrendous boat trip, stood with necks craned, staring upwards, contemplating the climb. It was probably doable, and, interestingly, there was a kind of flat piece of terrain just in view with palms growing sparsely around the area. As Ben had seen him do several times in the past month at Sunset Cove, Kai shot up between the rocks that poked out of the cliff with ease. He sent loose dirt skidding down behind him, and Isaac waited until this stopped then followed. Charlie went next, Ben finding himself bringing up the rear. The advantage of being last was having the opportunity of seeing how the other climbers managed. The downside was the thought of one of them falling and taking anybody with them that happened to be in the way.

Charlie and Ben did slide around a bit, but after ten minutes of scrambling, acquiring various cuts and bruises to their knees and the palms of their hands, they found themselves on a grassy plain, still sloping but not as vertical as the first hundred metres. The debris on the ground was wet from the torrential rain earlier, and actually finding something dry to set fire to was going to be pretty impossible.

"This is all soaked. There is no way it'll light." Kai was wandering around under the palm trees. He carried back three old, brown, coconuts. Placing them carefully next to a smooth rock, he walked away again and returned with a large stone big enough that it had to be held in two hands. By this time the others were all fascinated by his movements.

Kai sat on the smooth rock then hefted the big stone above his head and brought it down on the first coconut. Thinking he must be hungry, Ben was way off the actual reason for the activity. When a coconut husk finally gave way to Kai's bashing, it fell apart showing the fruit hidden inside. Kai repeated the performance until all the coconuts were open. He then picked up all the tinder-dry contents and made a small pile.

Indicating to Ben and Charlie to get some more kindling, Kai struck a match under the carefully constructed pile. The second one ignited, and tendrils of white smoke curled their way into the air. After that, it was easy to build an impressive bonfire. Once there was heat below to make them smoke, damp leaves and sticks were exactly what they wanted. It was obvious, really, a coconut is nothing more than a big seed. It has to be waterproof.

Ben wondered how long it would be before the Frenchman spotted the smoke coming from Black Cay. What worried him was that he couldn't see into Long Bay from where they had built the fire, so would Grammont be able to see the signal? With only a vague shadow of Kamaria visible to them, and the wind whisking it away once it rose a short distance, he doubted anyone on the main island would see the pale smoke three miles away, even if they were looking.

"Now what?" Ben asked.

"How much food did you bring in your bag?"

"Um, a couple of snack bars, some Cheetos and two bottles of water."

"Well, we'd better not eat it all at once." Charlie replied sarcastically.

Isaac picked up a big stick and hurled it at a cluster of green fruit hanging on a tree. Not dissimilar to a bunch of large grapes, they dropped to the ground. He collected them and handed them to Ben. Without saying anything, he turned his attention back to the tree and knocked out some more bunches.

Ben looked helplessly at Charlie. "What on earth are these?"

Kai obviously got the gist of the question by the lost look on his face and took then from Ben. He put one in his mouth and rolled it around a bit, before spitting out the green outer shell. He then chewed some more and spat out a stone which was buried at the centre of the fruit. Smiling and offering Ben the thumbs up sign of approval, he returned the rest to Ben.

"Go on, try them." Charlie urged.

Concerned about what they would taste like, he tentatively shoved one in his mouth and bit down. The green skin was easy to break through and the light, purple flesh beneath was sweet. The pip took up the bulk of the fruit, so as they all began to eat, Ben and Charlie learnt that there was a lot of work to be done to get a small amount of satisfaction. Isaac informed them that these were calledg ginups.

Beginning to worry again, they talked about the chances of Grammont seeing the smoke signal and what he would actually be able to do about it if he did. He had no form of transport except *Hardi*, and Ben knew that she was not an option to him. There was an old, beat up VHF radio in his cabin next to the parrot's perch, so maybe he could raise the alarm with that. Isaac announced that he was going back down to the beach to see if the motor was drying out, and Charlie went with him to check on the supplies in Ben's bag. Feeding the fire was as important as anything else that he could think of right now, so Ben and Kai stayed on the hill dragging palm fronds and lumps of rotten, wet, wood around.

Wandering a little further back each time, into the dense wooded area of Black Cay's western cliff, Ben realised that they were not even likely to be kept company by goats on this rock. Birds, lizards and probably other creepy crawlies that he would prefer not to think about (although now that he had, he was careful to look for scorpions before he picked up the fire wood), were the only inhabitants of this deserted island. He wasn't sure that even rats or mice were around. That made the four marooned teenagers the only mammals here.

With that scary thought in the forefront of his mind, he scrambled up a small incline in the trees. Still searching for likely things to set fire to, his attention was caught by a slightly out of place pile of stones. He'd seen people do this before at home, sometimes weird dudes that thought they were artists made totally random towers with flat rocks. This was kind of similar, but almost completely covered in moss and creepers. Looking back down at his feet for more loose stuff to burn, he kicked around for a couple more minutes, before finding himself standing back in front of the strange pile again.

Ben reached out and placed his hand on the top stone, pulling away some of the green vegetation covering it. This could just be a natural formation, but there was something a little eerie about the mound, uneven in shape but appearing to get vaguely narrower as it rose from its base on the ground. With the creeper gone from the top stone, Ben could move it, dragging it away with both hands and dropping it to the side. Tentatively, he did this again with two more stones, ripping the creeper as he worked. Lizards and ants were fleeing as he dismantled the tower; their home collapsing around them.

The remaining pile was now as high as his shins. For several minutes, he laboured at the task of reducing the pile to one giant stone that sat on the earth.

Had someone really piled these stones up? If so, who and even more importantly, why? Intrigued, but now a tad jumpy at the idea of someone being here before them, he braced his back to prepare to move the last stone. It didn't budge an inch. At this point, Kai, still not giving the slightest impression of apprehension at being stuck on a deserted island, bounced over to Ben. Not even bothering to make an attempt at explaining what he had already done to get to this rock, he gestured to Kai to give him a hand to dig the stubborn stone from its resting place. Eyeing him like he had finally lost the plot, Kai obliged, deciding he should help him out, even if he was crazy. After some grunting and kicking, they rolled the rock away. Now, there was an unorganised pile of recently moved stones around the boys and an empty spot of sandy earth next to their feet. Ben wasn't sure what he had expected to discover, but all he got was dirt!

Kai shrugged his shoulders, now convinced his friend had gone mad and wandered back to the fire. Ben was silently admonishing himself for being such a dork as he kicked at the soft ground. He rubbed his bare foot back and forth over the area he had uncovered then jumped back in surprise. Carefully bending down and touching the spot he had just found with his toes, he brushed dry dirt away.

It was black metal, he was sure of it. Using two hands now, he dug and pried with his fingers, exposing a patch of manmade material.

Amused that Ben was now on hands and knees, Kai walked back, standing over him with folded arms. He spied the object below the ground, and making excited noises, joined in the uncovering of a square, tin box. They had to find makeshift tools to dig away the bottom of the box as the earth was compacted so tightly around it.

After what felt like an eternity of digging, Ben lifted the container out of the hole. Heavy and obviously old, it had a top opening lid, locked by a key that would be inserted in the centre of the front edge.

"Kai, this has to be from a ship!" Frustrated that they couldn't open the lid, he turned around and spotted Kai who looked like he was doing a war dance, yelling and waving his arms around. He was actually calling Charlie and Isaac to get up there.

"Treasure! We've found treasure!" Charlie looked up from the beach, only aware that Ben was shouting something. She assumed he had seen a boat or some sign of life, so she stared out to sea trying to catch sight of their rescuers.

"No. Up here, quick!" Ben was madly waving his hand in a "come here" motion at her.

"Alright! Keep your knickers on. I'm coming." This had better be good, she muttered to herself as her first couple of vertical steps resulted in her sliding back to the beach again.

Ben was waiting at the edge of the opening and grasped Charlie's arm, pulling her the last few feet.

"What's all the fuss about? Did you see someone out there?"

"No, it's much better than that!" Not sure how anything could be better than being rescued from a small island with no food, shelter or communication system as a probable hurricane was fast approaching, Charlie was speechless.

"Look what I found over there in the trees." Ben pointed to the black box, dulled by years of being buried in the side of the hill.

"Is that all? You could have at least have found something to eat or a freshwater stream or something."

"Charlie, it was buried under a pile of stones. It's been there for a very long time. I think it's from a pirate ship."

Charlie strutted over to the unassuming object and went to pick it up. "Wow, it's heavier than it looks. What's in it?"

"I don't know. I can't get it open."

"When you have solved that far more important problem, you might want to help build the fire up, as its getting windier, and those black clouds look suspiciously like there's a thunderstorm brewing."

CHAPTER 31
MISSING

Frank Johnston's day was panning out very much as he had expected. If anything, it was actually worse. There was something going down, and he didn't seem to be included. He was getting the distinct impression that he was being blocked out of conversations. Painfully aware that the entire board of directors of DreamWorld, Inc. was flying in later in the day, with a major dinner meeting scheduled the following evening involving his company's entire legal team, he had to decide what to do.

The more Frank thought about it, the more torn he was between keeping his head down, thus getting the promotion he had worked many long hours for, which would give him the choice of anywhere in the world to make a home for his family, including staying here in this remarkably unspoiled part of it, or sticking his neck out even more than he already had and going with his instincts about a dirty deal in an underdeveloped and delicate community that was going to single-handedly destroy so much in one fell swoop.

It had been made clear to Frank that this contract was the largest they had won to date in this small branch of the firm, and to make waves, potentially putting the plans in jeopardy, would not do his popularity, or future, much good at all. So, did he want to help preserve a natural beauty that could never be replicated by a commercial, concrete resort or keep his job?

His mobile phone rang. "Frank, Ben's not back with Mr. Hamilton's boat yet. The old man has just walked down the beach to ask if I had heard from them."

"What do you mean? It's four o'clock, and the weather is horrendous on this side of the island. The guys are putting up storm shutters and moving computers off the floor. They reckon its going to come right over us. Isn't the sea rough on your side?"

"Yes, very. That's why I'm so worried. They shouldn't be out there. I've tried to call Ben's phone, but there's just a message saying it's turned off or out of range."

"Okay, don't panic. Let's sort this out. I'll drive over the hill now. No, wait I may need to get help from town."

Holding the cell phone to his ear, Frank's mind was blank. He had just been informed that his son and three friends were missing at sea, hours before a hurricane was due to pass over their heads. Then, as his mind began to clear and kick into gear, it also sunk in exactly how cut off he was. "Just sit tight and get all the stuff in off the porch. I'll call you right back." Jumping up from his desk, he grabbed the handset to his work phone.

Who did he call first? RNLI? Nope, there was no such thing here. No coastguard. No search and rescue organisation, just a shack that served as a local police station across the road from the ferry dock. He called the number. Speaking too fast, he began, "Yes, hello, my son is missing from Sunset Cove. He went out in a boat this morning and hasn't returned. I need help."

A slow, tenor voice replied. "What is your name, sir?"

Frank told him.

"Your son's name?"

Frank told him.

"Where was he going, sir?"

Frank began to say Scorpion Island, but hesitated as he wasn't totally sure where they were going that morning. He'd left in such a foul mood, he hadn't bothered to check. He instantly felt guilty for not knowing. "Well, they were going to get fish pots for Mr. Hamilton who lives up the beach and—"

"They?" the officer interrupted him, "Are you saying that it is not just your son who is missing?"

"Yes, he goes off with Mr. Hamilton's son and nephew usually, and he also has a friend staying from the UK right now, so she is missing, too."

The voice took on a condescending tone. "So, let me get this straight, sir, there is not one child missing but four?"

Beginning to lose his cool, Frank battled on. "Yes, exactly. Four teenagers. My thirteen-year-old son and his friend named Charlie and Isaac and Kai Hamilton, I think."

"You think, sir?"

"I know. Look, can you get someone to start looking for them? There's a hurricane coming."

"Mr. Johnston, I am fully aware there is a hurricane coming, that's why the fishermen have just finished preparing their boats in readiness. We have no way of searching on the ocean, sir. I would suggest that you get on a radio and listen in for any sightings. I expect they will show up, sir, young boys like to play around. They have probably forgotten the time and are around the corner as we speak."

This little speech did nothing to ease Frank's panic. He grabbed his cell phone and left the office, sprinting past the receptionist as he ignored her question about leaving early to prepare for the storm.

The small fleet of fishing boats were indeed tied up securely, most further around the harbour amongst the mangroves. Mangroves, unusual trees that liked to grow in salt water, provided natural protection from the worst of the wind and surge. Frank wanted to talk to Nelson and find a VHF radio. He had no real knowledge of these devices but vaguely understood that they were the accepted means of communication between vessels at sea.

It wasn't difficult to find the Rasta. He was squatting with the rest of the captains, drinking rum and talking about the storm to come. Nelson stood up when he saw the concerned look on the white man's face. Thankfully, he didn't give the impression of having had any rum. Frank quickly explained. The Rasta nodded and advised, "Man, they probably on Scorpion Island by now. Don't worry, they is good kids. They wait with the Frenchman until the storm finish then come home."

Taking just a tiny bit of reassurance from Nelson's laid back optimism, Frank pressed. "Nelson do you have a VHF radio? We could call the guy on Scorpion and ask if the children are with him."

"The radio on the fishing boat, man. Besides it no good from here. The mountain in the way."

"It can't transmit to that side?"

"No man, only cell phone, but the Frenchman, he don't have no cell phone."

Thinking for a moment Frank pushed on. "Can we get the boat round to Sunset?"

"No, the captain he tie her up, it's too dangerous now."

"That's what I am afraid of. What about a portable VHF radio? Does anyone have one here?"

"Only the folks on the yachts carry them, and the police maybe."

"Okay, Nelson. I'm going to the police station and then over the hill to Sunset Cove. Please make sure all your friends know that there are four children missing."

When Frank burst through the door of the police station, the police officer that had taken his report on the phone a few minutes earlier looked up from his magazine.

Without any small talk, Frank demanded, "Do you have a portable VHF radio?"

"We did have one handheld, but it was mashed up last month, and we're still waiting for a new one to come."

Cursing under his breath, Frank's anger finally escaped. "So how do you propose searching for two visitors and two of your own young people who could be fighting for their lives as we stand here doing nothing!"

"Please, sir. I understand your concern, but we have to be patient and trust in God."

Frank left the officer, hoping God was paying attention this afternoon because it looked like Ben and his friends were going to need all the help they could get. He could do nothing but head over the hill to the beach house and help his wife close up everything. As he reached the peak of the mountain that separated New Town and Sunset Cove, he stopped the old pickup and looked out to sea. The vague shape of

Scorpion Island was surrounded by white water, even from this distance, looking very angry. The three-mile passage between Kamaria and Scorpion was coated in white horses topping off high waves. Frank could see no signs of life nor imagine anyone driving through that kind of sea in a small, open boat. Unnoticed by the Englishman, a single gull, nicknamed Humphrey, flew low over his truck as it fought its way directly into the storm building around Scorpion Island.

Penny, of course, was distraught. Even Ruby sensed that something was wrong as she was repeatedly calling her big brother's name and pointing at the raging sea. Frank explained his efforts in town to his wife who collapsed onto a chair, gripping her own shoulders with her hands.

"We have to do something Frank. We can't just sit here."

"Yes, I know, but I'm not sure what," he said. "I think I should go and talk to Beck Hamilton, he deserves to know what's going on. Stay here, I won't be long." Not giving her too much of a chance to object, Frank let the screen door crash behind him. Sandy, acting very strangely, followed close behind. "I guess they didn't take you today, boy?"

The dog looked at Frank as if he knew exactly what he had just said. His expression was sad, his ears pulled back and his gait, slow. He, too, kept turning his head towards the sea as if he expected his beloved young master to come swimming in at any moment.

"Trust me, you would not want to be out there Sandy." Frank rushed up the beach, deep in thought.

Beck Hamilton was outside his front door waiting for him.

"Good afternoon, Beck. I'm so sorry that we find ourselves in this horrible situation. I take it you've seen no sign of the children?"

Shaking his head he looked up at the clouds. "Hurricane coming, and them boys and that there girl have got themselves lost."

"Nelson says that they are probably on Scorpion Island with the Frenchman. I hope he's right. Ben's cell phone is not ringing, but I guess it could have gotten wet and they are fine, just not able to talk to us."

Beck nodded unconvinced. "They in for a rough night."

Frank was at a loss for what else to say. The old man seemed resigned to waiting to see what would happen.

"I'm going back to the house. I'll let you know as soon as I hear something."

CHAPTER 32
HURRICANE DOLLY

The fire was roaring and sending some seriously black smoke up now. They were becoming experts in choosing ingredients that made the most fumes. Ben kept returning to the box, trying to prize open the lid. The rest of the time he spent imagining what could be in there, maybe gold coins or a pistol, or, trying really hard not to think about Pirates of the Caribbean, someone's body part, maybe.

On Scorpion, Michel Grammont was preparing for a bad storm. He didn't know what it was called, but he knew it was coming. His livestock needed to be shut up next to the cabin and drinking water and fuel for the generator topped up. He kept glancing down the beach at the sloop still sitting in the relative calm of her mooring inside of the reef. He knew that when the ocean really caught hold with the force of the hurricane, waves would push their way over the natural barrier, and the boat would be at their mercy. But he was not going to lose too much sleep over that boat, perhaps it would put an end to his pain if she did founder. Anyway, there were other, more important tasks to attend to.

The palm tree closest to his home was laden with coconuts. If he left them there, they would turn into flying missiles, causing damage. He needed to climb to the top and knock them off onto a safe piece of ground. Climbing palms was something that Nelson had taught him years earlier. He remembered Lottie gently making fun of him as she watched, saying he must be part monkey to be able to climb that well with just his hands and feet. The memory, like all the others, came unexpectedly and never without his heart being squeezed.

The tree was swaying dramatically at about fifteen metres above the ground, and Michel wished he had thought of doing this yesterday before the wind got so strong. He had directed most of the huge fruit onto empty space below, so resting for a moment, he looked up to his right. Black Cay was still partially hidden from this height, but something had caught his eye. He scanned the area for a second glimpse of what he could have sworn was smoke.

Yes, there it was again, but how could that be? There was smoke coming from a point just out of sight on the side of Black Cay. He knew immediately it was a signal but from whom he had no idea. Sliding down the vertical palm, he began to have his suspicions. Those kids would have wanted to prepare the sloop for the storm. Especially the English boy; he always seemed so intense. From the ground, the smoke was lost, but after a few minutes of looking, he caught sight of it again. Had he not gone up the coconut tree, he never would have noticed the signal.

How irresponsible could those annoying children get, stranded on a deserted cay with a hurricane about to hit? Striding back to the cabin, he reached for the radio handset he kept on the wall inside the door. The VHF ran on batteries, charged by the generator. He switched it on expecting the usual static noise before he adjusted the squelch knob on the front of the unit. Nothing happened. Turning it off and on again made no difference. The radio was dead. Grammont had used it just days earlier. Confused at the lack of response, he peered underneath the radio. It was fairly easy to see the problem. Many wires of all different colours and thicknesses entered and left the receiver; however, most had been chewed or severed by a blunt instrument.

Sensing that she should keep her head down for a while, after having great fun with the machine on the wall, Sunny the green parrot flew off her perch into the darker depths at the back of the cabin.

"Don't let me catch you, bird, not if you value that scrawny neck of yours."

Grammont's fishing boat had given up years earlier. The sloop was the only floating vessel on Scorpion. How could he possibly do anything about these kids without a motorboat? Even if he had one, he stood no chance of landing anywhere on Black Cay's shoreline. They would have to wait it out until he could get word to Kamaria or someone else came looking for them after the worse of the storm had passed.

Collecting the coconuts he had thrown from the tree, he allowed his imagination to cut in. What if one or more of them were injured or worse? They couldn't have any supplies, and there was no shelter on that barren place for them to sit out the hurricane. With about an hour and a half of daylight left, the only possible solution was the sloop. He had promised himself he would never set sail in her again.

A voice seemed to be pushing its way to the front of his mind. "You can't leave them, Michel. They are children. You still have time to take *Hardi* and bring them back to Scorpion where they will be safe. They must be so frightened. Please, try for me." The voice was gentle and very familiar. It made tears spring to the backs of his eyes.

He looked again at the sloop waiting for him then spoke to the wind, "You leave me with no choice, my love."

Grabbing a long piece of floating line and an old life ring that had been washed up years earlier, Grammont sprinted the length of the beach. Wading towards the sloop, he hesitated once, looked back at Long Bay and then heaved himself aboard. Dispensing with the jib, he began hoisting the main sail. He left one reef in the sail as

Eye of **the Storm**

he tied off, making the canvas less powerful than normal. He was heading out into forty knots of wind, and the thunder clouds over his shoulder promised more to come very soon.

Even with the reduced sail area, the boat leapt over the breaking waves as he passed the reef. Fighting the sail and the tiller, he headed for Black Cay. As he sailed, he tried to collect his thoughts, remembering the last time he had helmed *Hardi*. Now, thirteen years later, he had no intention of losing anybody.

As the boat smashed over or through the huge waves, he could make out the dory on the beach behind the flats. Impressed that they had the brains to make shore here, he looked for signs of life. The fire was bright and there were two, no three figures close to it. Where was the fourth he wondered? There, that had to be Isaac, kneeling by the engine.

Giving up on Ben and the box lid, Charlie looked for the hundredth time out to sea. Her heart hit her mouth so hard, she opened her lips but no words came out. Eventually as her voice returned, all she could manage was to scream, "The *Hardi*. Oh my God, it's the *Hardi*."

Shooting to his feet, Ben looked from Charlie to the wonderful sight of the beloved sloop, sailing proudly over gigantic seas towards them.

"It's Grammont. He must've seen the smoke." The implications were not lost on him. Even in his rush to push Kai and Charlie down the slippery slope to the beach, Ben knew what it must have taken to get this man in his boat again.

Isaac had also seen the approaching rescuer and was waving frantically. By the time they had all gathered by the dory, Grammont was sailing back and forth weighing up the possibilities of picking the stranded group up without putting himself in the same dangerous position. Not thinking, Ben started to wade out onto the flats.

"Ben, wait. You'll stand on an urchin." Kai was now pushing at the front of the dory.

Too far away to communicate, Michel watched a pantomime unfold on the shore as he tried to figure out what the kids would do. They appeared to have decided to push the small boat back over the flats. He could only assume that the engine was useless and probably the cause of the original problem. He had envisaged having to pick up swimmers, but this was a much better idea, it would keep them together and give him a larger target.

Just about to begin the slow process of crossing the flats, Ben hesitated and ran back to the stony beach. He'd slid down the incline from the fire with the box in his arms. He wasn't going to leave it behind now. Grabbing it, he placed it in the bow. Charlie shot him an angry look and shook her head.

"It may be important. We can't just leave it behind."

"Whatever. Can we please go now? I can see lightning over there."

The waves at the entrance to the flats towered above the crew of the dory. Isaac let out a soft moan and shrank lower into the bottom of the boat. *Hardi* came into view, and Grammont slowed her down within shouting distance and told them to hold their position and he would do another pass and throw a line.

Ben yelled an okay with both his thumbs up and hauled on a paddle to try and keep the dory from being picked up by the surf and hammered onto the reef. As he watched *Hardi* tack and sail back at them, she was so close to the deadly breakers that he wanted to call out to Grammont to go back to safety. He didn't, though. They had gotten this far, but he suspected that they would have only one chance at getting this bit right.

Hardi passed by close enough that Ben could see the Frenchman's drenched face in detail. His jaw was fixed, and his features strained with concentration. Standing up with the tiller between his legs and the mainsail flogging noisily, he threw a coiled, yellow rope. It unwrapped in midair and landed upwind of the dory. Ben knew this was deliberate; the Frenchman had aimed exactly where the long line landed to make sure it was blown down onto the stricken boat. As Kai and Ben frantically paddled towards the drifting lifeline, Charlie reached out and grabbed at it. As soon as her fingers curled around the plastic rope, Ben ordered her to wrap it around the cleat at the front. He was sure that if she held it for too much longer, she would be pulled from their boat and dragged into the roaring sea, head first.

She did as she was told and then seconds later, there was a snatch that sent them falling back onto Isaac's frightened form. Getting his balance, Ben looked for Grammont. He was momentarily hidden in a trough between two waves. As he came back into view, he shouted at them to hang on.

Hauling in some mainsheet made *Hardi* gather speed. Before he could reach the children, he had to make sure that both boats were out of immediate danger from the reef. The dory did not like being towed. They had to jump back and forth, trying to stop the submarine effect as it climbed and fell, making them feel as if they were riding a frightening, wet rollercoaster.

Grammont could see that the small boat would not last much longer. He had to stop again and haul the kids close enough for them to climb in. He strained, hand over hand, his strength depleting much too quickly for his liking. With them twenty feet away from the sloop, he secured the line.

"Ben, pull yourself to me now." Happy to do something, Ben took up the strain and pulled. Each time he hauled an arms length in, some was taken back by the waves, burning his hands on the rough rope as it did so. Kai took the towline and carried on, making more headway than Ben.

Eye of the Storm

Finally, the dory was alongside *Hardi*. The swell threw both boats around but not necessarily together, so the next challenge was to cross the gap without falling in or being trapped between the hulls. Charlie went first. As the boats collided on a wave, she leapt across and up as Grammont caught her arm and dragged her the rest of the way. He mentally counted: one.

Kai, as usual, was the most nimble, landing on his feet in *Hardi* with a grin: two.

Ben looked round for Isaac, but he was motionless in the middle of the bucking powerboat. "Come on, Isaac, move! We have to get out of here!"

The boy looked up and with horrific panic in his eyes, shook his head.

Looking to Grammont for support, Ben heard him shout, "Grab him. Get him to me!"

Before anyone could react, a spectacular shaft of light split the dimming sky. It was dusk, the diluted sun had disappeared, and the thunder rattled around them as if chastising them for being out on the sea so late. Ben tugged at Isaac's petrified arm. He reluctantly rose and stumbled to the side of the dory. He cried out in terror as he lost his balance. Ben caught him and forced him toward Grammont's waiting arms. Isaac was pushed and dragged to the relative safety of *Hardi* by brute force and determination: three.

Waiting for the next wave to lift the dory again, Ben jumped. He saw the faces of his friends sitting huddled on the floorboards in *Hardi*'s protective grasp and then something went wrong. The boats parted and his hands slipped. He felt the brush of Michel's fingertips on his as he fell into the boiling waves.

Pale blue, rolling water full of small bubbles turned Ben over and over before he could work out which way was up. Eyes wide open, coughing and thrashing for the surface, he made it to air.

"There! There he is!"

Before the next wave hit him and he was under again, he caught sight of Charlie's forlorn face at the stern of the disappearing *Hardi*.

Grammont's mind was racing. The only long line was tied to the dory. Even if he cut it, by the time he reached the old life ring that he'd thrown in the bow of the boat whilst he'd rigged, it would take too long to attach and throw. They would lose sight of the boy forever. "Lottie, get the life ring!" Without any more hesitation, he stood on the gunwale and dived overboard in the direction Ben had last surfaced. Coming up for air, the Frenchman lunged around screaming Ben's name.

"Where is he? Can't you see him?"

The three left behind on the sloop were desperately scanning the confused sea for a sign of their friend.

"No! I don't see—Wait! There, over there to your left!"

Michel prayed for a second wind as his lungs were screaming for more oxygen with the exertion of keeping his head above water. Still seeing nothing but the walls of water trying to take him back to the reef, he yelled at Isaac to throw the floating ring where they had last seen Ben. It landed and then he saw him.

Ben was giving up. He came up for air but was so tired he figured it better just to have a sleep now. Grabbing the orange sphere, Michel kicked for Ben's prone body. Rolling him over, he whispered something, then pulled the boy through the centre of the ring. Tugging Ben's face high enough to breathe fresh air, Grammont was relieved to see his chest heave as the boy began to cough. The child would survive if Michel could get him back to the sloop. This wasn't, however, going to happen. They were too far away and the wind was creating a larger gap by the second between the swimmers and *Hardi*. Taking a deep breath, Grammont yelled one more time.

"Lottie, sail the boat. Sail the boat away, turn her around and come back for us."

Not believing what she was hearing Charlie cried, "I can't. No. I can't. Please swim!"

"I won't make it, Lottie. You can do this, now get on with it." Grammont turned on his back, cradling the boy and the floatation device to his chest. He needed the buoyancy as much as Ben did. Lightning crackled across the darkening sky above.

Gathering herself, she thought aloud. "Okay, I can do this. Just a basic man-overboard drill, right? I've done them before in Mirrors."

Kai jumped to her side, understanding what was happening in his uncanny way. She handed him the mainsheet and indicated that he should pull in the flogging sail. Steering away from Ben and Michel, she fought back the horror of losing site of them. Making Isaac point at the spot where they bobbed up and down, she counted the boat lengths. She'd have to go far enough to turn around and be able to stop alongside them. The dory was still hanging from the stern. She would try and get it close to them so they could grab it. Talking to herself constantly, she pushed the tiller across and sailed back towards the desperate pair.

"Where are they now, Isaac?"

"I can see them. There." Spotting a flash of orange, she realised she was going too fast. If she wasn't careful, she'd overshoot them or run them over. Kai let go of the mainsheet at her frantic hand-opening signal, and *Hardi* slowed quickly. They appeared on her windward side. Grammont was waving madly. As if an invisible force had picked it up and placed it perfectly, the dory stalled directly in front of the survivors.

He reached for the dory with one arm, and with his last ounce of energy, Michel ducked under the water and launched Ben into the bottom of the boat: four. He had nothing left now. All the Frenchman could do was hang on to the stern as Kai and Isaac hauled them alongside.

Kai jumped neatly into the dory as Charlie held *Hardi* in a hove-to position. They passed a very weak Ben over the side as gently as possible and laid him down on the cabin roof. Kai went back for Grammont and helped him in. Making sure the Frenchman transferred safely, the deaf boy waited. As he was about to jump over for the last time, he noticed the black box tucked under the bow seat. Retrieving it, he pushed off the seat and landed in *Hardi*.

Exhausted, it was all Michel could do to form the words, "You sail her home, Lottie."

As they fought their way through the darkness and the still-increasing wind and waves, Ben began to recover. He helped Charlie with the helm, and between them, they attempted to guess the gap in the reef by the light from the forked lighting all around them.

"Just sail her up the beach. It's her only chance now."

Without question, Charlie aimed at the sand and Ben held onto the main. "Hold on, we're about to hit!" Everyone braced themselves but were still thrown forward by the power of the hull digging into wet sand.

"Well, she just did a hell of a job saving our skins, so maybe we should spare a little time to make her safe from the storm. What do you say, guys?"

Slightly stunned at the Frenchman's words, Ben leapt to unsteady feet and started dropping the sail, wrapping it tightly with the mainsheet as he went.

"Isaac, untie the line from the dory. We can use it to tie her down to those trees over there." In the dark, Isaac turned to the back of the sloop; he picked up the yellow towline and pulled, expecting the heavy resistance of the waterlogged powerboat. The line came so quick it hit him in the face.

"Man, it gone. The boat. It gone!" They all turned and looked at the line as he pulled it over *Hardi*'s side. Dangling on the end was a stainless steel cleat that used to be bolted to the front of Mr. Hamilton's dory. In the rush to get back to Long Bay, none of them had noticed that the boat had broken free.

"That's that gone then," was Grammont's only comment.

Isaac looked dismally at the cleat as he declared sullenly, "My uncle's gonna kill me!"

Charlie tried to cheer him up by suggesting that Beck Hamilton would be so pleased to have them back in one piece, he wouldn't be worried about the boat. This didn't help, and Ben had a feeling that Isaac was pretty close to the mark. His uncle was gonna kill him!

Michel disappeared into the darkness as they tied things down wherever they could. He returned with a hammer and chisel. Without a word, he climbed back aboard and walked to the stern. Bending down he lifted a floorboard, exposing the ballast stones. Moving two away, he positioned the tip of the chisel on one of the planks. Raising the hammer high above his head he dropped it hard on the chisel handle.

"What the, what's he doing? He's banging a hole in the boat!" Charlie ran to the stern followed by the others, but Ben had already guessed what was happening.

Grammont explained as he worked, "It's okay. Relax. We need to let her take on water, otherwise the waves and wind will wreck her. If she is on the seabed, she'll be safe—too heavy to knock over."

Letting this very alien technique sink in, Charlie went quiet.

"Look, this is all we can do for her. I think we deserve some food and warmth now, don't you? Let's get out of this blasted thunderstorm!" Michel walked off, followed by four exhausted young adventurers. One of them carrying an old, black box.

CHAPTER 33
THE DORY

Frank and Penny were beside themselves with worry. Darkness had closed in, and the thunderstorm continued to grow closer, making them all jumpy. This was the first time that either of them had been in such an awful situation over their children. Nothing in the past had prepared them for the feeling of helplessness and not knowing what was happening. Oh sure, Ben had fallen down and hurt himself a couple of times, once he had ended up in the casualty department with a broken wrist, having to be plastered up for a fortnight. Tonight, however, was the first night that both of them had spent away from their son. His phobia of sleeping apart from his parents had tied him to them whether they liked it or not, and right now, Penny wished with all her being that Ben was lying on his bed chatting to Tony online.

They had considered contacting Charlie's parents and tell them what was happening, but Frank had persuaded his wife to hold back until the morning with the hope that the children would be found unharmed and any news relayed back to the UK would have a happy ending. Ruby was upset and confused, wanting her brother to come home. The thunder and lightning did nothing to help her mood as she restlessly tossed and turned on her cot.

Both adults leapt up as there was a knock at the door.

A voice called out "Inside!" which prompted Sandy, who had been lying under Ben's window on the deck, to go berserk. Nelson recoiled as the dog skidded round the corner, barking like crazy.

Frank shouted at him, which did enough to quiet the animal as he sniffed the air around the Rasta.

"Man, that dog, he hates me!"

"Sorry about that. Come in." Closing the screen door in Sandy's scowling face, Frank directed Nelson to an empty chair.

"Did you hear anything yet?" Penny hadn't bothered with pleasantries. She was too frantic to hear any news.

"Yeah, I just come from town. Jack Hamilton, Isaac's father, dropped me by you. He gone to see old Beck."

The news wasn't coming fast enough for Penny. "So, what did you hear?"

"Well, this American yacht coming in to shelter from the hurricane found a boat drifting." Frank looked at Penny, and then with horror in their hearts, they turned back to Nelson. "And?"

"I went to the dock when they brought it in. It's Beck's own."

Penny took three whole seconds to comprehend what the man was saying to them.

"No sign of the children?" Frank reached out for Penny's hand as in answer to this question.

Nelson produced a black rucksack that they recognised instantly as their son's. A wailing noise came from his wife's throat as Frank tried to hold on to her shaking body.

"This just means they are ashore somewhere safe. They're both strong swimmers. They'll be okay." Speaking words that he didn't believe himself, he looked back at Nelson who had gotten up, not wanting to be in the way. "Can we get a helicopter searching at first light do you think?"

"Yeah, they done that from the airport before. Talk to the police inspector; he arrange them things." Nelson walked into the howling night. He had not mentioned that Isaac, Jack's son, could not swim.

Desperately trying to put things together in his head, Frank debated with himself, "Surely, they would not have all fallen overboard, and if the boat had capsized then it would have been upside-down when the yacht found it. The bag wouldn't have been in there, that's for sure."

"So, where are they, Frank?"

"I think Scorpion or maybe along the coastline a bit from here. If they had to climb onto rocks, they will have to stay put until it gets light." Imagining the children perched on jagged rocks in the middle of the storm made Penny cry again. Ruby came sleepy eyed into the room and crawled onto her Mum's lap. They all sat hugging each other while Hurricane Dolly pushed away the thunderstorm.

CHAPTER 34

THE BUCCANEER'S TREASURE

Michel Grammont didn't have much in the way of furnishings and possessions, but what he did have he proceeded to lift off the ground. "The rain can come down the mountain so fast behind us that it can't spread out into the ground quick enough, so it floods the cabin floor. If this doesn't happen, there is a chance the sea may push so far up the beach it comes in the front way. Either way, we are likely to get wet feet."

There was a long kind of daybed thing that was already raised on pieces of wood, and Charlie and Ben fell, shattered, on this. While the others helped the Frenchman with a huge sea chest that he wanted to lift onto rocks, Ben spied the VHF.

"You have a radio! We have to call someone to tell our parents we're safe!"

"I've already tried. The thing is busted, thanks to the parrot. It seems she wanted to try a little do-it-yourself electronics. Look for yourself."

Ben glanced under the radio and groaned. He could imagine his mum and Dad going spare with worry. He hated that feeling. He didn't want them to hurt because of him. He suddenly became very homesick. Charlie was reading his thoughts as she wondered if the Johnstons had contacted her parents in England. She hoped not.

Grammont disappeared again. He came out with some shirts and shorts of his that he handed around. Finding them much too big but dry, Ben encouraged the others to change into them. Charlie hadn't been given anything, and she had gone outside the cabin when the boys were getting changed. When she came back in, Michel shyly beckoned to her to follow. Glancing over her shoulder at Ben, who just shrugged, she did as she was asked. She found herself in a tiny bedroom just big enough for a double bed and a chest of drawers. Gesturing towards the cabinet, Grammont explained that if she looked on the left hand side, she could probably find something appropriate for a girl. Without giving her a chance to respond, he left.

Carefully opening the top drawer, she saw layers of folded tops, the drawer beneath held shorts, plain ones mostly light tan or khaki in colour, but they were all women's sizes. Torn between upsetting Grammont by wearing his late wife's clothes and her desperation to be warm and comfortable, she hesitated. If he hadn't wanted her to see, he wouldn't have invited her in here, so she picked out what she needed and changed. Carrying out her wet stuff, Grammont gasped as she walked past him. He said nothing more.

It was after ten o'clock at night, and they all realised just how hungry they were. They dined on goat stew and homemade bread, which although it didn't sound very appetizing, was the best meal Ben had ever had. He seemed none the worse after his near-drowning experience, but he was finding it difficult to recall all that happened in the water.

After dinner, not able to contain himself any longer, Ben got up and went outside to where he had left the black box. No one noticed as he came back in cradling the antique. All were dozing in the chairs with the exception of Grammont. He looked from the box to Ben and back to the box again. Saying nothing but allowing a slow smile to spread across his face, the Frenchman got up and turned away.

Surprised that he had not insisted on looking at it immediately, Ben stood and watched Grammont's back as he did two things. He reached for a dark bottle that Ben guessed was rum, pouring some of the fiery liquid into a short glass until it came halfway up the side. Then he took three steps to a wooden cabinet on the wall and opened it. As he turned back to Ben he had a glass of rum in one hand and a large, ancient key in the other. "So it was on Black Cay all the time, eh?"

Confused, as he was expecting this to be a complete surprise to Grammont, Ben stuttered over his explanation of where he found it. "So, you knew about it, sir?"

Drinking from the glass, the Frenchman smiled again. It was tired and somehow sad, but it was definitely a smile. Ben was not used to this expression on the eccentric guy. Mind you, he had just saved Ben's life risking his own in the process, so he probably shouldn't think of Grammont as eccentric, even in his mind, anymore.

"Ben, my name is Michel. I think we should try to get on to first-name terms now, don't you?"

"Sure. Do you know what this box is, then?"

"I most certainly do. Would you like to try the key?"

Thrilled but scared to see what may lie inside, Ben declined. "No thanks, Sir. I mean, Michel. You should open it. But do you know what's in it?"

"I have a good idea but no, not completely. I just suspect that I am familiar with the last owner."

"So, was it a pirate then?"

"Of course. None other than the original, Monsieur Michel de Grammont, buccaneer and commander of an infamous and feared fleet until the hurricane that shipwrecked him here on Scorpion Island four hundred years ago. I found the key many years back, but the ship's box had escaped me until now. He hid it well, burying it on Black Cay.

Ben placed the box on the table, and Michel offered the lead key up to the lock. This was really happening, and Ben had to remind himself that Captain Jack Sparrow was not going to come bursting through the door any minute. The key turned in the lock without effort, and Grammont left it in place as he lifted the lid.

Picking up his glass, he looked at Ben. "Go ahead, tell me what you see."

A very spooky feeling came over the room. Ben glanced up at the buccaneer's portrait, half expecting to see it come to life, like in a *Harry Potter* story. Reaching inside, he touched a document folded twice and sealed with a red, wax emblem of some kind. He lifted it out, like it was made of fragile glass.

Nodding to himself, Grammont announced, "The ship's articles. I thought so." Underneath the parchment was an array of small items.

Between them, they spread the contents out on the table in a row. There was a handful of what Michel described as Spanish doubloons—blackened, gold coins with an irregular, vaguely rounded, edge. A bundle of letters tied with twine, a small portrait of a formally dressed family gathering, a satin pouch containing dried snuff and a tiny dagger decorated with red, green and translucent gems.

Charlie stirred on the cushioned seat, opening her eyes for a moment, not knowing where she was. She dragged herself up, dropping down hard again onto a wooden chair next to Ben. "Is this really what was in that old box you found?" Now wide awake, with the burning knowledge that the last person to touch these personal effects was a notorious and ruthless buccaneer, Charlie gently touched the portrait and the gold coins.

Grammont stood and walked to his bottle of rum, topping up the glass before saying, "Make yourselves comfortable, you two. I think it's time I explained his story."

Returning to the soft seat, Charlie curled up against Ben's shoulder with her feet tucked up underneath her as she sleepily waited for Michel to take another sip from the glass that he held with both hands. Isaac and Kai were sound asleep, both snoring as they dreamt about their day.

The Frenchman sat opposite the two tired teenagers with his drink on the table close to his right hand. Trying in his mind to separate his own life story from that of the pirate's, he looked up at his ancestor's portrait for support and began, "Michel de Grammont was born in 1650 in the southwest of France to an aristocratic family. At the tender age of fourteen, he challenged a young military officer who was courting his sister to a duel."

Ben broke in, "He was the same age as you, Charlie."

"Yeah, you should be grateful I don't have a brother."

Looking peeved at being interrupted, Michel continued. "The young Michel easily won the confrontation, and amazingly, as the young officer lay dying, he gave the brother and sister the majority of his estate. Soon after this incident, Grammont was drafted into the French Navy. Loving life at sea, he rejected his upper-class upbringing and adopted the coarse dialect of the seaman that surrounded him.

"During one of his naval voyages, Grammont and his crew captured a Dutch ship which had been nicknamed 'The Purse of Amsterdam' because of the amount of money and precious cargo it carried. Following this escapade, he spent several days gambling away his share of the loot in the taverns of the French Antilles. Finding a lucky streak, Grammont won enough gold to purchase his own ship. Returning to France, he resigned his position with the navy and opted for the life of a pirate."

Shifting his weight in the chair, Michel nodded at the picture on the wall. "That portrait was commissioned by the captain during his most ruthless years. They say that when the artist had finished, he was forced to walk the plank for his troubles. The most lucrative of his expeditions happened between 1678 and 1686, hanging around South America and the Mexican coast, raiding and taking hostages for reward. In fact, he was so successful, the King of France tried to stop Grammont's illegal activities by offering him the title of Lieutenant of the King for the Province of Santo Domingo."

Ben opened his mouth to ask where that was, but closed it again thinking it may be better to save the questions for later.

Michel continued, "He accepted the position, but it didn't slow him down for long. Assembling 200 men in three ships, Grammont sailed for another planned raid, this time to St. Augustine, Florida."

It was weird, Ben had always imagined one-on-one, bloody fights as pirates boarded ships laden with gold and jewels, not taking whole communities hostage. "During the trip, a heavy storm forced the fleet to change course. Running for safety, Grammont became separated from the other ships, and the French authorities never heard from him or his crew again."

Ben moved and in doing so, woke Charlie. She opened her eyes briefly, moaned something and closed them again, nuzzling into Ben's shoulder. The only of the four awake now as the sounds of Dolly howled around the tiny cabin, Ben looked over at Michel, demanding more of the story. "So he was near Scorpion when the storm hit him, then?"

"Yes, Dog Leg Reef took the original *Hardi*, breaking her into splinters and drowning all the crew but Grammont who was probably unconscious and half dead by the time he was washed up here on Long Bay."

192   Eye of **the Storm**

Looking through the crack of a shuttered window towards the beach, Ben saw that everything was black now, but his imagination had no problem picturing a floundering pirate ship in a storm as the waves rolled her over onto the cruel coral, snapping her masts like twigs. First-hand knowledge of being in waves probably only half the size today, gave him a very good idea of the carnage that would have ended many lives and crushed the ship.

"Did you find the wreck when you came here?"

Michel nodded, draining his glass. "I've found small pieces of the wreck and some items that were onboard over the years, nothing for a while though."

Looking around inside the cabin at the driftwood that Sunny used as a perch and the step that he walked on each time he entered the room, the penny dropped in Ben's tired mind. These were all bits of the Buccaneer's flagship.

Reading the boy's mind, Michel smiled dryly. "Yes, all this junk is from my great, great, great grandfather's vessel."

Against his will, Ben's eyes were becoming more insistent on closing.

Seeing this, Michel stood and simply said, "Enough for tonight. It's been a very long day, and you need to sleep Ben."

Not able to object, Ben lifted his feet and stretched them as best he could onto the shared daybed. Charlie moaned again and turned her head away from him, taking the pressure off his shoulder. Although he would not have moved her deliberately, he was quite glad she had shifted her weight. His arm had been numb for ages. Instantly, the fair-headed boy was fast asleep.

Michel waited for many moments, watching over all the teenagers in his cabin. His thoughts returned to the rescue, and the gentle voice revisited him. "You and *Hardi* saved them all, my love." Looking for the source of the voice in the direction of his bedroom, he knew he would not see her. He didn't need to. He could feel her presence everywhere around him. Not bothering to undress, he lay on his bed, somehow knowing that the morning would bring a fully fledged hurricane to Scorpion Island.

CHAPTER 35
THE EYE OF THE STORM

Unbeknownst to the inhabitants of the cabin on Long Bay, Dolly had been officially declared a category two hurricane. Those with radios, computers and TVs were told that sustained winds of one hundred and ten miles per hour had been recorded, and the eye was expected to pass just twenty miles north of Kamaria early the next morning. Frank had moved his drowsy wife and young daughter to the double bed in the hope that at least they would get some sleep. It was after one o'clock in the morning, and the rain was torrential. Sandy was behind the chair, having had to be persuaded to come into the house. Frank was sure his unusual reluctance to shelter from the rain was because he knew Ben and Charlie were missing, and he should be on guard, ready for when they returned. The dog's instincts were strong, but there was no way the animal could begin to know just how much danger the children were in right now. The forecaster had explained in the eleven o'clock bulletin on the radio that they should expect to take a direct hit from a category two—and rising—hurricane.

There was not much moon. What should have been visible was blocked by storm clouds. So until first light, which was about five fifteen the next morning, Frank could barely see the closest palm tree, let alone any further down the beach or out to sea. He could, however, hear the roar of the wind that was punishing anything that could be bent or lifted, accompanied by the gradual building of the crashing waves that were advancing up Sunset's beach.

He had been promised by the Kamarian police inspector that a helicopter, with a pilot experienced in search and rescue, would fly at first light, assuming that the weather permitted. He had also been advised that he should stay on the ground, ready to act on any information. This, Frank knew, was going to be a piece of advice very difficult to abide by.

Frank had closed his eyes a couple of times during that long night, but each time he'd forced them open again as his frantic imagination thrust images at him of rolling waves and drowning children. At five o'clock, the diluted sun began to illuminate the breaking waves hammering onto the beach and the palm trees bent double under the strain of the wind. Throwing water in his face from a plastic gallon jug, he prepared to go and find his son. The drive into town was treacherous as he avoided rock slides and several fallen trees, sliding to a screeching halt as the light pickup lost its grip on the wet ground outside the police station. Half expecting the place to be deserted still, he was pleasantly relieved as the inspector opened the door in greeting.

"The pilot has agreed to fly, but he won't have much time in the air. The winds are already gusting way over his recommended limit."

"I'm going with him."

"No, sir. That's not possible. He won't take you." Frank stopped in his tracks as he realised that Mr. Hamilton was already in the tiny police station.

"Good morning, Beck."

"Let's hope God, he think so," was his simple, but heartwrenching reply.

Frank began to argue the point about flying but realised that it was pointless and would only delay the helicopter from taking off and scanning the area. "Okay, just get him in the air."

Glancing at a large round clock on the wall, the officer said, "He should be taking off as we speak."

While he waited, Frank called his wife to let her know that the helicopter was flying. She already knew. Even over the sounds of the hurricane, she had picked out the mechanical noise of the rotating blades as the chopper flew low over the beach house. This had happened just moments before the cell phone rang. She stood in the doorway and prayed aloud as the flying machine grew smaller against the black sky.

"Bring them home to us, please God."

Something flying around untethered outside the vulnerable cabin woke the occupants abruptly from their dreams. All four of them looked around at their primitive surroundings, wishing they were in their respective beds and that today wasn't happening. Nature calling, the boys left the cabin, and Charlie wandered around lost. The Frenchman appeared, dressed the same as the previous night and explained about the bathroom. It was the wooden construction behind his home, and she could visit it when she needed to. Realising the power in the wind now, she decided to go sooner rather than later as the miniature building looked like it was ready to take off.

All assembled back inside, the four discussed the possibilities open to them in contacting their families. There were none. They were stuck on Scorpion until the storm left, and by then, they had all decided, their respective parents would have had triple heart attacks.

Michel rushed in yelling, "Get out here now!" Not waiting to be told again they did, tripping over each other in their haste. "Look there!" Michel pointed at the sky behind them.

"Where?" Ben asked.

Charlie exclaimed in delight, "It's a helicopter, Ben. Look!"

They all looked, and there it was, a blue chopper that Isaac recognised as the one that flew short trips to neighbouring islands and had also been known to airlift hospital patients to the mainland.

"They are searching," Michel explained. "We have to make sure that he sees all of you. Go down to the water and wave. Don't stand too close together; make sure he can count you."

Needing no further encouragement, the four did as they were told and stood in a row grinning and waving. The chopper spotted them immediately. Flying in an arc, he returned low enough to wave back at the stranded children. Grammont made sure that the pilot could see that he was also present allowing him to relay to the families that they would be safe with him on Long Bay until the hurricane had passed and a boat could be sent for the group.

Waving over his shoulder, the pilot headed for the airport on Kamaria. As he flew, he radioed the police station. Frank heard static and an intermittent call from the VHF behind the counter as the inspector picked up the handset.

"Four children safe on Scorpion Island."

This was all either father needed to hear. Old Beck Hamilton slowly nodded his head in silent prayer.

Frank punched the air screaming, "Yes!"

The smiling inspector held up a hand as the pilot continued. "The Frenchman is there. They will be safe until the storm has abated. Alpha—Romeo—one—eight—returning to base—out."

"All's well, it seems."

Frank dialed Penny's cell phone. "They're safe! They're on Scorpion with the Frenchman." Drawing breath for the first time since he'd heard the pilot's report, he began to think.

"Thank heavens. Are you sure?"

Penny was crying down the phone, and Frank could hear Ruby yelling "Ben, Ben, Ben!" in the background.

"Yes, the pilot saw all four of them on Long Bay."

"Couldn't he bring them home?"

"No, there's nowhere to land. They'll be picked up by boat as soon as the seas calm down."

"But, will they be okay there with the hurricane and everything?" Frank had this feeling that the danger had passed for the youngsters, and now it was just a matter of time and patience before he would see his son again.

Turning the ignition key in the rusty truck, he began to climb the hill into the clouds, suddenly aching to be back in Sunset Cove. The local radio was still airing bulletins to the community every hour, notifying them to close all windows and shutters, lash animal shelters and boats down and remain inside until the hurricane had passed. The announcer advised how dangerous it was to venture out onto the roads until the all clear was announced. This could be a day or more later.

The windswept beach came into view as he crawled down the road that bore a much closer resemblance to a ravine. Before making a dash for the beach house, Frank sat with the engine running and his windscreen wipers working on overdrive. Scorpion Island was a pale shadow fading in and out on the horizon. They would be okay there, wouldn't they?

The torrential rain was horizontal and stung their skin. Ben had never experienced so much wind. The gales that sometimes ravaged the south coast of England in the winter seemed puny compared to Hurricane Dolly. With the helicopter returning to Kamaria to report his findings, they could all relax a bit, knowing that their families understood they were safe.

"Can you see *Hardi* from there?"

Charlie was sitting close to a shutter at the end of the cabin, peering out through a gap in the wood. "Well, kind of, but not really. I can see she's still there, but that's about it."

Michel threw the cabin door open, immediately slamming it shut behind him as he shook like a dog. Even in the second it took him to jump through the opening, water flooded the floor around him.

"Sir," Ben said, still unable to get his head around calling the Frenchman by his first name, "Do you think we should check on *Hardi*?"

"She'll have to get on with it now. It's too rough out there for you." Michel had, in fact, already wondered about the boat himself. Yesterday's events had brought back his old feelings for the sloop, and he was concerned that even though she would be full of water now, sitting a metre or so under, he knew there was a chance that she could be rolled and then pounded by the waves that were already finding their way viciously over the reef.

"But you were just out there, couldn't we go and check her? We'd be careful."

Michel scoffed, knowing first hand that this thirteen-year-old boy was not into being careful at all.

"I can't stop you. If you are going to go, find some heavy tree branches to use as props on both sides of the hull; it may just stop her from getting turned over."

Ben stood up motioning to Isaac and Kai to get ready. "Brilliant! I am sure we can do that." So pleased to be out of the stuffy cabin and doing something useful, he moved towards the door.

"Here, take my knife and these jackets." Ben pocketed the folding knife and shrugged on a waterproof, hooded top. Kai couldn't do much until he had persuaded Sunny to get off his shoulder. She was obviously not amused about losing her human perch and ran over his head back and forth from arm to arm as the boy tried to gently detach her. As Grammont came towards her, she finally gave up and flew across the cabin to a dark corner where she had stashed a pile of seed.

"Charlie, do you wanna stay here?" As soon as he said this, Ben knew it was a mistake to even dream that his girlfriend wouldn't want to be involved.

"Excuse me? Why would I want to do that, Benjamin Johnston?" She always did that, used his full name when she was angry at him.

"I just thought…nevermind. Whatever."

Michel handed her another waterproof. Its cut gave away the fact that it had belonged to a woman. He tapped the barometer on the wall by the door. "The pressure is still falling. If you are going, you'd better get on with it."

With Isaac grumbling about "another crazy idea from Ben the genius," they piled outside.

The small amount of beach remaining was covered in a carpet of natural debris, either washed up or fallen from the hill. The rollers were huge, gathering their momentum on the shallow reef. They grew before the children's eyes, finally collapsing and delivering thousands of gallons of charging water high up onto the sand.

Heads down, their bodies leaning into the ferocious wind, they made slow headway. Speaking was pointless with the noise of the storm and the strength of the wind that took your breath away as soon as you opened your mouth. When they risked raising their hooded heads, they could just see the boat. If he made slits out of his eyes, Ben could make her out, as waves filled her then dragged themselves back out again.

Reaching the sloop, they discovered two of the lines they had fixed the night before were free, not surprisingly as the trees were gone. Isaac busied himself finding other anchor points on limbs of bush that looked sturdy enough as the others scoured the area for timber to use as poles. *Hardi* was already leaning to her starboard side. Watching the wave pattern, Ben calculated that every half a dozen breakers moved her some more. The props had to be pushed under that side first. A lot of the branches they dragged up snapped straight away, but some seemed to be holding. Everything took three times as long in these conditions, and Charlie was freezing cold—a strange sensation to have in the Caribbean.

If it could possibly get worse, the weather was doing just that as they wrestled with the last two branches. They were still attached to the tree, and Ben had to hack at the green wood with Grammont's knife. Sheet lightning that had been flashing in the distance all morning was growing closer, fast. They had been outside for an hour, and in that time, the average wind speed had increased to sixty miles an hour. The even higher gusts were becoming very scary. Unbeknownst to them, one hundred and fifty knot winds were circling the outer edges of the system just forty miles southeast of Scorpion. It wouldn't be long before the full might of Dolly would be on them.

A deafening thunderclap ricocheted around the bay. Charlie was lacing more line around the mainsail that, even though packed well, was beginning to look like it would be shredded. She was waist deep as she worked in the hull, not enjoying the strength of the waves as they tugged at her. Finishing her job, she leapt from the bow of the boat between breakers, soaked to the skin, stumbling to her feet on the moving sand. Ben and Isaac had pushed the last prop into place on the port side while Kai kicked a rock on top of the end of a pole on the opposite side of the hull.

What happened next was instant and yet drawn out in front of them like a movie recorded in slow motion.

A spectacular bolt of fire shot from an invisible source within the clouds. The fork of lightening fizzed as it found its target: *Hardi*'s rigging cracked loudly beneath the energy of the strike. Static electricity buzzed through Ben as he stood mesmerized, watching the tapered tree trunk used as *Hardi*'s mast begin to crumple.

The ten-metre pole fell towards the starboard side of *Hardi*, away from Isaac and Ben but aiming directly for Kai. He wasn't moving. The mast was falling, and Ben was yelling, but it dawned on Charlie that he couldn't hear. He still had his back to the danger. She leapt into the air, hurling herself at him, winding them both as she took him down. The wooden mast, buckling in the middle, collapsed around Charlie and Kai as they lay face down in the shallows. Rigging wires and big splinters rained down on them, the mast landing inches away where Kai had stood a moment before.

Isaac and Ben both arrived at the same time and cleared stuff away from the two still lying on the beach.

Unwrapping herself from Kai, Charlie slowly sat up with a dazed look on her face and announced, "That was a close one!"

It took Kai a little longer to figure out what had happened, he examined the smashed mast then slowly nodding his head, grinned at Charlie. With the thunderstorm ringing in most of their ears, the exhausted team ran as fast as they were able, back to the relative security of Grammont's cabin.

Eye of **the Storm**

It was the last time that any of the residents of Scorpion Island or Sunset Cove ventured from their boarded up refuges for hours to come. Hurricane Dolly unleashed gusts that would knock over a man and gave birth to seas capable of crushing concrete. The rain fell from the mountains seeking the ocean below in raging torrents, slicing open the soft earth, creating gullies the size of highways.

Two o'clock that afternoon, after a day spent cringing as stuff flew past—or sometimes into—the cabin walls, a mopping up routine was well established between the four of them.

The wind eased so quickly that the silence seemed loud. They all sat speechless looking at each other's amazed faces. Grammont came out from his room with a book in his hand. "It's the eye."

"What do you mean the eye?" Charlie went to open a locked shutter.

"No, don't! It's not over yet. It's the eye of the hurricane; it means that right now the centre of the storm is directly over our heads."

Ben whistled, impressed. "Wow, that's awesome. It's so still and quiet. Can we go outside now?"

"Yes, as long as you stay very close to the cabin. She'll come back as suddenly as she left."

They bounded for the door, full of pent up energy, eager to breathe fresh air.

"Be careful not to let Sunny out. She will be blown away when the wind returns."

Charlie turned to Michel and asked, "So, are you saying that we are only halfway through?"

"Sadly, yes."

"Come on, Charlie, let's make the most of it while we can." Ben pushed her out the door, and Isaac and Kai followed behind.

The four youngsters had taken no more than three steps each before they stopped, staring around them. It was the weirdest sensation ever. One minute the palm trees were bent double and you couldn't venture out in fear of being physically blown away, the next, nothing. No birds, no wind, no rain, nothing. The beach was strewn with palm fronds, but there were also huge coconut trees fallen too. They looked heartbreaking, lying there like dead animals. Michel had followed them outside and gone directly to check his goats who were warily peering out from their shelter. There wasn't much left of it, but the surrounding trees were still providing enough protection if the livestock stayed hidden.

Ben had just started feeling the vague effects of a watery sun doing its best to burn through the clouds, when a gust of wind cooled his face. As he turned towards it, realising it was coming from the opposite direction than they had grown used to, it increased like someone had turned up a ceiling fan.

Michel came from the back of the cabin. "Let's go, everyone. It's time to close the cabin down again!"

Dejected, they all lowered their heads and trooped in behind him.

Eye of **the Storm**

CHAPTER 36
DREAMWORLD, INC.

On Sunset Cove, Sandy was scratching at the corner of the beach house door.

"Okay, okay. I guess you can go out, Sandy." Penny reached for the door handle.

"Maybe we shouldn't let him go yet." Frank called from where he was playing Legos with Ruby.

"Why not? It's remarkably calmer now."

"I think it's the eye of the storm. John warned me about it a couple of days ago. It means it's right over us and will pass quickly and then we'll get the other side of the system."

Disappointed, she looked down at Sandy. "Well, what do you think, boy? You want to risk it?" Sandy's response left no doubt that he did, so she let him out. After less than five minutes, Penny heard scratching at the outside of the beach house. The wind had picked up, and the trees were rustling again. Sandy walked in and settled back onto the blanket behind his chair and fell asleep.

The second part of that Friday in August was long and boring for Penny, Ruby and Frank. Late afternoon, however, the cell phone rang. Puzzled, as he didn't think anyone had the number other than Ben and Penny, Frank grabbed at it. "Hello?"

"Frank, it's John. Do you still have a house over there?" It was his friend and colleague from work.

Trying to hide his disappointment that it wasn't his son calling up for a chat, Frank replied. "Yeah, we're doing okay. What about you guys?"

"Not bad, some flooding in the back of the apartment, just hope they don't keep the power off for days like last time. So, anyway, thought I should remind you that the DreamWorld board of directors are holed up in the hotel in town and expecting a dinner meeting tomorrow at six p.m."

Amazed that John could be talking about work under the circumstances, Frank realised that he hadn't actually told anyone about Ben and Charlie being missing. He'd run from the office when he'd gotten the call from Penny and never gone back.

"Actually, John, I'm not sure I'm going to make dinner." He went on to briefly explain what had happened.

"Why didn't you call us?"

Frank couldn't think of an answer to that one, other than the fact that they wouldn't have been able to do anything, but he resisted saying that.

"We need you to be at this meeting. They are going to have a fit if they think you are boycotting because of this ridiculous petition Ben got involved in."

Frank's anger started to rise in his throat. His son could have drowned yesterday, and this idiot was panicking about a contract while there's a hurricane raging over his head. Raising his voice into the tiny receiver of the mobile, Ben's dad spat, "First, I will bring my family back together. Then and only then will I begin to consider DreamWorld, Inc!" Frank Johnston hung up in disgust.

Stomachs were rumbling again in the Frenchman's cabin on Long Bay as they smelled more goat stew being heated over a basic, gas camping stove. Ben and Charlie had been examining the treasures from the black box while he filled her in on the bits she'd missed of the original Michel de Grammont's life story.

Charlie gazed at the family portrait, imagining having to wear skirts with wooden hoops and tight bodices laced up the back. The picture showed a mother, father, brother and sister. Michel looked about fourteen or fifteen. "What was the pirate's sister's name?"

"I don't know," Ben said.

Grammont served the food in bowls on the table, being careful to move the collection of handwritten letters still tied in ribbon to a shelf. He answered Charlie's question, "Her name was Bernadette. She lived a long life in France, tending to their estate, eventually marrying but never having any children. Although she was brought word informing her Michel had been lost at sea that year, she continued to hold his shares in the wealth she had accumulated, in case one day he returned. In a way, she was right. He had survived, but he never left Kamaria. He eventually died of weakness and infection left over from his original injuries sustained on Dog Leg Reef."

Ben realised that the spoon topped up with steaming stew he was gripping had been hovering in front of his open mouth for the whole time Michel had spoken. Kai was sniggering at him as sauce dribbled down his hand. Isaac had obviously been trying to work something out and wasn't sure whether to ask about it or not. Eventually he could resist no longer, "Your great, great, great grandmother, she from here?"

Charlie, beginning to understand the underlying reason for the question, opened her mouth and blurted out what Isaac was thinking, "So, you're part black?"

Ben stopped in mid-chew, and Isaac just stared at Charlie. Laughing at the embarrassed children trying to be politically correct but failing miserably, he responded. "Yes, she was, and that means that I have a little Kamarian in me."

"Me always think you were clear-skinned, not white." Ben didn't really know what that meant, but Grammont didn't seem to mind Isaac pointing it out.

"The buccaneer lived with a Kamarian woman and fathered three children during the last of his years."

Kai had been sketching during the long hours shut in the cabin, using anything Michel could find for him to draw on. He'd finally given up with scraps of paper and found an old, leather bound notebook and donated that. Glancing over his shoulder, Michel saw sketches of *Hardi*'s mast collapsing in the lightening strike and incredible images of Charlie, her long hair flying symbolically around her head, leaping to Kai's rescue, the incident cleverly portrayed as if she were a hero in a comic book.

When the team had reached the cabin after the near disaster and explained to Michel what had happened, he had commented little, knowing that as an "act of God," there was nothing anybody could have done, he was just glad they were all in one piece. The sooner he was able to pass them back to their parents, the better.

Darkness arrived earlier than normal as if the sun had just given up trying and shut down. Although devastation seemed to have occurred outside, the cabin was still standing as was the beach house on Sunset. Both homes had suffered roof damage, and kitchen utensils were littering the floors catching drips from small leaks. The darkness always seemed to make things worse, and with no power, the Johnston family suffered the most, having to sit by candlelight and prepare any food on the gas hob on top of the stove. Microwaves and fan ovens don't do too well without electricity.

On Long Bay, there had never been any mains power, so Michel was much more at ease. Other than having to brave the elements to top up the fuel supply in the generator, nothing was unusual about his living conditions. The youngsters made an effort to coordinate sleeping arrangements just a little better than the previous night when they were simply delighted to be under a roof. Isaac and Kai had collected cushions and laid them out on the floor. Michel brought lightweight blankets and sheets out for them and they made themselves as comfortable as was possible in the tiny space. Ben opted to do the same thing and made a bed on the floor, gallantly donating the couch to Charlie. Although appearing to be a gentleman, if the truth was known, he wasn't really ready for sharing sleeping spaces, even with his girlfriend.

General chat and shuffling around began to fade around eleven o'clock that night. Ben lay on his cushions and closed his eyes. Grammont was sitting in the far corner of the room with a glass of rum, reading the letters that had been hidden underground on Black Cay for over four hundred years.

Then it dawned on Ben. He was not at home with his parents. He was about to sleep somewhere else without them. Last night had been so traumatic that he had not had the time or the energy to consider it that way. Now, he was preparing to go to sleep without his parents next door. His eyes sprung open. Was he about to burst out crying or have a panic attack like before? Ben held his breath and waited for his insides to start freaking out like they had in the past when he'd tried to be away from his family. His heart beat harder, but that may have been due to the fact that he was not breathing.

He was going to be able to do this. Since there was no choice in the matter, and he was surrounded by friends, he would be okay. Closing his eyes again, he saw images of his mum and dad and Ruby floating around. He knew they understood he was still alive, but he also knew that they would still be frantically worried, as they had to endure the hurricane on Sunset Cove wondering about him. This hurt. He wished he could call them and say hi. That wasn't possible, and now he couldn't sleep. Sitting up, he watched Michel by the light of an oil lamp lost in the ancient letters.

"Who are they from, sir?" Ben whispered across at Grammont.

Looking up startled, as if he had forgotten they were all there, Michel spoke, "Bernadette—the Buccaneer's long-suffering sister."

"Oh, are they hard to read?"

"No, not once you get used to the writing, it's a little flowery but legible."

Taking a sip of rum he said, "I take it you can't sleep."

"I keep worrying about my mum and dad and sister."

"Come, sit over here. Otherwise, you will wake the others."

Michel attempted to go back to his reading, but he got the distinct impression that this boy wanted to talk, even if he was too polite to interrupt. Not the best at chitchat, Michel made an attempt, "So what have you got up to on Kamaria, when you aren't over here bugging me?"

Caught a little by surprise at this question, Ben struggled to recall anything much other than his sailing days on *Hardi*. "I have to look after my sister sometimes so my Mum gets a break, but I like to go snorkeling and exploring the hill when I can." Michel gave the impression of being bored already with this conversation then Ben thought about DreamWorld, and his blood began to boil.

"Actually, we got a petition signed by hundreds of Kamarians last week during the carnival."

Peering at Ben over the top of his reading glasses the Frenchman asked, "Petition? What on earth for?"

"There's this American corporation that has been hanging around, preparing to buy up pieces of land on Sunset Cove, and they want to buy Mr. Hamilton's land, but he doesn't want to sell, and they say that he will have to as they are going to build a huge resort on the beach, and Isaac's cousins want their fathers to sell, but Isaac and Kai and Mr. Hamilton they don't as they want to build homes on the land and go fishing and stuff." The statement came out in a long mouthful without pause for breath.

"You seem rather worked up about this. Why do you care?"

"Well, you see, sir, there's a really cool fort up behind Mr. Hamilton's house with a carving on the wall of a big ship. And there's a sugar mill that used to make rum." Ben inadvertently glanced at Grammont's glass. "And well, the reef is so beautiful and full of fish, and I know that if DreamWorld get their way, Sunset will be ruined by the developers who don't care about those things. They'll just want hotels and restaurants and stuff." Ben stopped for a breath. "And also, you know that ruin on the top of the hill? Well that's a church that the slaves built after emanci… um, emanci… well you know, after they were set free. So, Charlie and I, we had this idea to get a petition up and take it to the corporation and maybe they would listen. My Dad helped. He's a lawyer, but it was difficult for him 'cause his firm is handling the deal."

"What did they say when they saw the petition?" Michel seemed to be sitting up just a little straighter now and had removed his glasses, looking at Ben closely.

"Not much, I don't think. They told my Dad they would take it into consideration." Ben dropped his head despondently as he remembered that he had got the impression from his father that nothing would change, even with the petition.

Michel continued to study the boy's dejected features but said nothing further. As the Frenchman grunted and seemed to want to go back to his letters, Ben said goodnight and headed back to his portion of the floor. His head hit the pillow and his eyes closed. He woke up at daybreak on Saturday.

Frank shook his head, attempting to clear it after another disturbed night. The weather had definitely improved. Still overcast, the winds had dropped dramatically, and all he could see as he opened the door was destruction. Trees felled, rivers cut into the sand still running with rainwater off the ravaged hillsides. Sandy bounded outside, cocking his leg and sniffing the air. The dog trotted down to the water's edge, where the swell still insisted on crashing on the sand, and studied the horizon. Frank could see Scorpion Island much clearer than the previous day, and the channel between them carried fewer white-topped waves. Leaving Sandy on the beach to investigate the rubbish everywhere, Frank went back inside, kissed his wife and daughter and left for New Town to arrange the rescue of his eldest child and his friends.

Nelson was easy to find. All the local fishermen were hanging around the dock very animated as they compared notes over damage to their homes. The town had been generally spared, some buildings being hit harder than others, but all of them suffered water damage to furniture and fittings. Settees, tables and chairs were already drying out together with rugs and clothes in the front yards or over the balconies of the homes, shops and offices.

Frank needed to negotiate a fishing boat to be prepared to make the trip to Scorpion Island and rescue the children. It wasn't difficult to sort out, and Frank, in advance, rewarded the boat owner with a wad of money for his time and effort. Frank, Nelson and the captain that had taken Ben the first time he had set eyes on Long Bay headed out into moderate seas. The boat rolled its way around the coast and across to Scorpion.

The youngsters were more than ready to get off Scorpion by now. They had gone down to *Hardi* and checked her, retrieving bits of the mast and the wire rigging. It would take some effort to get her sailing again, but even Ben's biggest concern this morning was his family. They all wanted a hug from their mothers, even if they wouldn't admit to it out loud. Charlie was homesick, and for the first time remembered that she would be flying out in just three days.

When they saw the boat approaching, Ben had never been so pleased to see the familiar face of his father as he waded ashore. He surprised himself as he cried on his father's shoulder, saying "Sorry, Dad" over and over again through his sobs. Frank thumped Isaac and Kai on their backs, smiling at them, trying to reassure them both that they were safe now. Charlie received a kiss on the cheek and a squeeze. Frank Johnston was so delighted to be standing on Long Bay surrounded by these precious children that he couldn't stop a tear escaping and running down his own cheek.

Grammont hung back as the greetings were made. Frank strode over to him, hand outstretched, to thank the man for all he had done, unaware of the drama two afternoons before when this tall stranger had saved his son's life.

They all piled into the fishing boat, and even the captain had a smile on his face. Waiting for his dad to finish with Grammont, impatient to see his mum, Ben couldn't understand what was taking so long. Eventually, Frank shook Michel's hand again and nodding his head made his way to the waiting boat. They were on their way home.

The afternoon in the beach house was spent clearing up wet things whilst Ruby bounced all over Charlie, and Sandy bounced all over Ben. Penny kept bursting into tears and hugging her son who, after a while, was seriously wishing she'd give it a rest. The friends explained as much as they could—and dared—about the adventure. Frank kept saying, "I wish I had known he had pulled you out of the water, Ben."

Grammont was alone again. It felt much safer, not having to look after a bunch of children. That's what he kept telling himself, anyway. In fact, it was unpleasantly empty. He sat at his table with Sunny the parrot walking pigeon toed in circles on the rough oak top. Talking to the darkness, Grammont asked, "What do you think, my love? Do I help the lawyer and his son?"

That evening, DreamWorld, Inc. met with their lawyers minus Frank Johnston. Ben couldn't work out why his father had such a smug look on his face.

Eye of **the Storm**

CHAPTER 37
GAZUMPED

Dolly had moved on. The hurricane left in her wake a gentle swell and a resculptured beach. In many places, Charlie and Ben walked on stones, the sea having stripped the top layer of sand away. Mr. Hamilton told them that this had happened many times in the past, but the sand always built up again.

"Sea put it back," he said.

The pair had walked the length of Sunset Cove, ending up at his shack. Kai was pleased to see them but was quickly told by his uncle to get on with his chores. Isaac was still over the hill with his family, probably getting told the same thing, Ben thought to himself.

When the two returned to the beach house, having promised to look after Ruby, Frank was in his work suit and Penny a smart skirt and blouse. "Where are you going, Mum?"

"We are going to church."

Thinking he'd misheard, as he could have sworn she had said "church,'" he repeated the question.

Frank confirmed his wife's original statement.

"That's nice, Mr. Johnston." Charlie glanced at Ben pulling a 'they've lost the plot' look.

"We'll be back in a couple of hours or so. Please try and do something boring like stay on the beach. No more adventures Ben."

Already noticing that the tears had worn off this morning and been replaced by frequent digs from his father, hinting that he should be feeling guilty for getting them all into the mess in the first place. He told himself it was best to take them on the chin as this brief annoyance was better than new, permanent rules being put into place.

As they were leaving, Penny turned to her husband and asked, "Frank, did you tell Charlie that we have confirmed her flight for Tuesday morning?"

"Everything's okay for that, Charlie. Your parents are meeting you at Gatwick. Ben we've booked you on the same flight. We thought it would be nicer for you both to fly together." Not waiting to hear anymore of the stuttered 'but, but' coming out of his son's mouth, Frank put the truck in gear and drove away, waving merrily as he disappeared around the corner.

"Sorry, Ben. Got to go. Have to be in church!"

"I don't believe it. They're sending me home early!"

"I take it you don't want my company on the long flight back, then?"

"You know I didn't mean it like that. It's just that I had another week, and I'm not ready to go back to England, yet. I have things to do here. That only leaves me one more day."

Thoroughly disappointed, Ben was not interested in Ruby's games. He threw himself off the deck and stomped down to the sea. His eyes settled on Black Cay where the buccaneer had gone to bury his possessions. He still couldn't work out why there and not Scorpion. He wondered what Michel was doing. Probably fixing the goat pen and clearing up after the storm. He really needed to go back to Scorpion Island one last time to say goodbye.

Thinking back to yesterday morning, he had been so pleased to see his dad, Ben hadn't taken the time to explain to Grammont how grateful he was to him, not just for the rescue and saving his life, but also for the things about his past that he had shared. Ben had got the distinct feeling that was the first time anyone had heard the full story. Just as importantly, the thirteen-year-old wanted to say goodbye to *Hardi*. She had been his friend for the summer and had looked after them, including saving them from a hurricane. The least he could do was make sure she would be okay. Would Grammont be able to get her clear of the water on his own? He had to get back over there before Tuesday morning. Not knowing what else to do, he grabbed some snorkel gear and went for a swim—alone.

The hurricane had caused almost as much devastation beneath the waves as on top. Sea fans and pieces of coral that were not already washed ashore were lying broken on the sea bed, the water was still churned up, messing up the visibility. Generally, life underwater was not a whole lot cheerier than on the surface right now.

Frank and Penny turned up with satisfied looks on their faces around midday and some basic supplies for lunch from the reopened market in town. Ben started to protest his early departure to his dad.

"A couple of things have cropped up over the past few days, all good, but it just means you will be better going home with Charlie. Take the disgusted look off your face and sit down for a moment."

Ben pulled out a chair from the table, deliberately scraping it across the floor, making an ugly noise. He stared outside at his mum, Charlie and Ruby playing on a clear spot of sand.

"Firstly, I have had emails from Tony's dad saying that they have enrolled him into Edgington College with you."

If Ben hadn't been so angry, he'd have been delighted at this news, as it was he just snapped, "Good."

Frank ignored him and continued, "Secondly, I have some very urgent business to attend to over the next forty-eight hours and then subsequent paperwork that will tie me up at the office for at least two more weeks. Because of your escapades over the weekend, I am not a very popular employee right now and have to spend some time sorting this out."

Ben interrupted, "So what does all that have to do with me? Mum was going to come home and take me to the new school."

"Now Tony's parents are meeting you at the airport, and you're staying with them for the last few days before you travel to Edgington."

Feeling that old panic rising at the thought of being on his own, he pushed it away knowing in his heart that he would be okay with that from now on, but he still asked, "Won't Mum or you come with me to school?"

"Mum will be there the day you get settled in, and then you have to be at school for three weeks before they allow you to have a weekend at home."

"Sounds more like prison to me."

Losing his cool with his son, Frank battled on, "Look, Ben, I take it you would like to return here to Kamaria at Christmas?"

"Of course I would." Thinking that Christmas was light years away, Ben stared at his feet.

"Then you will have to show some patience and understanding. I can only assume from your time spent on Scorpion that you no longer mind sleeping away from us, and that's wonderful, if the hurricane did no other good, at least it helped you over that."

"It's just that I want to say goodbye to everyone. I should thank the Frenchman for everything, and what about Isaac and Nelson? I've only got tomorrow now to do all that."

Frank did genuinely feel sorry for Ben as he struggled to deal with the fact that he was going back to the "real world" and so many new experiences. He knew his son would be fine, but there was no way of comforting him. Ben had to work through it himself.

"Tomorrow morning we can all go to town. You can catch up with Nelson, and you'll find Isaac either there or down the beach right?"

"Yes, but what about Mr. Grammont? I want to make sure *Hardi* is okay."

"We can do that, too."

"How? I don't have a boat to get there." Ben's pleading eyes tempted Frank into explaining more but he resisted.

"Just give me a break, Ben. Trust me, it'll all work out okay!"

Later that day, Ben sat on the old, fallen tree trunk, still there surrounded now by several more felled by Dolly, his arm slung around Sandy's neck.

"I wish you could come to England with me, Sandy. You'd love running in the fields around my house, but there's no beach, and I guess you would get a bit cold." Penny had already put the mockers on taking the dog to England. She had explained what he would have to go through just to be allowed into the country, and then how alien it would be to him, living in such a strange environment. She had, however, conceded that he was a part of their family, albeit the Caribbean one, and his dad would look after Sandy, making sure he was cared for when Frank was in the UK.

It was just all sinking in too fast, leaving Kamaria, Sandy and the *Hardi*, not to mention his human friends. This was a new feeling for Ben. He was so incredibly sad, it really did hurt inside. It wasn't fair, he'd never wanted to come here this summer, but they'd made him, and now they were dragging him away.

The other weird feeling was about Charlie. He couldn't quite work it out, but he thought he would rather go back to having her as a friend than a girlfriend. She was beginning to annoy him, and he didn't want to have his arm draped around her constantly anymore. He knew she was upset with him, but he just couldn't help it. He was far too concerned about his dog and a broken sloop to worry about her right now. Jumping to his feet, he started to run along the beach. "Come on, Sandy, let's go and find Kai."

Monday morning dawned along with a depressing feeling of having to do things like pack his case and say goodbye to people. His parents were still acting weird, but Ben wasn't interested in finding out why. All he knew was this was his last day on Sunset Cove. Charlie kept trying to cheer him up which only made him more miserable.

"Okay, here's the plan, guys," Frank said. "I have an early, emergency meeting at the government administration offices, so we all need to be ready to head into town in fifteen minutes." Anything but have to face the finality of his packing, Ben nodded, and Charlie scooted into the bathroom.

The five squeezed into the pickup, Ruby trying her luck at sitting in the back with her big brother but to no avail. New Town was bustling. The fishing boats were being untied from the mangroves, and a ferry had just arrived, spitting people out of its insides as it bobbed up and down gently on dock lines.

Ben could see Nelson and the captain on their boat moving fish pots back on deck from a hiding place in the cabin below. Isaac was onboard, too. Frank parked the pickup outside his office and jogged inside. He returned almost immediately with a bulging briefcase and kissed Penny on the cheek. Ben was sure he heard his father say, "Wish me luck." His mum and sister walked round to the market, and with Frank already striding off in the direction of the government building, that just left Charlie and Ben—alone.

"I'm going to the dock to wait for Nelson to bring his boat over."

"I'll come, too."

"Whatever," was the only word of acknowledgment she received. They sat, not talking, with a significant gap between them and watched the men as they prepared their boats, ready to head out and lay the fish pots, now the storm was gone.

Ben stood and caught the line that Nelson tossed, tying it to a free dock cleat. Following suit, Charlie reached for the stern line that the Rasta hurled at her but, mostly due to bad aiming on his part, she missed. Ben tutted and shook his head at her unkindly.

"What is up with you, Ben? I just missed the rope. It's fine now, or do you want to check my knot? What are you, God's gift to boats all of a sudden?" Not waiting for a reply, she stormed off in the opposite direction.

"Hey, man, your woman giving you trouble!" Jumping the gap with a third line, Nelson watched Charlie stomp up the road with all the body language of an upset sumo wrestler. Isaac appeared, carrying a casting net. A flashback of the day the boys met on the rock further around the harbour zoomed through Ben's mind.

"Hey, what's up?"

"Lots. I have to fly back to England tomorrow morning."

"Man. that sucks." Dumping the contraption at his feet, with a huge grin on his face that made his dark eyes sparkle, he explained the latest news to his friend. "The Captain, he give me job, so I can save cash for my own fishing boat."

"Don't you have to go back to school?"

"Tests come soon, but then I have a fishing business."

"That's great, Isaac. I'll be back at Christmas. I get three weeks off school then, so maybe the captain will let me come fishing, too?"

"Cool man. Me go catch bait fish." Picking up a bucket and the net, he began to walk barefoot towards his favourite fishing spot. Turning to Nelson, Ben checked to see if he was going to be here all morning then he yelled at Isaac, "Hey, can I come?"

"Yeah, man, maybe you get it right this time." Isaac laughed as Ben caught him up and punched him on the arm.

Two hours later, the pair made their way back along the edge of the harbour, one with a bucket and one a casting net on his shoulder. Isaac was keen to get the bait fish he had caught to the boat and leave on an afternoon trip to set pots and try their luck at some trolling on the way. Ben could see just how much his heart was in the industry, providing food taken from the sea to families and restaurants on Kamaria. It was all Isaac needed from life—his own fishing boat and eventually his own home.

Ben had been getting pangs of guilt about Charlie while he was messing around with Isaac. He didn't mean to upset her, he just needed some space right now. He thought he had better go find her, so he said goodbye to his friend with an elaborate handshake, Caribbean style, and ran off in the direction of the hotel and stores.

His mum was sitting outside the hotel at one of two tables provided on the side of the road, Ruby was playing with something in the dirt by her feet. What blew Ben's mind was the person she was talking with. Michel Grammont was sat at the table with her. So deep was the conversation between them that neither noticed him approaching until Ruby yelled his name.

"Did you find your friends?" his mum asked.

Struggling to find his voice, he tried to take in the fact that not only was the Frenchman on Kamaria, but he was sitting with none other than his mother. "Er, yeah I did. Hi, Mr. Grammont. It's good to see you." He felt awkward and almost a little jealous, as up until this moment, the eccentric hermit was his, not his mum's.

"Yes, you should be surprised to see me. This is the first time I have been to the main island for about thirteen years." Looking back at Penny he continued, "Well, I think we've completed my business, and I have definitely had enough of the metropolis for one day. Let me say goodbye, Mrs. Johnston, I am sure we will meet again in the not-too-distant future." He offered his hand to her, and she took it in both of hers.

"I will never be able to thank you enough for what you have done for us in many ways, Monsieur Grammont. Please take care of yourself." Smiling at her, he turned to leave.

"Sir, are you going back on Nelson's boat?"

"Yes, Ben, but I have promised your parents that today, Scorpion Island is off limits to you."

"I'll come with you to the dock," he said then asked, "I was wondering what will happen to *Hardi* now?"

Smiling again (he seemed to be doing a lot of that today), Michel explained;"I have already asked Nelson and Isaac to come out in a couple of days and help me bail and lift her clear of the water. I will repair the hole I made and then look for a new tree to shape a mast from. Don't worry, I won't leave her to rot away."

Relieved at this news, the tension in Ben began to ease away. He said goodbye to Nelson as he untied the boat, but just as the Captain was manouvering her sideways off the dock, an impulse made Ben leap aboard and without hesitating (in case he changed his mind), he wrapped his arms around the stunned Frenchman's neck and said, "Thank you, Michel. Thank you for everything". With the gap widening between the rugged hull and the dock, Ben jumped back ashore, only just making it.

Eye of **the Storm**

Looking into the young boy's unhappy face, the buccaneer's great, great, great grandchild replied, "No, Ben, thank you. You've no idea what you have brought back to me this summer."

Everyone, even the captain, waved at Ben as the boat gathered speed, black smoke gushing from the exhaust, engulfing the stern. Tears rolling down the boy's face, he stood on the end of the dock and watched until the old boat disappeared from view. A gentle touch on his shoulder brought him back to reality. Charlie stood beside him watching the last of the boat's wake dissolve back into the sea.

"Charlie, look I'm sorry about earlier. It's just that I don't want to go home, and I didn't mean to take it out on you."

Looking nearly as upset as him; "It's okay. I understand. Let's just take it slowly for a while. We both have to go back to England and different schools and stuff. Do you want to go see if your mum and dad are ready to leave?"

"Yeah, sure. Come on. My mum's over there."

Penny told Ben, "Your father has a meeting in half and hour, so he said for us to go back to Sunset, and he'll get a ride over the hill when he's finished later. That way you kids can have a swim, and I'll begin your packing for you, then you can finish it off later, okay?"

Feeling better than he had since being told the news about leaving, Ben grabbed Ruby's hands and spun her around so her feet left the ground. Squealing for more, Charlie took a hand and they walked to the truck swinging the toddler between them.

Frank walked into the public meeting room flanked by Beck Hamilton, his brother, Jack, and Father Peterson, Head of Kamaria's Anglican Church. Feeling like he had been dropped into a scene from an old spaghetti western, he wondered if he should be walking like a gunslinger with his hands poised over each pistol, ready to draw. However, Frank wasn't using guns today; his chosen weapons were a whole lot of money and the element of surprise.

The meeting had been confirmed during the Saturday evening dinner attended by DreamWorld's board of directors and Frank's firm of lawyers. It was designed as a public display of united ideals between DreamWorld, Inc. and the Government of Kamaria. The press was invited, and, in fact, the occasion had attracted international interest from agencies understanding the importance of this large step in the advancement of tourism on Kamaria.

Not ones to miss out on a show, many Kamarians had taken seats provided theatre style, in the community centre. Most of these audience members had signed Ben's petition. The top table was surrounded by display boards decorated in artist impressions of the planned five-star resort on Sunset Cove. The pictures spoke for themselves.

Suited American executives sat, sweating, next to the Minister for Land and

Resources and his Permanent Secretary. Between them lay a folder containing four copies of a contract selling one hundred and twenty acres of what was currently government-owned land, to DreamWorld, Inc. A surveyor's map pinned behind the heads of the signees showed this parcel of land in red, it surrounded the Hamilton family's smaller but crucial plots presently left white.

A welcome speech by the Minister had already taken place, and as the four men walked into the hall, the Chief Executive Officer of DreamWorld was thanking the government and people of Kamaria for "embracing their presence and development plans." Chairs moved, and there were muffled conversations going on in the audience as the guy tried to rattle through his scripted speech. He looked as if all he wanted to do was get the contract signed and escape as quickly as possible, back to some air-conditioning.

"Therefore, it gives me great pleasure to invite the Minister to sign with me and cement a long-term relationship of prosperity between DreamWorld and Kamaria." The developer passed the fountain pen provided for the occasion across to his counterpart.

"Actually, if the Honourable Minister would allow me a minute of his time, I come bearing vital news that even he has not been privy to this morning." Everyone turned to stare at the owner of the voice and his serious-faced companions. Anyone taking notice of the table of officials at this moment would have seen the false smile slip from the CEO's sweaty face and the Minister look slowly from the lawyer to each of the Hamilton Brothers, finally resting his gaze on Father Peterson.

Press photographers, all of a sudden interested in the unexpected entry of the unlikely looking group, began clicking their cameras in the direction of the back of the room. The volume of chatter from the audience rose markedly.

Frank raised his hand and continued, "Sirs, if I may, I have been asked by the Chief Minister of Kamaria to explain some changes he has agreed upon this morning and deliver a signed contract to the Minister for Land and Resources for his information." The chatter fell away as Frank walked towards the top table followed in tight formation by his gang.

The Minister threw his hands in the air in mock surrender and sat down. DreamWorld's board of directors were in a huddle looking like they were about to begin a game of American football. Frank reached the table and turned to the audience, enjoying every second now.

"Minister, members of the press, ladies and gentleman, perhaps I should remind you all of this document." Frank reached into his case and pulled out with difficulty, the thick pile of papers signed by the majority of Kamarians and a few visitors, during festival week. "This is the petition started by my son and the children of Beck and Jack Hamilton expressing concern over the development of Sunset Cove by

DreamWorld, Inc. It was signed by three quarters of the population of this country, so I can continue with confidence, knowing that the Chief Minister has taken note of your wishes and decided to accept a second offer for the purchase of the land described in the original agreement.

The CEO couldn't stand it any longer. "What on earth are you talking about, man? There hasn't been any other offers, and besides, the arrangements were made weeks ago." Stabbing his finger at the paper in front of him, he said, "This contract still stands."

"I'm very sorry to have wasted your valuable time, sir, but I am delighted to say that the one I am holding is for the eyes of the Minister only and shows closure on the sale."

Smiling at the audience, Frank added, "It doesn't take a lawyer to understand the basic rule of going with the highest bidder, now does it, sir?" The crowd were chuckling, enjoying seeing these suits squirm.

Frank gave the new contract and accompanying letter to Beck. "Perhaps you would like the pleasure of handing the Minister this, Mr. Hamilton." Beck did as he was asked, and a complete hush fell on the community centre as the two pages were read in silence.

After what seemed like an eternity, the Minister rose from his chair again, folding the papers tidily into his own briefcase. "Well, it falls on me to thank DreamWorld for their time and efforts, but on this occasion, we must politely turn down their proposals and begin to put into place this new and inspiring challenge." The mouths of all the executives dropped open. They certainly had never been treated like this before.

The CEO, gathering his wits about him spoke once more. "Honorable Minister, I feel the least you could do is explain to me and the waiting audience what this is all about."

"Yes, sir, I would be delighted. I have been asked by the Chief Minister to hold back the name of the individual responsible for the funding of the purchase, but to explain his specific conditions of contract to all present." The Minister drew breath and began to sum up the covering letter hastily written by Frank this morning and signed by the leader of the country.

"The land purchased will be placed in a trust, legally guarded by a group of specially selected, local trustees that will report to and advise the owner of any major issues. The trust will ensure that this land and plots belonging to the Hamilton family bordering it, shall not be used for development other than family homes and small cottage industries relevant to the area and only when they are shown to be appropriate to the nature of Sunset Cove. No matter who proposes to lease land from the trust, their project must provide proof that it will in no way compromise or endanger the environment or raise conservation issues on either the land or under the sea, including impact on the whole of the bay and hillside and all coral reefs and fish life contained in it."

Drawing a long breath as the audience "ooed" and "ahhed," some clapping their hands in approval, the minister bent to retrieve the contract, checking for information he had left out.

"Ah, yes, let me see. Within the agreement, it has been suggested that the old fort and the sugar mill be declared national parks, preventing them from further decay and preserving these important pieces of our heritage (that I may add, seem to have been overlooked by these developers), for future generations to enjoy and study. I believe that Father Peterson is present to demonstrate his promised commitment in seeing to it that the ruined church on the hill overlooking Sunset Cove, built by our ancestors the slaves, be restored and protected as a place of worship once more."

The crowd loved every word. They clapped and cheered, and the reporters frantically scribbled notes pushing their mini voice recorders as close to the Minister as they could reach. They began firing questions at the top table. The obvious one was, "Who was behind this huge investment?" They were not to find out, and with nothing more to do or say, the winners and the very sore losers left the hall.

Frank shook the hands of the Hamilton brothers, promising them he would keep them up to speed in the days and weeks ahead, and made his exit. Several Kamarians slapped him on the back as he made his way towards the sunshine. He smiled and thanked them but kept walking. His last task that day was to report back to his firm and hope they didn't sack him on the spot. During the Minister's unrehearsed speech, he had spotted his boss at the back of the room, and then he was gone. Probably to change the locks on Frank's office door.

"You had better have one awful big cheque in your pocket, Frank Johnston, because you just threw away our largest client ever."

"Give me two minutes to explain."

Sitting down heavily in his leather swivel chair, the Managing Director sighed and said, "Okay, let's have it."

"My client came to me asking to stay anonymous and what with the scheduled signing this afternoon, I didn't have time to bring you up to date."

"How much, Frank?"

"Five thousand dollars over the DreamWorld offer, per acre." The MD did some mental arithmetic.

"That's pretty impressive, but the problem is, Frank, we would have earned enough money out of the ongoing deals with an American company, constantly burying themselves in donkey dung each time they messed up a bit of the environment, to keep us going for years."

Frank continued, "We have exclusive, legal control over the trust and all its transactions. All leases and day to day dealings go through us."

Frank's boss sat up straighter. "Oh, I see."

"This means we earn more commission out of the original sale, we will be on a retainer from the trust for as long as you desire, and we are doing something worthwhile for the environment of Kamaria."

"How on earth did you pull this one off, Frank?"

Laughing he admitted, "Well to be honest, I didn't. Ben did."

Wearily shaking his head, the director admitted, "I don't think I want to know anymore. You gonna tell me who this multimillionaire is then?"

Frank pushed the signed contract across the shiny desk, "Here, check it out for yourself."

Eye of **the Storm**

CHAPTER 38
NEW HOMES

They drove to the tiny, single runway airport in silence. Sandy rode in the back with Ben. Penny had opted not to come with them but to say goodbye to her son at the beach house. She and Ruby waved as they watched the truck turn the corner and disappear from view.

"See you in a few days, Ben." Penny had yelled as Ruby jumped up and down.

Charlie and Ben were friends again, their special summer cementing that part of the relationship for a lifetime. Charlie couldn't bear to sit in the back with Ben as every time she looked at him hugging his dog she started to cry. Frank checked them in and talked to the flight attendant who would see them through their stopover further south in the Caribbean before boarding the jumbo jet bound for Gatwick, London.

The previous evening, they had celebrated the news about Sunset Cove not being ruined by DreamWorld, and Frank had explained some of the details about the new trust and its conditions for future development. "Progress has to happen, Ben; it just needs to be done carefully, with the needs of the local population at the top of the list. Sustainable development will allow Kamarians to be proud of their traditions and way of life while still encouraging visitors to experience the real heart of the country, not just another luxury resort that could be anywhere in the world. It means your reef and ruins will be protected. Isaac can set up a fishing business, and all the children will be able to build homes on land that has belonged to their families for centuries." Frank looked at his son. "Thanks to you, the people woke up and said no to a corporation. Because of the trust, another DreamWorld won't ever be able to attempt the same takeover again."

It was all so incredible that neither Ben nor Charlie could think of anything to say.

Now all that was left was to say goodbye to his dad and, much worse, his beach dog. Sandy knew something was very wrong. He hung around Ben's feet, tripping him up and whining for attention. For the last time before Frank shut him in the cab of the pickup, Ben hugged the dog and whispered in his soft ear. "I'm coming back, Sandy. Wait for me, and be a good boy. Don't chase Mr. Hamilton's chickens, or he'll use that machete on you." Sobbing, Ben let his dad take the makeshift leash from him.

"Ben, there's something here for you and Charlie. I was asked to wait until now before I gave them to you. Open them when you get on the plane, okay?"

"Who are they from?"

Frank had handed them both small parcels wrapped up in brown paper and string. "I have a feeling that will be obvious once you've unwrapped them." He hugged his teenage son hard. "I'll be back in about a month. See you then. Be good, Ben!"

Charlie squeezed the lawyer around the waist. "Thanks for everything, Mr. Johnston."

"You're very welcome Charlie. Look after him for me."

Smiling through her tears, she said, "Sure, he'll be okay."

With a last glance at Sandy whose head stuck out the passenger window, tongue hanging out, ears back, not understanding the need for the goodbyes at all, the children climbed the steps of the five-seater plane. "Call me from Antigua, Ben."

Rooted to the spot until the light aircraft vanished into a cloud, Frank finally returned to the pickup and made a fuss of the confused dog as he talked. "Well, I wanted a summer to remember for my son, and I think he got that, Sandy. Maybe this really is a place where dreams can still come true."

His cell phone rang half an hour after Frank had got back to Sunset. The Beach House felt empty as he and his wife sat on the deck watching Sandy gently play with Ruby. Frank knew that the parcels would have been opened, and the two youngsters would now be proud owners of a little piece of history. He warned them to keep the treasures very safe, as Ben explained about his gold coins and Charlie's miniature dagger.

A cryptic note had been enclosed with Ben's parcel.

Dear Ben,

The letters that you found sent to the buccaneer from his sister confirmed and provided proof of a large fortune accumulated over four hundred years of investment. I know I can trust you to keep a secret. Rest in the knowledge that because of your discovery, Sunset Cove will remain the way it is now, for your children and theirs to follow.

Yours truly,
Michel de Grammont

Now that Ben knew where the millions had come from to rescue Sunset from DreamWorld, Frank saw no harm in telling him on the phone that Grammont had committed to making sure that Kai was given an opportunity to go to art school and a new Boston Whaler had been ordered for Beck Hamilton to replace the boat lost in the hurricane.

"Ben, before I say cheerio, there's one more thing." Ben's mind was beginning to swim with all this sudden incoming information!

"What's that, Dad?"

"The reason that your mum is staying just a few more days is so that we can jointly sign a lease for an acre of land here on the hill at Sunset."

Silence.

"Ben, are you still there?"

"Do you mean we are going to build a real house there?"

"Yes, a home that we can all return to from our traveling. A family home on Sunset Cove."

Turning to Charlie in the seat next to him, as they buckled themselves into the long, overnight flight to Gatwick, Ben said, "There's just one thing I can't work out. I remembered yesterday when Grammont grabbed me in the water that day, before he pulled the life ring over my head he said one word."

Charlie was reading a book and only half listening. "What was that?"

"I'm sure he called me Matthew."

Charlie took a moment to register the significance. "I didn't tell you, did I?"

"Tell me what?"

"The graves I told you about, his son's name, it was carved on the stone. His name would have been Matthew."

Landing into a grey, cold London wasn't much fun. Charlie spotted her parents first and ran and hugged them both. She returned to Ben and kissed him on the cheek. "Thanks for a great summer, Ben."

"Yeah, see ya."

Tony was leaning against a post the other side of the customs barrier. "Hey, how was it?"

"Pretty good."

"You should've been at Tesco's this summer, it rocks."

Placing his bag on the floor by his feet, Ben looked at his English friend's pale face and replied, "Rocks, you have no idea about rocks. Keep Christmas open, and I'll show you some rocks."

THE END

Eye of **the Storm**

About the Author

Alison Knights Bramble lives in Tortola, British Virgin Islands where she has been a sailing school principal since 1997. In 2009, Alison and her husband Colin initiated the formation of Special Olympics BVI to which she dedicates most of her spare time. When not on the sea, Alison is either in the classroom or reading. *The Eye of the Storm*, her first novel, is a culmination of experiences and inspirations collected while living and working in "Nature's Little Secrets," the BVI.